What Reviewers Say About B

KIM BALDWI

"'A riveting novel of suspense' seems to be a very overworked phrase. However, it is extremely apt when discussing Kim Baldwin's [*Hunter's Pursuit*]. An exciting page turner [features] Katarzyna Demetrious, a bounty hunter…with a million dollar price on her head. Look for this excellent novel of suspense…" – **R. Lynne Watson**, *MegaScene*

RONICA BLACK

"Black juggles the assorted elements of her first book, [*In Too Deep*], with assured pacing and estimable panache…[including]…the relative depth—for genre fiction—of the central characters: Erin, the married-but-separated detective who comes to her lesbian senses; loner Patricia, the policewoman-mentor who finds herself falling for Erin; and sultry club owner Elizabeth, the sexually predatory suspect who discards women like Kleenex…until she meets Erin."– **Richard Labonte**, *Book Marks, Q Syndicate, 2005*

ROSE BEECHAM

"…her characters seem fully capable of walking away from the particulars of whodunit and engaging the reader in other aspects of their lives." – *Lambda Book Report*

GUN BROOKE

"*Course of Action* is a romance…populated with a host of captivating and amiable characters. The glimpses into the lifestyles of the rich and beautiful people are rather like guilty pleasures.…[A] most satisfying and entertaining reading experience." – **Arlene Germain**, reviewer for the *Lambda Book Report* and the *Midwest Book Review*

JANE FLETCHER

"*The Walls of Westernfort* is not only a highly engaging and fast-paced adventure novel, it provides the reader with an interesting framework for examining the same questions of loyalty, faith, family and love that [the characters] must face." – **M. J. Lowe**, *Midwest Book Review*

RADCLY*f*FE

"…well-honed storytelling skills…solid prose and sure-handedness of the narrative…" – **Elizabeth Flynn**, *Lambda Book Report*

"…well-plotted…lovely romance…I couldn't turn the pages fast enough!" – **Ann Bannon**, author of *The Beebo Brinker Chronicles*

Visit us at www.boldstrokesbooks.com

BATTLE FOR TRISTAINE

TRISTAINE BOOK TWO

by

Cate Culpepper

2006

BATTLE FOR TRISTAINE

ISBN 1-933110-49-X

THIS TRADE PAPERBACK IS PUBLISHED BY
BOLD STROKES BOOKS, INC.,
NEW YORK, USA

FIRST EDITION: JUSTICE HOUSE PUBLISHING 2004
SECOND EDITION: BOLD STROKES BOOKS, INC., JULY 2006

CREDITS
EDITORS: CINDY CRESAP AND SHELLEY THRASHER
PRODUCTION DESIGN: J. BARRE GREYSTONE
COVER ART: TOBIAS BRENNER (http://www.tobiasbrenner.de/)
COVER GRAPHIC: SHERI (graphicartist2020@hotmail.com)

By the Author

The Clinic: Tristaine Book One

Acknowledgments

My sincere thanks to Radclyffe and her great team at Bold Strokes Books, especially my editors, Cindy Cresap and Shelley Thrasher. I appreciate the fine talents of Tobias Brenner and Sheri, the creators of Tristaine's images. Thanks also to this story's first editors, JD Glass and Jay Csokmay. As always, the support of the women of the Tristaine mailing list has been both saving grace and guiding light.

DEDICATION

For my mother, Joyce L. Culpepper

Don't be dismayed at goodbyes. A farewell is necessary before we can meet again. And meeting again, after moments or lifetimes, is certain for those who are friends.

Richard Bach
Illusions

CHAPTER ONE

Writing in one of these things is illegal in at least half the Cities in the Nation. Personal journals were outlawed even before personal computers. I've never understood how domestic terrorists could exploit some school kid's diary, but that's been the law as long as I can remember.

Shann tells me not to worry about it. "If we're captured," she said, "You'll be shot for treason long before anyone gets around to charging you with journal writing."

I've never even littered.

Brenna brushed a leaf from the page of her journal and focused on the tall Amazon at the edge of the grove. Jess was hauling a roped parcel of dried meat several yards up an aspen to keep it from predators. She was intent on the narrow platform as it rose in even stages toward a high branch.

Brenna lost herself for a moment in the subtle dance of muscle in Jess's tanned forearms and the glossy hair she shook from her eyes to check the plank's ascent. Brenna forced her gaze back to the notebook in her lap.

I'm losing track of time out here. The battle in Caster's camp is a dim memory now when I'm awake.

It took Jess and Camryn several days to heal enough to make the hike through the foothills to this meadow. That journey took a week, and we made camp here over a month ago. How long has it been since we escaped from the City? Six weeks? Impossible.

Shann knows more about healing than I do, but we couldn't get Jess through a night without fever for what felt like months.

Brenna tipped her head back to catch the light breeze that feathered her hair across her forehead. The nights had already turned cold, but their refuge was not so high in the mountains that it missed the last blush of summer. The hushed morning trill of a wood thrush joined the music of sparrows in the surrounding trees, and Brenna was filled with a pleasant lethargy.

Shann wants me to record my dreams in here as well as keep a diary. I think that's redundant because I can't seem to stop talking in my sleep, so everyone's heard all my dreams anyway.

The Amazons have decided I'm some kind of latent mystic. Even Jess seems convinced of it.

Practicing mysticism, I should add, is still illegal in every City in the Nation.

For the first time, it might be possible to listen for what Shann calls my inner voices and think of something other than brute survival. We've all been so focused on finding food, tending the wounded, and keeping watch for these last weeks. But our immediate needs are being met. One advantage of Tristaine's Amazon heritage is the woodlore her daughters have retained. Everyone but me seems to know enough about fishing and hunting to keep us decently fed.

All of them teach me when they can. Shann deserves her reputation for saint-like patience, based on how she taught me about Amazons this summer. She's a walking encyclopedia on Tristaine, and she's generous about finding time for me. If you need to take a speed course about an Amazon clan, it really helps to have their queen's undivided attention.

Kyla keeps me from poisoning anyone when I cook, and she's teaching me to track. She's better at night tracking than either Camryn or Jess, which gratifies us both to no end.

Camryn is friendly now, but she still keeps her distance. She answers any question I ask, then drifts politely away. We're closer than we were before the battle at Caster's camp—digging a bullet out of someone's leg will do that—but I still can't call her Cam to her face.

Mostly, I learn from Jess—everything from how to skin a boar (she's impossibly sexy even when skinning a boar) to freehand fighting techniques. She started drilling again weeks ago. Sooner than I liked, but I can see her strength coming back. She takes us all through three hours of defense training a day now. Even Shann joins us sometimes, and she moves really well for a woman in her forties. I've got a lovely hematoma on my hip the size of a fist.

Kyla's musical voice interrupted Brenna's meditation on her bruise. "Hey, Jesstin! Shann's eyes are bothering her again."

Kyla and Camryn paused on their way into the forest. They carried empty packs for gathering herbs and edible greens, and Cam cradled one of their two rifles.

"Does fennel have three leaves or four?"

"Small yellow blossoms," Jess called, tying off the pallet with an efficient slipknot. "Know what you're picking, Ky, or you'll poison our lady, rather than ease her eyes."

"We'll look for ambrette too, Jess, fer you and yer monthly crrrrankiness." Kyla's trilling imitation of Jess's brogue broke Camryn into cackles, and Brenna smiled as they disappeared into the trees. Their adolescent teasing reminded her so vividly of Sammy.

As far as we can tell, Caster is laying low in the City. We haven't seen or heard signs of aerial surveillance for weeks. I'd like to think we've seen the last of her, but stone-cold sobriety won't let me kid myself.

Shann wants me to get the basic facts about our recent history down. If this journal survives us, she wants Tristaine to know what kind of enemy they're dealing with.

Caster was the most eminent scientist in the City, and the Clinic where she worked was the best medical research facility ever funded by the Government. I'm putting all this in past tense because I assume, believe, and devoutly pray that our escape changed all that. Caster was banking heavily on the Tristaine Study. She staked her reputation on its success. Without Jess, there's no study. Now there's just one disgraced and very pissed-off scientist.

The Military funded the study to find a way to force the Amazons of Tristaine out of their mountain village. They were becoming folk heroes in the City, and that made them dangerous. Steady streams of women were stealing over the City limits to join the clan. Any kind of political unrest is anathema to the Government, and in the popular imagination, Tristaine was becoming a sort of renegade promised land.

The Feds had Jess captured and hired Caster to devise a method to gain an Amazon's compliance. They wanted to find a way to render an Amazon passive and controllable. They had no idea who they were dealing with. None of the tortures used on political prisoners were able to turn Jess. I know Caster would have killed her trying, and Jess would rather have died than betray her clan.

Shann wants us home in Tristaine before the first snowfall. The Amazons long so much for their mountain village. I long for it too sometimes, and I've never even seen it.

Every night before we sleep they tell stories about Tristaine. Every morning, I wake up next to Jess, my head on her breast, and I hear her heartbeat, steady and strong. Then I remember kneeling over her on the floor of Caster's lab at the Clinic, pounding on her silent chest and screaming.

Brenna dropped the pen as a shiver coursed up her spine. This couldn't be what Shann intended, this futile dwelling on the past. And it was easier to shelve those memories now that Jess was strolling up the rise toward her. Brenna studied her easy stride, her broad shoulders, her rugged face pleasantly flushed with exertion.

A shame she's working in the brush today, Brenna thought, *or she'd be shirtless. That golden tan. . .*She felt her ears blush.

A certain swagger entered Jess's walk as she climbed the short rise. She decided to allow herself that indulgence. That fond, almost hungry light in Brenna's green eyes merited a small strut. Jess felt a come-hither smile of her own drift across her face.

She settled her long form onto the grass beside Brenna, a bare arm brushing against her, connecting them with a friendly warmth. Their silence was comfortable as they enjoyed the mild morning sun.

Brenna shifted against the log and examined the swell of Jess's bare shoulder. The skin there was smooth now, with no lingering trace of the multiple stunner burns inflicted in the Clinic. The colors and lines of the small tattoo, the glyph that identified Jess as an Amazon warrior in Tristaine, were clear and vibrant again.

With the tip of one finger, she lightly traced the image of three arrows in flight, then bent to rest her lips against her lover's shoulder for a moment. Jess's skin was warm and salty.

"Brazen hussy." Jess's light brogue made something delightful of those words. "Lipping me in broad daylight now, like a wanton guppy."

"Amazon ego, Jesstin." Brenna flipped open her journal again. "I wasn't kissing you. I was sucking on you for nutrients. I'm hungry. If you really loved me, you'd haul down that pallet of boar again and make me a nice ham sandwich."

Jess scrunched lower against the log and closed her eyes. "And while I'm carving boar, who will protect my fair wench from rampaging lions?"

"All right." Brenna sighed. "I did ask you once, probably while I was weak from hunger, about the possible presence of lions in these woods. To my unending mortification. But never mind, I'll pass on the boar. The only reason Shann lets you out of cooking duties, Jess, is you can't turn out anything remotely edible."

"I make tasty eggs."

"You burn eggs to cinders, honey."

"Aye, I do," Jess admitted. She squinted at Brenna. "You really want me to make you a pig sandwich?"

"Nah, stay put." Brenna gave her a friendly nudge. "I can wait for Camryn and Kyla to bring home a nice salad. Maybe they can find me some hallucinogenic mushrooms out there." She turned to a fresh page in her journal. "I'm going to need them if Shann expects me to play fortune-teller for Tristaine."

"A little weed might help." Jess cracked open an eye. "I'm serious, lass. You need to relax, if you're to see what's coming. I don't think you've relaxed since you were five."

"How would you know what I was like when I was five?" Brenna asked as she scanned what she'd written. "Me and Sammy were growing up in a City Youth Home, and you were growing up in the mountains, in some Tristaine kindergarten, learning to shoot pigs with your toy arrows and getting high at recess."

"I was such a cute little tyke." Jess chuckled, stretching against the log. "With my tiny red eyes."

"I'm sure you were. Ah, Jesstin, this is so much—gaaaah!" Brenna slapped the notebook shut. "I have no idea what Shann wants from me. Do I look like an oracle to you?"

"Why not?" Jess turned her head on the rough bark and regarded her with affection. She understood all too well how City life could bleed the confidence out of the strongest woman, and Brenna had spent more than two decades there. "You never belonged to the City, Brenna. If they hadn't gotten their hooks into you young, you'd have been drawn to Tristaine years ago. Your sister Sammy too, most likely. If the two of you had grown up among us, we'd have nurtured a seer's talent, and you wouldn't doubt yourself now."

Brenna stroked the cover of the journal. "I guess I'm lucky Shann doesn't see me as a sorceress, or you guys would expect me to float us back to Tristaine on a cloud."

"Shann knows women well, adanin." Jess smiled, her eyes drifting shut again. "If she's wrong about you, she's wrong. But if marking your dreams and recording our story might help us preserve Tristaine someday, is it so much to ask?"

She didn't seem to require an answer, so Brenna opened the journal and went back to scanning the few paragraphs she'd written. A shadow swam across the white page, and she flinched violently. Jess put a steadying hand on her wrist.

"Brenna, I'm sorry." Shann's gray eyes held real regret as she joined them. "I didn't mean to startle you."

Brenna pressed a hand against her pounding heart. "Why

can't Amazons learn to rustle some grass when they walk, like normal people?"

"I heard her coming ten yards back," Jess said helpfully. "Shann has enormous feet. She's hard to miss."

"True," Shann agreed. She hopped up on the fallen log and walked its length, her arms spread for balance. "Dyan despaired of teaching me stealth decades ago, Brenna. And I despaired of teaching Jesstin to cook. And lo, it came to pass that Tristaine's Amazons lived in harmony forever more."

Shann walked the log with her tongue clenched between her teeth in concentration. Strands of silver shone in her light brown hair, but at the moment, her posture and expression were almost childlike with pleasure.

Jess peered at Shann's feet. "We'll want to patch those boots before we break camp for Tristaine, lady. They're falling apart. You can't scale cliffs in those."

"Cliffs?" Brenna repeated politely. "Ah. Are there many of them between here and Tristaine? Cliffs?"

"Yes, there's one rather daunting ridge, even on the kindest route." Shann pivoted, wheeling her arms slightly for balance, then started back down the log. "But," she stepped over a small protruding branch, "I made it over alone, even with my enormous feet."

Brenna slid the thick spiral notebook back into her pack. "Jess says it'll take us about three days to hike from here to Tristaine, more or less?"

"If Gaia grants us good weather." Shann nudged Jess's dark head aside with her toe to clear her path.

Brenna was finding it impossible to hold on to the feeling of safety she'd enjoyed earlier. A sneaking cold began to creep through her, despite the sun's rays on her back. "How can we be sure Caster's not just nesting up there, waiting for us?"

"We'll scout our routes carefully on the way," Jess replied. "Once we get close to Tristaine, there'll be sentries posted at regular intervals. They'll warn us of anything waiting in the village. You're stepping on my hair, Shann," she added.

"Oops. Enough time has passed with no sign of us that Caster might consider us well and truly banished, Brenna. At least beyond the border of the County." Shann stood balanced on the log in graceful silence for a moment with her hands clasped behind her. "In any case, our home calls to us, and we need to return soon. Jesstin and Kyla and Camryn haven't known Tristaine's peace since they were captured—"

"Camryn," Brenna said.

Shann glanced down at her. "She and Kyla are hunting herbs, Blades. They'll be back soon, hopefully with enough wild onions for a—"

"C-Camryn," Brenna said again, and she laid cold fingers on Jess's arm.

Jess heard the fear in Brenna's voice and sat up.

They heard the dull, flat crack of a rifle shot, deep in the trees.

Jess was on her feet and pulling Brenna erect as Shann jumped from the log. They raced down the grassy rise toward the tree line where Camryn and Kyla had entered the forest minutes before.

Jess and Brenna ran full out, quickly leaving Shann behind. Acid coated the lining of Brenna's stomach as she snapped through the snarled greenery of the forest floor. She was acutely conscious of Jess, beside and slightly ahead of her, leaping a waist-high bank of brush without breaking stride, searching for any path through the dense trees ahead.

They heard a frenzied squealing—not just one inhuman voice, but several, a chorus of chalkboard shrieks that chilled Brenna's blood. Camryn's rifle sounded a second time, then a third.

The wild boars had lost one of their pack to Jess's arrows the day before. Brenna had been unpleasantly surprised by the dead creature's total lack of resemblance to the City's domesticated swine. It was four feet of smelly, bristled brutality, its gray tongue lolling between two deadly looking tusks in its lower jaw.

Now the rest of that wild porcine tribe were bursting through the green foliage all around her, their tusks slashing fat leaves to green slivers in their terrorized flight. Brenna dodged, narrowly avoiding one gray-black torpedo streaking toward her, and called back a sharp warning to Shann.

She heard a solid thwacking sound and an explosive grunt, and as she followed Jess through a tangled curtain of vines, she saw Camryn. The young Amazon had reversed the empty rifle in her hands and used its solid oak stock as a club against the head of the last charging boar.

The blow was powerful, but it didn't stun the huge creature entirely. It was enough however, to dissuade it from another lunge, which was fortunate since Camryn had no leverage for a second swing. Her bad leg gave out beneath her, and she sprawled onto her knees in the sparse grass, keeping a white-knuckled grip on the rifle barrel.

Jess's solid kick was enough to send the addled boar into a shuffling, grunting trot after its brothers.

Over her pounding heart, Brenna registered the trampled greenery and the high, thin squawking of birds startled out of their morning's peace. Only a few feet away, blue-winged flies had already settled on the two dead boars in the high grass.

Jess helped Kyla stand, and Brenna tried to make sense out of Kyla's stammers as Shann joined them, panting.

"They j-just attacked, lady." She was as pale as ash. "You can let go of me, Jesstin. I'm okay."

Brenna went to Cam, who struggled upright, using the rifle as a crutch. Like Kyla, she was covered with dirt and a frightening amount of blood. It took Brenna a moment to reclaim her bedside manner.

"Sit down, Camryn!" She grabbed the girl's arm just as her leg buckled again and helped her awkwardly lower herself to the grass.

"I shot him, then he jumped on me, but I'm fine." Camryn's teeth rattled like castanets, looking past Brenna to Kyla, who was staring just as wide-eyed back at her. "This is his blood on me—the pig's. It's not my blood."

"What happened, Cam?" Jess raked her fingers through her hair and willed the faintly sick aftermath of an adrenalin surge to pass. "Weren't you watching?"

"Wild boars happened, Jesstin. This isn't a City park."

Shann knelt beside Brenna and Camryn. "Blades? What do you think?"

Brenna finished her examination of Cam's trembling extremities and sat back on her heels with a nod of relief. "You're all right, Camryn. A few bruises, but nothing too serious."

"There were seven of them," Camryn told Shann. "Seven boars. I didn't even see them, lady, until they swarmed us."

She looked about twelve years old, Brenna thought. Almost as tall as Jess and a member of the same warrior's guild, Camryn, though ordinarily inscrutable, was as pale as Kyla now that the crisis had passed.

"I shot two," Camryn continued. "Ky helped me bat one off. The others ran. Jess kicked out the last one before you got here."

"Those tusks are like razors, adanin. They could have cut you both down." Jess was still angry. "You weren't on a nature hike, Camryn. We knew this pack was out here."

"And our little sisters fought them off." Shann's voice was low as well, but her gaze on Jess was more intense than Brenna had seen before. "One rifle against seven animals. They did well, Jesstin. Let it be."

"I kept distracting her, Shann." Kyla's voice was still high and breathless, and she kept her hands pressed tightly to her thighs, as if to contain herself. "We found some henbane. No fennel, but a patch of fiddleheads, lady, for your eyes. Cam, I'm s-so sorry."

"It wasn't your fault, adonai." Cam looked bleak.

"Let's get you both back to camp." Shann's tone warmed as she extended a hand to Camryn and helped her stand. "We'll make you a fine pork dinner, adanin, a fitting end to this morning's saga."

"Ah, Artemis, you guys are gonna be so pissed," Kyla whispered. Tears rose in her eyes. "I'm sorry. Don't yell, Jess."

"What are you on about, Ky?" Jess's tone was milder, but Brenna eyed the red-haired girl uneasily.

"I might as well..." Kyla sighed. "Look, I can't move my hand off my leg to walk, okay, because if I lift it—" She demonstrated by removing her palm from her thigh.

An alarming jet of blood sprayed from it, and Brenna shot to her feet.

Jess lunged and caught Kyla as she fainted.

❖

The supplies in the medical kit they had smuggled from the Clinic had been all but depleted after the clash with Caster's men. Brenna was able to form a rudimentary tourniquet, which sufficed long enough to get Kyla back to their holdings, but once there, she used the rest of their suturing thread to close the wound.

"That's the last of the sulfa, too." Brenna dropped the empty vial into the kit with fingers that were still wrinkled from repeated washing in the frigid water from a nearby stream. Her hands had been coated with blood by the time she'd gotten the wicked slice in Kyla's thigh securely closed. She looked at Shann, troubled.

"It's a bad cut, Shann. Not long, but very deep." Brenna kept her voice low, and both Jess and Shann stepped in closer to hear her. She glanced over her shoulder at Camryn, who sat by Kyla's pallet, holding her wife's hand as she rested. "I'm worried about infection. A wound like that needs a long course of antibiotics, and as of now, we're fresh out."

"What about permanent damage?" Jess asked. There were fresh lines of tension around her eyes.

"Not that I can tell." Brenna finally had good news. "I don't think any nerves were affected. She has full sensation and mobility. It's just a damn deep cut. Can we use anything out here against infection?"

"We can find herbs in the marshland just south of us that purify the blood." Shann tapped her thighs thoughtfully. "But they can be toxic, and Dyan was allergic to most of them. That doesn't mean her blood sister will have the same reaction, but we'll want to watch her closely."

"She'll need healing time before we travel." Brenna brushed Jess's arm and felt the tightness in the fine muscle. "We were planning to leave for Tristaine soon, but would a few more days do any harm?"

"It might harm Tristaine." Jess regarded Shann. "Our clan has been without their queen too long, lady."

"Ky, it doesn't matter," Camryn said behind them. They turned and caught her tender expression as she lifted her wife's hand. "Will you please stop worrying about such dreck?"

"It will." Kyla looked obstinate, one of her more characteristic features, and Brenna was relieved to see a spark of returning spunk in her wan patient. "I'm going to have a gigantic scar like a big zipper running right up my leg. And did I get it in battle? *No,* no battle wound for Kyla. Kyla had to go get herself bit by a *pig.*"

Shann settled on the grass beside the pallet, and her serene smile warmed Brenna's jangled nerves. "Don't dismiss the skills of our resident medic, little sister. Blades stitched you as carefully as a Tristainian quilt-crafter, and your zipper will hardly be noticeable."

"Thanks, Bren." Kyla summoned a smile and played with Camryn's fingers. "Hey, Cam, at least our legs have matching deformities now. Except around the storyfire, you'll brag about a bullet making your scar and a dumb *pig* making mine."

"It was a really big pig." Camryn couldn't smile. She was still as pale as Kyla.

"We'll swear it was a giant python around our storyfires if you wish, adanin." Shann's finely veined hand stroked the girl's damp brow. "She's still a bit shocky, Bren."

"I'm okay." Kyla yawned, shivering.

Brenna knelt and pulled the army blanket higher around Kyla's shoulders, then felt her hands and took her pulse at the throat. "Your color's still a little off, Ky, but your circulation's picking up, and your heart's strong and steady." She glanced at Shann. "I think those breathing exercises really helped."

Shann was revered as a healer in Tristaine, but all Brenna's City training rebelled at reliance on natural medicine. The use of wild plants as remedies was suspect enough, but guided visualizations and patterned breathing? To a certified Government medic, these techniques seemed the primitive milieu of witch doctors. But Brenna couldn't deny the benefit of Kyla's intent focus on Shann's voice earlier, when it distracted Ky from the burn and jab of the stitching needle, and her comparative comfort now.

"I was so stupid to keep yapping at you like that, Cam." Kyla's eyelashes fluttered. "If I'd just kept my mouth shut, we'd have heard them coming. If Dyan were here, she'd serve me my head on a platter. Apple in my mouth."

"I should have kept better watch, Ky." Camryn's thumb moved in repetitive circles across the back of Kyla's hand. "Dyan wouldn't blame you."

"True enough." Jess stood over them, her arms folded. "Dyan was a wise woman. She'd blame the big pig."

Brenna caught Shann's small smile at Jess. Camryn kept her gaze on Kyla's limp hand.

"Clouds moving in." Jess studied the small circle of sky above the treetops surrounding their camp. "We'll want to store some dry firewood in case those turn ugly."

She bent and rested her lips on Kyla's forehead, then straightened and disappeared into the pines.

Brenna looked after her and worried her lower lip with her teeth. It took a moment before she felt Shann's nudge.

"We could use fresh water, Blades. Would you mind a trip to the brook?"

"Sure, of course not," Brenna contradicted herself absently. "We'll let Kyla rest for a while, Camryn. You need to get cleaned up, and Shann should check you over again. Be right back."

❖

Jess chopped a dead limb from the fallen tree, wrenched its dry, stringy branches from the trunk, and tossed them onto a growing pile. The open collar of her blue shirt was damp, but the sharp blade still bit powerfully into the dry wood with each swing. She turned at Brenna's voice.

"One should not sneak up on a hatchet-wielding Amazon warrior." Brenna stood just outside the copse of aspen, her hands clasped behind her. Jess nodded, and she came closer and settled on a wide stone blanketed with moss.

Jess went back to her chopping, bits of bark dancing in the dappled sunlight of the glen.

"A pity Jode couldn't have slipped a chainsaw into our packs," Brenna observed, "before he helped us escape from the Clinic."

Jess shrugged. "Standard camping gear's all he and Pam had time to put together for us, but this'll do."

"You want to take a break when you're through here? You've been pushing pretty hard the last few days, Jesstin, and it looks like we won't be able to start for Tristaine right away."

"Amazons heal fast, and we want to be ready. We need to gather some vines that might be strong enough to rope us when we hit that ridge."

"You really think we can carry a wounded girl safely over miles of mountains? Not to mention cliffs?" Jess could hear the uncertainty in Brenna's tone. "Two women and two newly recovered warriors?"

"Five Amazons," Jess corrected. She hacked at another branch.

"I'm no Amazon, Jess."

"You weren't born one," Jess acknowledged. "But then, most of us weren't. Shann herself was born in the City. And it's miles of hills, lass, not mountains. Tristaine is remote, but there's only the one ridge to worry about."

"One's enough." Brenna was quiet for a moment. "You know, Dyan probably could have erected a fully equipped critical care unit in the time it's taken you to chop our kindling."

Jess was puzzled. "Sorry?"

"I never met Dyan of Tristaine, but I can picture her perfectly." Brenna leaned back on her hands on the sun-warmed rock. "She was seven feet tall, gorgeous, sexy, brilliant, fast, strong as ten horses—"

Jess emitted a soft bark of laughter. "Dyan was five-six, broad as a barn, freckled, and plain as dirt. Young Kyla got more than her fair share of the looks in that family. But smart, strong. Aye, Dyan was that. And more."

"I know. She was on Tristaine's high council. She led your warriors. She was Kyla's blood sister and Shann's wife. And Camryn's hero, and your best friend."

Jess straightened and lowered the hatchet to her side. She raked her damp hair out of her eyes and looked at Brenna.

"Jess, I don't mean to preach about this. But I think Camryn's back there blaming herself for what happened to Ky, because she thinks she's not living up to some standard Dyan must have set for all of—"

"Ah, Cam's beating herself up because I half-flayed her in front of her sisters." Jess grimaced and rested her foot on the log. "Dyan would have snatched me baldheaded if she heard me pop off at a scared kid like that."

"Look, that's what I mean." Brenna rested her elbows on her knees. "Dyan's memory is all around us. She's like a ghost you're afraid of disappointing."

"Bren, it's not Dyan." Jess swung one long leg over the log and sat, gingerly. "Aye, she was one of the best of us. We love her, we grieve for her, and we'll miss her forever. But no one here is trying to walk in Dyan's boots, lass. It couldn't be done."

"Okay. You're not trying to live up to some impossible standard, then." A breeze blew Brenna's hair across her forehead as she surveyed Jess clinically. "But I can swing that hatchet almost as well as you, Jesstin. And either Shann or I could have helped you carry Kyla back to our camp. So why do you insist on pushing yourself like this right now, when your back's killing you?"

Jess sighed. Hiding the occasional twinge was difficult when married to a psychic healer.

Brenna pushed herself off the rock and went to the log. She swung around and sat behind Jess on the rough bark, clasping the broad shoulders.

"I've got a passing familiarity with this body now, so even if I weren't a brilliant physician, I could tell you're hurting by the way you move."

She slid her hands beneath the thick hair and wrapped them around the base of Jess's neck, probing the dense muscle carefully.

"You don't have to do everything yourself, Jesstin. Correct me if I'm wrong, but this feels an awful lot like empty Amazon macha."

Jess didn't answer for a moment. She studied the glen, unwilling to give in to the pleasant warmth Brenna's hands were coaxing into her rigid neck. When it finally seemed reasonable to believe that no Government troops were going to leap from the trees at any moment, Jess lowered her shoulders beneath her lover's gently insistent touch.

"Aye," Jess said slowly. "Maybe it *is* Amazon macha. But it's not Dyan we're trying to live up to, adanin, me and Cam. Or not only Dyan. You called us warriors…You know what that means to us?"

Brenna's hands smoothed the planes of her upper back now. "Well, I know you and Camryn are pledged to Tristaine's warrior guild, and Dyan was your leader. That means you're part of your village's fighting force, your army?"

"We fight," Jess affirmed, shivering with the tendrils of pleasure spun by Brenna's strong fingers. It was important to her to get this right. Jess talked to Brenna as easily as she prayed to her Mothers, but the complexities of Tristaine's culture were difficult to explain. "But an Amazon warrior is more than a soldier. We protect Tristaine's women in times of peace too. We make sure they're safe. Whether the threat's a flooding river, or rabid bats, or a mad Government scientist."

"Or a charging boar," Brenna finished. Her hands stilled. "There are rabid bats in Tristaine?"

"Aye, they have their own guild." Jess grinned when Brenna tweaked her ribs. "Camryn and I, we're the only warriors here, Bren. Shann's our queen, you and Ky are both dear to us. We have to stay alert."

"Jesstin, that's sexist as hell." Brenna moved her hands lower on Jess's back. "I saw Shann put a bullet through a man's head before he could kill you, and both Kyla and I have been in Caster's talons and escaped whole, just like you and Cam. We're not delicate little—"

Her probing thumbs hit a particularly painful kink, and Jess tightened, her left shoulder rising.

"You found it," Jess pointed out.

"Sorry," Brenna murmured, smoothing the stiff muscle with the flat of her palm.

"I'm not calling any Amazon frail, Bren." Jess rose, shaking off Brenna's restraining hand. She reversed herself on the log so she sat facing her. "You're strong, and you have a brave heart. I know that. I love that."

She lifted Brenna's hand and held it, sifting through her fingers. She opened them and held her palm to her damp chest. "But this—you—are precious to me, adanin. I'd give my life to protect you. That would be true even if I'd never taken a warrior's oath." Jess searched Brenna's face. "Let me do what I think I must to keep you safe."

Brenna stared at her silently for a long moment. Then she smiled, the love in her eyes rich and tender, and cradled Jess's face in her hand. "I accept your protection. And I thank you for it. But just know this, Jesstin. When I was ten, this bully at the Youth Home pushed my sister Sammy down, twice. I broke the bitch's nose. Does that tell you anything?"

"I should always be nice to your little sister."

"Nope." Brenna skated her fingers up Jess's throat and wrapped them lightly around it. "I'll always have your back, Jesstin. In any fight, you won't need to look around for me. I'll be right beside you."

Jess covered Brenna's hand with her own and leaned in to kiss her. They were getting better at this now, with weeks of sweet practice.

Brenna's lips moved, warm and pliant beneath Jess's searching ones, then parted to admit the slow sweep of Jess's tongue. They breathed softly, drinking in each other's taste, their mouths warm and pliant.

"Yer sure you've got no use for Amazon macha now?" Jess drawled and kissed her again.

Brenna explored the planes of her face. "You're gonna tell me. . .that's who's kissing me, right? The macha Amazon?"

"Ah, no, lass." Jess skated her lips over Brenna's lifted

chin and down her taut throat. "It is indeed yer own sweet Jesstin, smoochin' you here on this log. But it's the macha Amazon warrior doin' this."

Strong hands gripped the front of Brenna's blouse and ripped it open with one yank, baring her breasts. Jess lifted her gaze from naked cleavage to blue sky and grinned. "Thank ye, Lady Gaia, for this bounty I am about to receive!"

Brenna laughed, a high, breathless sound that was equal parts surprise and pleasure. Jess shifted closer to her, and the soft fabric of her shirt warmed her bare breasts. A flush rose in Brenna's cheeks.

"I'm makin' ye blush." As always on such occasions, Jess's brogue was deep as syrup. She leaned forward slowly and Brenna leaned back.

"Maybe it's aggression you're seeing, and I'm getting ready to pop you one in the nose," Brenna suggested, leaning further back. "Hey, Camryn taught me that base-of-the-palm-to-the-nose thing. It looked real, real, painful—"

Brenna sputtered into silence as Jess employed her best time-honored technique for shutting her up. Jess's kiss grew forceful, as she bent Brenna down on the log. She covered her with her upper body, holding her down against the rough bark. Her hands found Brenna's breasts and circled them lightly, their erect nubs tickling her palms.

Jess squeaked, and Brenna lifted her head.

"My back," Jess gasped.

Brenna frowned and began to sit up. "Damn it, Jesstin, I told you—"

"All better now." Jess's grin was gamine, and her body relaxed instantly, pressing Brenna back down on the log.

"You rotten punk," Brenna snarled, slapping Jess's shoulder.

"Amazons heal fast." Jess lowered her head and continued healing.

❖

"I'm not the one who brought up pythons, Jesstin. Shann brought up pythons."

"Brenna?" Jess scanned the snarled branches overhead. "If you're eaten up by a rabid lion, or ambushed by a giant snake, I'll make Camryn suck the poisoned blood from your—"

"Blech. You and what army, Amazon?" Camryn yanked on the vine Jess pointed to and snapped it free of the branch above.

Brenna measured the coil of vines looped over her shoulder, frowning. "You really think these things are strong enough to catch an adult female in free fall? Of average height and weight?"

"We'd best stop at the canyon on the way back to camp and test them." Jess threw Camryn a bland look. "Cam, you and I are still too shaky from our battle wounds, so Brenna will have to tie these to her ankles and jump off the—"

"You're having a good time with me, aren't you?" Brenna slapped Jess's shoulder. "I'd like to see you navigate gridlock City traffic at rush hour, Jesstin."

"Blech." Jess shuddered. "I'd rather test the vines."

She began kicking a path through the high grass of the thicket, and they started back to camp. Brenna waved a hand to disperse the small winged creatures scattered by their progress. She stifled a yawn. Her dreams had been especially vivid the night before, and sleep had come in discordant snatches.

More important, though, Kyla had passed the night well. Her wound showed no sign of infection, and the pain was localized and manageable with Shann's mild herbal tea. Camryn was still quiet this morning, but that wasn't unusual. Brenna had come to recognize silence as her natural state.

"I'm not sure how we'll find Tristaine, Bren." Jess rested her rough hand on Brenna's arm and guided her around a snarl of brambles. "But if the village is quiet, we'll do what we can to get a message to Samantha in the City."

Brenna drew in a quick breath. "Hey, I'd like that, Jess. A lot."

"We'll have to be careful. They might be watching her. But we still have some people in place in the City. One of them can contact her eventually."

"Wait...and risk getting caught?" Brenna's hope dimmed. "If

Caster found out I tried to contact Sam, Jess, it would be bad for her and her husband. She's about to have a baby. I'm not sure I want to take any chances."

"I bet she'd want you to take a chance." Camryn walked a few steps behind them. "Your sister, I mean. She's probably real worried."

They stopped and waited until Cam reached them. Brenna noted she was limping slightly.

Jess's palm was gentle on the back of Camryn's wiry neck. "I think you're right, adanin. Your Lauren would want to know the truth, if it was you missing."

Camryn nodded. She'd given Brenna her only picture of Lauren for safe storage in her journal. Cam's younger sister had been lost in the same ambush that killed Dyan.

The sun was touching the western ridge by the time they reached the meadow adjoining their camp. Even in fall, the golden grass was still flush with the rich growth of high summer, and they waded through knee-high waves of it.

Brenna heard the faint screeing of some new species of grasshopper—probably carnivorous—and scanned the ground uneasily. Her ears pricked again at a new sound, a musical trilling whistle that rose from the far end of the meadow.

She looked up to see Shann, standing on a large rock near their base camp. She was too distant for Brenna to discern her expression, but her head was tilted, and she seemed to be searching the skies.

"Hey, do you guys…?" Brenna turned and saw that Camryn and Jess had stopped several yards behind her. They looked like mirrors of their elder sister, their eyes trained on the cloudless blue expanse above them. The soft screeing sounded again, and this time Brenna followed their gaze skyward.

"What is it, Jess?" Brenna frowned. "Are you hearing a plane?"

"No, a gyr."

"You're hearing a jar?" Brenna squinted.

"A gyrfalcon, Brenna," Jess answered. "It's a kind of bird."

"Thank you, Jesstin. I know a falcon is a *bird*—"

"I see her!" Camryn pointed.

Brenna tried to follow Cam's finger. She picked out the tiny silhouette before many City women could have. Her weeks in the mountains under the Amazons' tutelage had sharpened her senses.

She heard Shann's eerie musical whistle again.

At first the falcon was a tiny, dusty thread flapping against the blue bowl of sky above them. It circled, descending in lazy spirals toward the far end of the meadow. Brenna shaded her eyes and traced its path.

"Watch your footing." Jess's hand brushed Brenna's back in passing, making her jump. "The field's pocked with gopher holes, and a twisted ankle won't bring Tristaine's tidings any faster."

This cautionary lecture was lost on them all, including Jess. Brenna wasn't sure yet why they were running, but her own tension matched the sense of urgency emanating from the two Amazons. For one thing, she wasn't wild about watching a bird of prey dive-bomb the unprotected head of Tristaine's queen, who waited motionless on the distant rock.

Brenna jumped over a furrow, then caught her breath as the falcon slowed its descent. Its glossy silver wings sent up a backdraft of chill mountain air as sharp, curved talons stretched toward Shann's upraised arm. The gyr touched down with surprising gentleness, leather tethers trailing from its leg.

By the time they reached Shann, she was smoothing its breast feathers with the backs of her fingers. She spoke to it in a low, crooning tone, her eyes shining with pleasure. Brenna, ever practical, noted with relief that beneath the falcon's fierce claws, Shann's forearm was wrapped in several layers of thick denim.

"Isn't she beautiful? Her name is Talfryn, Brenna. It means 'the high end of the hills.'" Shann smiled proudly. "Look at her wingspan, Jesstin. She was just an eyas when you were taken!"

"Aye, she's lovely, Shann, really." Jess clawed her tumbling hair out of her eyes. "What does she say?"

Shann handed her a small folded paper, then gathered the bird's trailing jesses and wound them around her wrist. Jess shook open the parchment carefully and studied it. Brenna felt a stab of misgiving as a look of unpleasant surprise flitted across Jess's rugged features. She handed the tattered square to Camryn and Brenna.

The creased parchment felt like soft cloth in Brenna's hands. Red lines interlaced with black to form a twirling symbol that covered a third of the worn sheet. The drawing made no immediate sense to her. No eventual sense either, to be accurate, but something in the strong, blocky design chilled Brenna. The news wasn't good, whatever it was. She looked up to see Shann studying her face.

"Lady, we should leave for Tristaine tonight." Cam looked like she wanted to bolt.

"It's only a secondary alarm, Cam. There's no immediate danger. Jesstin? My arm's wearing out." Shann waited while Jess wound her jacket around her forearm, then transferred the large falcon to her with the ease of long practice.

Brenna still openly gawked at the bird, transfixed by its alien, prehistoric beauty. Both Shann and Jess handled the exotic creature as naturally as Brenna had once punched numbers into a cell phone.

"Blades?" Shann shook out her arm. "How soon do you think we can have Kyla ready for hard travel?"

"Wait, I need to sum up." Brenna ducked slightly as the bird flapped its wings, presumably for balance. Its talons looked wickedly sharp. "This big messenger pigeon is named Talfryn, and she was sent here from Tristaine. She somehow found us in this one little field, in the middle of a huge mountain range. And she's carrying a message in her beak from your village that says, 'Come home, there's trouble.' We don't know what kind of trouble. That's where we are, right?"

"The scroll was tied in Talfryn's jesses, but otherwise, well done." Shann smiled. "I love watching your eyes when you're learning something new, little sister. There's such life in them."

"Thank you," Brenna sighed. "And that's all the parchment says?"

"Yes, that's all this glyph tells us." Shann nodded. "Tristaine is endangered and we're needed. It's a matter of leaving a bit earlier than we hoped. We'll not be able to spare Kyla the recovery time she needs, but we can rig a pallet to carry her."

"At least," Brenna said faintly. "If we're going to be climbing mountains."

Shann's voice was working its usual calming magic on Brenna's nerves, but she thought she could detect a subtle tension in the lines of Shann's body. She couldn't read the language of her movements as easily as she read Jess's, but Brenna had learned to trust her clinical eye.

Shann turned to her second. "Jesstin? What's your counsel on the urgency of Tristaine's message?"

"We can break camp in the morning. I'll rig a stretcher for Ky tonight." Jess stared into the falcon's gold eyes, an odd smile lifting the corner of her mouth. Then she glanced around. "We make fine targets out here, sisters. Let's find some shade."

Maybe it was just an adrenaline- and falcon-fueled energy surge, but the moment Jess spoke, Brenna's upper arms prickled. She felt vulnerable in the wide expanse of the pasture, and she quickly closed ranks with the three Amazons as they moved toward the trees containing their camp.

Brenna felt Shann's hand on her arm. "How much time does Tristaine have, adanin?"

"At least a week, I think." Brenna blinked. "Wait. How much time before what?"

"It's all right, Brenna. You answered me." Shann smiled at her, then wound her arm around Camryn's waist. "Let's show Talfryn's message to your adonai, Cam."

Jess had turned to wait for Brenna several yards up the muddy path. The powerful falcon rested easily on her raised forearm, and the muscles in Jess's shoulders stood out in stark relief beneath the last red rays of the sun. The trees overhead sent dappled shadows across the strong lines of her face, and Brenna felt that small, secret muscle in her sex relax.

Brenna's City friends would say she avoided fanciful thinking, but in her eyes, Jess was rendered an engraving out of myth, gold-edged and timeless.

Jess lifted an eyebrow, and then her smile turned roguish. As her insolent gaze slid slowly down Brenna's throat to fasten on her breasts, Brenna felt her nipples stiffen and rise. She strode past Jess, muttering invectives, and they returned to the fragile safety of their camp.

CHAPTER TWO

Brenna ignored the dampness of the soaked earth seeping into the seat of her jeans. She was almost too tired to register her discomfort or do much else besides sit, slumped on the muddy hill and nodding inside her musty poncho. The rain had let up ten minutes before, but she had yet to muster the energy to push back her hood.

The incessant rain that had plagued them for three days had finally stopped, a blessing the Amazons attributed to a benevolent goddess. This was fine with Brenna. She was willing to worship anything that could turn off the maddening drizzle for a few hours.

At least she had pleasant scenery to enjoy, stupefied or not. Jess had found high ground to lay their holdings for this brief rest, out of the worst of the runoff from the storm.

Brenna sat on a moonlit hill, the ghostly globe the Amazons called Selene visible overhead as scudding wisps of cloud swam across its surface. A silvery vista of treetops lay below her, a deep gray-green blanket stretching back unbroken miles.

Brenna set the softly glowing lantern behind a stump, blocking its meager light from the valley. She took such precautions automatically now. Living among mountain women was helping her adapt to the wild through osmosis.

She lifted the edge of the heavy spiral notebook in her lap and stifled a shivering yawn. Her body was exhausted, but her nerves were stretched taut. Sleep was not impossible, but felt unlikely. When it did come, it was too filled with chaotic dreams of battling and dying horses to bring true rest. If she couldn't sleep, she might as well try to write.

Brenna glanced over her shoulder as she fumbled through the journal to the first clear page. Shann boiled some kind of root mixture over the remnants of their fire. Jess was a silent shadow several yards above their camp, sitting watch on a high rock formation that looked out over the valley. The two blanketed forms that were Camryn and Kyla were motionless, and Brenna hoped that meant they slept. Shann caught her eye and smiled as she stirred the small pot. Brenna smiled back, with more assurance than she felt, and turned back to her journal.

What we thought was a three-day hike might take twice that. The terrain we're covering isn't brutal, but carrying injured, it's treacherous and hard to navigate in this bloody downpour. At least the rain cuts down on those tiny, demon-bred, buzzing gnats that target my eyes and drive me to psychosis when the sun is out. May each and every one of them fry forever in some horrific little bug hell.

Kyla gets more and more quiet as we travel. At first, she griped about being treated like an invalid, but lately she just closes her eyes, grips the wooden poles bracketing her pallet, and hangs on. She worries me.

We trade off litter-bearing duties. Shann and I try to make sure Camryn and Jess don't push themselves too far, but there's precious little we can do to spare them. Cam's limp is pronounced at the end of a night's travel, and Jess has got to be simply worn out.

She's everywhere, laying traps to catch enough protein to keep us on our feet, hacking out trails through snarled vines, moving swiftly ahead of us to scout out our next route. The damn woman either refuses to sleep or honestly can't. It seems whenever I open my eyes I see hers, shadowed but alert, moving restlessly over the camp. Keeping watch.

We'll reach the ridge tomorrow.

This time Brenna did hear when Shann walked up behind her. She scuffed her feet with such earnest warning, Brenna had to smile. Shann spread her poncho on the wet grass beside Brenna and pointed sternly. Brenna lifted herself with an effort and sat on it as Shann lowered herself beside her.

"Oof," Shann groaned and snugged her jacket over her knees. "Sweet Artemis, when did I become an old woman?"

It seemed a rhetorical question, so Brenna grunted something sympathetic and accepted the steaming bowl Shann handed her. She sniffed it curiously.

"Arsenic root," Shann said quietly. "It'll give us enough strength to make Tristaine. But it will alter our gene structure. We'll all have testicles when we arrive." She gazed out over the valley, then looked at Brenna again and snorted with laughter. "Brenna, it's onion soup!"

"Oh." Brenna blushed again, grateful for the dark. "Sorry, Shann. But arsenic soup would be fine with me right now, if I could sit down while I drink it."

"Poor Blades." She swept her fingers gently across Brenna's forehead. "You're never one to complain, but I know how tired you must be."

"We're all pretty spent." Brenna warmed her hands around the bowl. "Kyla's hurting."

"Yes. There's not much more we can do for her tonight. Tristaine's infirmary will have stronger analgesics than we can risk in herbal remedies." Shann rested her elbows on her knees as she absorbed the moonlit view. "Though I believe we passed a patch of dynamite hallucinogenic mushrooms, about half a league back. They'll do in a pinch."

Half a league, five minutes, I'm there, Brenna thought. The prospect of fading out for a while on a gentle, drugged wave held strong appeal at the moment. She wondered if the craving for a drink would ever leave her entirely. She had made no reference to that desire in her notebook, but it still occupied her thoughts daily. She drained the bowl of fragrant soup in one swallow.

Shann regarded her for a moment. "You have questions, I think."

Brenna readjusted her stiff legs on the poncho to give herself time to focus. She realized she still looked for Caster's mind-twisting in Shann's quiet authority, and still felt a wave of disorientation when she couldn't detect it. In their weeks together, Shann often sought Brenna for private counsel and usually began their talks with that same gentle invitation.

"Yeah. Several dozen." Brenna flipped through her journal for a clean page to take notes. Then she relaxed her fingers around the pen and looked up at Shann. "Jess said something, weeks ago, about Tristaine being divided since Dyan's death. What's that about?"

"There was division even before we lost Dyan." Shann folded her hands in her lap and almost visibly ordered her thoughts. "The City has always feared us, Brenna, for the many generations of Tristaine's existence in these mountains. And now there are those among us who believe that cooperation with its Government is the only way to ensure our survival."

"Cooperation?" Brenna was puzzled. "How can anyone in Tristaine believe that? You guys scare the crap out of the Government, Shann. That's why the Military hired Caster in the first place—to wipe out Tristaine. Amazons are legendary in the City. Women keep defecting to your village in droves."

"Hardly droves." Shann smiled. "But we've had a small, steady stream of City women join us through the years. And it's our newest sisters, those who've come to us in the last decade or so, who seem most willing to trust the Government's offer of peaceful assimilation."

"They really think they'll be allowed to keep their culture intact under City rule?"

"They believe cooperating with the City is our only hope if we're to keep Tristaine intact, period." Shann's velvet voice was troubled. "Our sisters aren't evil or stupid women, Brenna, but I fear they're dangerously deluded. And one of them, Theryn, sits on our high council. Dyan's reputation was enough to keep her faction in check while she lived—"

"And now Dyan's gone." Brenna softened her voice. "You've been away from Tristaine for months. Are you afraid this Theryn is trying to take over? Is that why they sent for you?"

"The glyph Talfryn brought us means rising tensions, yes." Shann turned her mild eyes on Brenna. It seemed there was no one else in the world more worthy of the queen's respect and attention at that moment.

"This will be the Tristaine we bring you to, little sister," she continued. "I wish we could offer you the feminist utopia that was our grandmothers' dream, but Amazons have learned that finding sanctuary must always be a process, rather than an achievement. Do you understand, Blades?"

"Yeah." Brenna nodded. "I do. But I have to admit, the stories you guys tell me about Tristaine, it really does sound like some kind of paradise sometimes. Hearing that it has its problems is probably a good thing, right? It'll help me keep some perspective."

"Tristaine is a paradise, peopled by very human women." Shann smiled and covered Brenna's hand with her own. "With all the joy and angst inherent in that simple phrase."

"Ooh, I like that," Brenna murmured, scribbling neat notes in her journal. "'A-n-g-s-t.' But, yeah, Shann, I see what you're saying. I've always known we're not through with the City. Or with Caster. And I realize I might not be universally welcome in Tristaine. Don't worry. I never sugarcoat my prospects. I know what to expect."

"You've had to, I imagine." Shann studied her silently for a moment. "What's going to happen in Tristaine in three days, Blades?"

Brenna looked up at her, puzzled, then closed her journal with a rueful sigh. "Shann, I don't know why I said anything about a timeline. I didn't even realize you were asking me about the village."

"And you didn't know what was happening to Camryn before the boars attacked, only that she was in danger." Brenna grimaced, and Shann smiled at her. "Don't try to force it, adanin. Our Grandmothers are slow to share their secrets."

"I'm sorry, Shann, but your Grandmothers, being dead for umpteen generations—"

"Shann, Brenna?"

They both turned as Jess's low voice reached them. They couldn't see her, crouched as she was on the rock overhang above the camp, until she moved. Brenna followed her raised arm to the blankets where Camryn and Kyla lay. Camryn had lifted herself on an elbow and bent over her partner.

"Help an old lady." Shann took Brenna's arm.

Brenna's own knees creaked as they hurried toward the small fire that still burned near their bedrolls.

"She hasn't slept." Concern roughened Camryn's voice and emerged as irritation. "I've been trying to keep her covered, lady, but she's—"

"Been changing my own diapers for years now," Kyla cut in and tugged the blanket from Camryn's grip. "I'm fine, people. You can stop hovering over me like wasps every time I twitch."

"Manners, little sister." Shann knelt beside Kyla. "Can we blame your foul mood on the pain in your leg?"

"Oh, Shann, I'm two days from my moons," Kyla grumbled, "and that's as close to an apology as you'll get from me. Bloody hell!"

Shann's eyes darkened as Kyla's hand tightened in her own, and Camryn stroked Kyla's hair until the spasm passed. Brenna managed a sympathetic smile for Cam. She knew all too well the helplessness she had to be feeling.

"We scale the ridge tomorrow, lady." In the shifting firelight, Camryn looked as if she'd aged ten years. "Do you think Ky can make it?"

"I'll be riding in that sling thing," Kyla mumbled.

"Blades?" Shann looked at Brenna. "Your thoughts?"

Brenna hoped the tsunami that roared through her stomach at the thought of the climb ahead didn't sway her clinical judgment. Another look at Kyla's ashen features convinced her. "Ky, you're hurting a lot as it is, and you haven't slept well. We might want to talk about taking just one day here to rest."

A stubborn line formed between Kyla's brows in a way Brenna now recognized as reminiscent of her blood sister Dyan.

"I'm crazy to get home too, adonai." Camryn cradled Kyla's free hand in her own. "But if Shann and Brenna both think we—"

"Look, I should get to decide this!" Kyla clenched her wife's hand with sudden strength. "I haven't seen Tristaine in half a season. I miss my sisters. And my dog. And if we can get there by the full moon, we'll be in time for the Festival of Thesmophoria, and I'll get to sing the Challenge, rather than that tone-deaf, immature, lame little toad *Deidre*. So *shut it*, Camryn. We're going home!"

Brenna blinked. Shann looked up at Jess, who stood over them with crossed arms, one shoulder braced against an aged cedar. Jess shrugged.

"We're decided then," Shann said pleasantly. She tucked the blankets around Kyla again. "If you rest tonight, Kyla, we'll face the ridge tomorrow. And the night after, we'll warm our feet at Tristaine's hearth."

She leaned forward and kissed Kyla's forehead, then laid a hand on Camryn's bony wrist. "Try to sleep, adanin. That means you too, Brenna, and take Jesstin with you. I have first watch."

❖

Brenna lay still while Shann finished feeding the small fire that warmed their circle. She tied her cloak around her shoulders and settled again on a moss-shrouded stone to begin her watch.

Brenna turned onto her back and scanned the star-spangled sky overhead. She could now pick out the Seven Sisters easily. Tristaine believed that particular star field composed the small campfires of the clan's seven founders, the women who first carved a crude camp above the City seven generations ago. Their names ticked through her mind like music: Kimba, Jade, Beatrice, Julia, Constance, Wai Yau, Killian.

According to Shann, the star representing Julia's campfire guided her, Tristaine's first—and only—seer and prophet. *I'll follow any star that gets us up that ridge tomorrow*, Brenna promised silently, not realizing she was praying. *If that star can wipe out a few zillion of those gnats, that's gravy on the meat loaf.*

She looked across the camp and studied Shann's austere beauty in the moonlight, made more poignant by the lines of grief that bracketed her mouth. She was studying the colorful glyph etched on her wrist, which identified her as an Amazon queen. Along with the design, the symbol of royalty, Shann's glyph consisted of the figures of three women—Amazons, presumably—and her fingers moved slowly over them now.

Not for the first time, Brenna wondered at the emotional burden carried by the leader and guardian of an endangered tribe of warrior women. One who had recently lost her own adonai—her wife and closest adviser—to violent death.

Brenna clasped Jess's forearm, which rested lightly beneath her breasts. She turned on her side, and Jess stirred and moved closer, warming her back.

"Ye haven't relaxed since ye were five," Jess teased in a sleep-thickened voice that turned her brogue to malt.

"I'm sorry, Jesstin," Brenna whispered, stroking the muscled arm holding her. "I finally got you to sleep. Don't let me undo my own good work."

Jess let the soft slide of Brenna's palm on her skin coax her awake. She breathed in the light scent of her lover's hair and rubbed her tense shoulder.

"You're tight as wire, Bren." Jess worked her left hand gently between Brenna's thighs. "How do City girls unwind after a long day?"

"Uh, not that way." Brenna grinned, then tapped Jess's arm. "Hey, listen. Kyla's snoring. Good. At least she's sleeping deeply enough to…Jesstin?"

"Darlin'?" Jess slid one leg over Brenna's and laid her arm beneath her breasts to hold her in place. Her fingers had moved beneath the waistband of Brenna's pants and softly stroked the furred mound between her legs.

"Jesssss." Brenna squirmed. "Excuse the hell out of me, but this is *not* the way to relax me, all right?"

"You're wrong, lass." Jess's breath brushed warmly across the side of her neck. "This works every time. It's an old Amazon remedy for easing tension and summoning pleasant dreams." Brenna could feel faint tremors coursing down her back.

She suppressed a gasp as the long fingers slid home, gliding among her suddenly liquid folds with insolent confidence. Her spine wanted to melt, but she was acutely aware that they were not alone. "Jess! We're at a *slumber party* here!"

"We're going home, my Brenna." Jess's voice and fingers stroked her skillfully, patiently, in a pattern proven to reduce her to shivering fragments. "In Tristaine, you and I will have a lodge of our own at last, and privacy. But we'll not do anything, then or now, that would shame us to have our sisters hear."

"Damn it, Jess, you know I can't—" Brenna bit her lip and tried to slow her breathing. "I can't just...whoa...do this quietly... this is the second time you've—"

"Shhhh, Bren, aye, you can be quiet, if I ask it," Jess whispered as her fingers moved faster now, with a tighter urgency. "Silent as a breeze..."

Brenna crested hard, and Jess was damnably right; the effort to keep silent only prolonged her pleasure. She timed Brenna sweetly and well, stroking her down slowly from shuddering climax to liquid peace.

Jess chuckled, gloating, and Brenna nudged her with a reproving elbow. She woofed into her soft hair. "Are you worried about tomorrow's ridge, lass?"

"Nope," Brenna sighed, melting back against Jess at last. "Piece of cake...sleep, Jess, now."

"Yes'm."

Across the camp, Shann smiled up at her seven Grandmothers, as tears traced the lines of her face.

❖

"Did you get hit?"

There was gruff concern in Camryn's tone, and Brenna made herself lower her hand from her eyes. "No, Camryn, I'm fine."

"Don't look down unless you have to," Cam advised her again.

"It's not looking down that gets me, at the moment."

Jess's ascent was kicking down enough small gravel to warrant proper eye protection for the women waiting on the ledge below. But apparently basic Amazon climbing gear did not include safety goggles. Or anything even faintly resembling a net.

They had one nylon rope they had smuggled out of the City, and Shann had brought another from Tristaine, made of some tough, sinewy fiber that seemed equally durable. But this high off the forest floor, Brenna found the twined vines that made up the rest of their suspension anchors woefully inadequate. She shaded her eyes to look up at Jess, then covered them again in spite of herself.

"She's climbing well, Blades." Shann patted her arm reassuringly. "Jesstin grew up in these mountains. She scaled heights like this when she was just a—whoops."

"What?" Brenna cried.

"Nothing," Shann said, steadying her quickly. "That outcropping there juts out too far to manage Kyla's sling, that's all. Jesstin's marking the second route for us."

Brenna looked for herself. She appreciated Shann's kindness, but refused to take comfort in anything she said. After all, it was Shann who had referred to this harrowing cliff as "a bit daunting." She peered skyward through her spiky bangs and sighted Jess again, working her way steadily toward the crest. Her movements were smooth and unhurried as she passed from one hold to the next.

Jess was climbing unanchored, laying rope and vine for the rest of them to use as she went. The lines would offer marginal security as they moved up the rock face, but if Jess slipped, nothing would stop her from plummeting down to the granite ledge where they waited, or beyond it to the valley below.

"She'll be fine, Bren." At Brenna's feet, Kyla managed a wan smile. Camryn tied off the last of the vines that would secure the makeshift sling designed to carry her over this treacherous stretch. "Jess is half mountain goat."

"More than that," Camryn muttered.

Brenna crouched cautiously on the narrow ledge and helped Camryn slide Kyla's bandaged leg into the folded blankets that comprised the sling. It was a clever contraption, strong enough to bear her weight, but leaving her uninjured leg free so she could distance herself from the rock.

"I wouldn't mind hitching a ride in this thing myself." Brenna eyed the sling with some envy as she checked the dressings on Kyla's thigh.

"It's how we carry babies and little kids," Kyla grumbled.

"And injured, sulking Amazons," Shann added. "Look, adanin." She pointed to a dizzyingly high spot up the cliff. "Our goat has triumphed."

Brenna craned her neck and saw Jess rise to her feet at the top of the ledge and slap dirt off her legs with her hands. She rested her fists on her hips and stood still a moment, scanning the forest below.

The goddesses who guarded Tristaine had granted them fair weather for the climb, which made Brenna weak-kneed with gratitude. She couldn't imagine scaling all this loose rock in a downpour. She tried to focus on anything other than imminent death and concentrated instead on the goal. She would glory in the sunshine and the soul-satisfying view that Jess, after her months of captivity, was sure to be soaking up at the crest.

"Blades." Shann laid a hand on her shoulder, and Brenna rose carefully.

"I'll get started." Shann steadied herself against the rock and looked down at Brenna, her eyes warm. "You're strong and agile, little sister. You'll be fine."

"I will be," Brenna confirmed, "if no queens fall on my head." She smiled up at Shann with more bravery than she felt.

"I'll swan dive past you, I promise." Shann bent and kissed her cheek, then gripped the nylon rope. She pulled herself up to the first long shelf that marked the route Jess had set for the climb. "Camryn, Kyla, move with care, please," she called over her shoulder.

"Lady," they chorused in assent, and all watched Shann's progress closely.

The order they ascended made sense to Brenna, at least after Jess had explained it. The strongest climber, Jess, went first to set anchoring points and chart the safest route to the crest. Shann climbed second to help guide Kyla's sling up the rock, while Brenna and Camryn shared Kyla's weight with Jess, who pulled the vines that raised the sling up the cliff's face.

"We're set." Camryn leaned in and kissed Kyla solemnly. She and Brenna would have to climb evenly up the rise to keep Kyla level. Jess had prioritized that necessity as she marked their path.

"Hokay," Brenna said to the stone wall before her. "I could be filling in requisition forms for Caster right now." That perspective helped her begin.

At first the climb was not the wet-palmed horror she feared it would be. Shann was right. She was up to this. Brenna had been an athlete even in the City, and long weeks without alcohol, with regular workouts and fresh air, had strengthened her. She moved slowly up the steep grade, finding holds where her hands and feet expected them, keeping her center of gravity in easy balance. She and Camryn watched each other carefully, glancing down to monitor Kyla's progress.

"Slowly, sisters." Jess's faint, low voice sounded above them like a benediction from one of the Seven. "This isn't a race."

"Watch the patch of loose shale here, Cam," Shann called down, panting a little as she lifted herself to the next hold. Camryn whistled acknowledgment.

Kyla was weathering the climb well. She used her free leg to kick off from the rock face, but otherwise moved as little as possible to keep the sling steady. Brenna heard a lilting melody below her as she pulled herself, gasping, over a snarl of roots.

"Oh, great, Ky's being funny." Camryn's breath was coming a bit harder too. "That's an old Amazon love chant she's singing. The words are 'don't let me go.'"

"Amazons have love chants?" Brenna squinted dust out of her eyes and peered upward for her next hold. She could see Jess, taking in line carefully as Shann eased herself around a tangle of brush. She and Camryn were better than halfway up the cliff's face, and she was beginning to believe she would live to see the sun set. "The

City has Reproduction Clinics. I think Tristaine is more romantic."

"We have reproduction clinics too," Kyla piped up, "but I bet they're a hell of a lot more fun than the City's."

"Save your breath down there!" Jess called.

A gritty scrambling of stone drowned out her voice, then Shann's sounded, sharp and clear. "Rock!"

Luckily for Brenna the instinctive thing was also the only thing she could do. Her forearm shot up over her head, and she braced herself against the cliff's face, making herself as small a target as possible.

Shann's foot had struck a loose shelf of shale, which broke off and hurtled toward them in dangerous chunks. For a moment, all Brenna heard was the impact of stone ricocheting off rock, and she hissed in fear for Kyla, swinging unprotected below them. An ugly thud and a muffled cry reached her scant moments later, and her eyes flew open to see Camryn reeling against her line, a hand pressed to her head and blood welling between her fingers.

"Shann!" Jess called.

"I'm secure, Jess!" Shann answered immediately, breathless but anchored again to the cliff wall.

"Brenna, Cam?"

Jess was answered when Camryn's line went slack and she sagged senseless in the halter securing her to the guide rope. Brenna lunged to the side and reached for her, but couldn't span the distance between them without losing her hold and snarling the rope that held the sling.

"Brenna, stay there!"

She heard Jess's shout through the tympani of her heart in her ears and craned her neck to search for Kyla.

"I'm okay, Bren!" Kyla had been able to shift her body so that most of her weight was taken from Camryn's line. Brenna felt the increased pull in her arms and legs.

"Cam, you talk to me!" Jess barked.

Camryn spun in a slow half circle, her hands trailing limply. A thin line of blood wended its way down her face.

"She's unconscious!" Brenna called to the group at large. She clenched both rock and line so tightly that the tendons in her wrists stood out like wires.

"It's all right, Bren. I've got her." Jess stood braced on the lip of the ridge, the nylon rope secured around a stone pillar. "You're tied off, all of you. Now keep your heads! Shann! Lady, can you reach me without my help?"

"I can, Jesstin."

"Then come." Jess gripped the rope and the woven vines that secured the sling.

"Brenna? Shann and I will help you lift Kyla and Cam. Camryn will be dead weight, but the harness will hold her," Jess called down in a clear, even voice. "Do you understand?"

"Maybe we could just c-camp here?" Brenna didn't even know if she was kidding. The ridge had changed from a benevolent challenge to a deadly trap in seconds, and she couldn't catch her breath.

"Jess." Brenna's voice shook. "Tell me what to do!"

"Brenna, lass, go easy."

Brenna looked up to see Shann lift herself safely over the edge of the cliff, then roll quickly to her feet. Jess was well braced and held most of Camryn's weight off the main line.

"We've done rescue lifts like this. Those knots are made to hold! You just need to keep climbing, adanin."

She tried. With every straining sinew and ounce of courage at her command, Brenna ordered herself to scale the rock. She forced her gaze away from Camryn's still form and found a sturdy ledge within reach. She heaved herself up to it, grunting with effort. The vines creaked alarmingly in her ears, and she looked down to check on Kyla.

"Good, Bren," Kyla's voice trembled, "don't worry about me. I'm fine down here."

Brenna's eyes locked on the yawning space that separated them from the forest floor. She felt as if the rock itself exhaled, breathing out against her in a cold, implacable wind to force her off its face. She gasped raggedly and clenched the rock in a spasm of fear.

"Brenna, Jesstin will help you lift," Shann called down, somehow her voice both calm and commanding as she laced the rope around the pillar. "Carefully, now," she cautioned.

Jess can't lift all three of us, part of Brenna's mind tried to reason through the chaos. *Shann's securing the slack in the line to brace us, Jess is taking half of Kyla's weight and most of Camryn's. I have to help her. I can do this. I'm strong enough. If I can just stay balanced. . .and let go of this bloody rock.*

"So, I must rescue your skinny butt *again*, Stumpy."

Brenna wouldn't have thought anything could penetrate her paralysis, but the strange voice that floated to her ears made her jerk in shock. She looked around wildly.

"Vicar, sweet Mothers!" Shann's tone was rich with relief. "Can you reach them?"

"On my way, lady," that new voice responded

Brenna watched a tall form rappel down rapidly toward them from the top of the ridge. She shaded her eyes as gravel clattered in her wake and tried to bring her breath under control.

"Yahoo! It's Vicar!" Kyla cried as she braced herself carefully against the rock with her hands. "She's one of us, Brenna. Vic is *so* cool!"

"Brace Camryn, Vicar," Jess called.

Brenna's jaw hung slack as a tall, muscular woman landed lightly on the rock beside her.

"Who're you?" the woman asked bluntly. Her *r*'s carried the same light brogue that flavored Jess's speech, and she was of similar build. However, Vicar's coloring was different. Intense brown eyes drilled into Brenna's, beneath a tousled mop of blonde hair.

"That's Brenna, Vic. She's adanin." Kyla's voice had begun to sound thin and reedy. "See about Cam. She looks really hurt."

"Aye, little sister." Vic gathered herself and pushed off the rock's surface, and Brenna felt a sick moment of vertigo until the line caught and curved Vic's flight. She swung past Kyla, then pulled herself up beside Camryn.

"Whoa, youngster, that's a wicked bump!" Vicar said. "All right, Jesstin, I've got her!"

"Hakan is here too, Kyla." Shann's voice reached Brenna. "The three of us can pull you up with Vicar's help. Brenna, are you ready?"

Brenna felt the sudden shift in her harness when Vicar took on most of Camryn's weight and balanced the sling carrying Kyla. Her body suddenly made sense to her again. She understood the amount of energy needed to move it, and the mountain no longer seemed to want to shrug her off its surface.

"We'll take it slow and steady," Jess called from above. Brenna looked up briefly to see her flanked by Shann and a third woman in dark clothing. All three of them held lines.

The climbers rose in gradual stages. Brenna moved methodically, trying to tamp down the demon of panic that still threatened to break free in her chest. The Amazon called Vicar climbed with ease beside her, even with Camryn slung over one broad shoulder.

Brenna got close enough to see Jess's face, and that both helped and hindered. The encouragement she saw in those cobalt eyes strengthened her, but her lover's pallor reminded Brenna of how narrowly they had skirted disaster.

Shann eased herself under the line and knelt on the ledge to help Vicar lift Camryn over the ledge. "Thank you, adanin!"

"She's coming to." Vicar clambered up and knelt by Shann. "I could hear her mutterin'. Are you all right, lady?"

"I am now, Vic." Shann spared her warrior a warm smile and clasped her hand. "Gaia's blessings on you and Hakan for your damn fine timing."

Jess pulled Brenna over the lip of the ridge. She felt Jess's strong arm slide around her waist, and she leaned against Jess for a moment before they finished lifting Kyla to safety.

Shann checked Camryn's eyes and probed the back of her skull. "Brenna, can you see to Kyla?"

"Sure," Brenna panted, as she fervently hoped blood would start to circulate in her fingers again soon, so she could feel the straps of Kyla's sling. The hammering of her pulse had finally started to quiet now that three feet of solid ground separated her from the ledge.

"Is she awake?" Kyla, too, was pale again, and her hands trembled badly as she fumbled with her straps.

"Getting there," Shann murmured, "here she comes."

Camryn grimaced then blinked. "B-Banshee bile," she stammered. "What hit me?"

"Your queen," Shann sighed. "Camryn, I'm terribly sorry. It was all my fault."

"Camryn, you idiot!" Kyla's tone was sharp despite her ashen complexion. "You could have ducked! You scared the crap out of me! Are you all right?"

"Stop shrieking at me, Ky. I'm fine," Cam mumbled and felt along her scalp gingerly. She blinked at the woman who supported her, then grinned. "Hey, Vicar!"

"Hey, bean sprout." The big warrior cupped Camryn's neck gently. "Don't you budge now till Shann gives the word."

"That small cut's already closing, but we'll watch you for concussion, little sister." Shann tilted Camryn's head carefully. "I want you to tell me if you feel dizzy or nauseous, or if your head—"

"Ah, Shann, up it comes." Cam groaned and leaned over Vicar, retching.

Vicar braced Camryn carefully until Cam started chuckling into her lap. Then she snorted laughter too and eased her upright again. "I see a season in a City Prison hasn't taught this brash little dyke any manners, lady!"

"I'd say throwing up on you is a pretty reasonable reaction, mate." Jess stood smiling down at them, winding the nylon rope into a neat coil.

The lines in Vicar's forehead relaxed. She got to her feet, and Brenna's jaw dropped again. There was definite filial resemblance between Jess and Vicar, but the blond Amazon towered over Jess's very tall form by a good three inches.

"You look well, Stumpy." Vicar took Jess's shoulders and appraised her keenly. "We've been worried about you."

"Warriors are masters of understatement," Kyla observed, and Brenna smiled at her.

"Nice save, Vic." Jess's eyes brimmed with tears. "My thanks, adanin."

The two warriors embraced, briefly but hard. Brenna was still amazed at how easily Amazons touched each other and the amount of love evident even in such fleeting contact.

"One or both of them are leaking, I take it?"

Brenna squealed in surprise and jumped a foot sideways when the low voice sounded behind her. The prodigiously muscled black woman called Hakan smiled at her politely.

"Poor Blades!" Shann laughed from her place beside Camryn. "We can't seem to stop sneaking up behind her. Brenna, meet Hakan."

Not especially tall, Hakan looked as if she could snap an aspen with her teeth. Like Vicar, she was dressed in warm, close-fitting furs, an ensemble unheard of in the City. She wore her glyph, an intricate twirling of silver lines that looked almost like a web, high on top of one cheek.

"Jesstin tears up easily," Hakan explained, extending sculpted fingers toward Brenna.

"She does," Brenna agreed as she shook the callused hand. "Thank you, H-Hakan, for your help."

"Did one of our gyrfalcons reach you, lady?" Vicar crouched beside Shann. "We sent all four by different winds."

"Yes, Vicar. Talfryn brought us the council's alarm."

"And the elders sent the two of you to find us?" Jess asked.

"Aye, Jess." Vicar nodded at Hakan. "We're one of three patrols the elders charged to track you down. We figured the southern meadow was our best bet." She grinned at Kyla. "We heard this youngster's sweet singing and swashbuckled over in the nick."

"Can our injured travel, lady?" Hakan asked. "Can we make for the village?"

"With all *prudent* speed, yes," Shann said before Kyla or Camryn could speak. "Tell us, adanin, what's happening in Tristaine?"

"Our source in the City says the Feds are about to move," Vic said quietly. "We can expect attack before snowfall."

Brenna saw a bleak look pass between Shann and Jess.

"We're preparing for migration, then?" Shann asked.

"Yes, Shann." Hakan's eyes on her queen were compassionate. "We await your order to evacuate the village."

❖

Except for the bite of cold in the air, Brenna was experiencing an odd déjà vu. A quiet stream of Amazons, moving with purpose through mountain splendor under a darkening sky toward an uncertain fate. Traveling with Jess and Camryn and Kyla after their escape from the Clinic had held this same element of anticipation and foreboding.

Shann walked beside Camryn, keeping an eye on her throughout the long night's passage. Jess and Vicar followed them, carrying Kyla's pallet. Hakan led their party through the high hills toward Tristaine, and Brenna figured she was paired with her for her own protection.

She still flushed with shame when she thought of the ridge. What if help hadn't arrived just in time, in the warrior-ex-machinae forms of Hakan and Vicar? Would she still be there, frozen to the cliff's face in a rictus of fear, useless and worse in her first true test before the women of Tristaine? None of them had blamed her for her paralysis, or even mentioned it, but without much effort, she could imagine scorn emanating from the silent warrior beside her.

Brenna shook herself mentally. There was self-examination and there was self-pity, and she was wandering perilously close to the latter. She made herself focus on her surroundings, the cricket-laden twilight and the path through the pass ahead.

She cleared her throat. "Do you need quiet, Hakan, to concentrate on the trail?"

"Not here." Hakan spoke for the first time in miles. "Closer to the pass, we'll need to watch for patrols."

"Patrols?" Brenna swallowed. "Patrols from the City or Tristaine?"

"Both," Hakan replied.

They walked quietly for a while.

"Hakan," Brenna said, "may I ask why you—"

"My line was born on another continent," Hakan broke in, "generations before my family migrated to the City. You'll see women of many colors in Tristaine."

"Actually, I was going to ask about your glyph, not your race." Brenna smiled. "But thank you for telling me. I've seen pictures of black people," she added. "There's a black neighborhood in the City, but I admit I haven't—"

"Black citizens are limited to their own borough." Hakan's voice was toneless.

"Yes." Brenna looked at her rugged profile. "I realize I won't get a grip on everyone's history until I live in Tristaine a while. Shann's tried to tell me about everyone's origins, but it gets confusing. Why Vicar and Jess speak with a brogue and no one else does, for instance, and who in Tristaine is really descended from ancient Amazons, from which continent, and how women who come from the City become Amazons. . ."

Brenna realized she'd begun to wave her hands, and she smiled shyly at Hakan and folded her arms. "You're from the City yourself?"

"I am. My mother brought me to Tristaine fifteen years ago, but I was raised in the Black Borough."

"Did you feel welcome when you came to the village?"

"After a time. Beginning a new life can be difficult." Hakan's boots were soundless on the uneven, rocky ground. "When I first came to Tristaine, I tried to earn my place by riding one of the clan's renegade stallions. I ended up on my back in the dirt with this huge brute lunging over me."

Brenna tried to smile. "Please tell me this isn't one of Tristaine's initiation rites. What happened?"

"I froze." Hakan chuckled ruefully. "Couldn't have moved if Gaia herself commanded it! Then your Jesstin jumped in and distracted the beast, while Dyan dragged me out of the arena. It was the first time I owed my life to them. Far from the last."

Brenna pressed her folded arms around a pleasant warmth in her chest. "Yeah, Jess can make quite an impression." She paused. "Thanks, Hakan."

"For?"

"Your story. You saw me freeze on the ridge. You know I've been there."

"And now you know I have." Hakan shrugged her broad shoulders. "As Shann says, Brenna, if we had no personal demons to battle, we would not need sisters. Shann was raised in the City too, by the way. Amazons are Amazons, wherever they're bred."

"That's true, isn't it? I'd forgotten Shann was City-born."

"And glad she was to shake its dust from her feet," Shann said behind them. She turned and called over her shoulder. "Jesstin, Vicar? Bring our wounded songstress so she can see her village."

Brenna had been so engrossed in her conversation with Hakan, she had missed the sense of anticipation rising in the Amazons as they approached the pass. Jess helped Kyla stand, then lifted her easily into her arms. The seven women moved through the lush undergrowth toward the low rise that dipped through the mountain range.

For a moment, Brenna feared another attack of vertigo, but the descending trail sloped in a gentle grade to the heavily wooded valley below. She came to a sudden stop, struck by the beauty of the moon rising over the shadowed pocket in the earth. Her gaze skated across the night sky, over constellations the Amazons held sacred, then down into the valley. In the midst of the trees, Brenna saw a gathering of fireflies—softly twinkling lights that might have been those stars fallen to earth.

The campfires of Tristaine.

Jess had stared out barred windows many sleepless City nights. The smog-shrouded lights of the City milked the stars of much of their brilliance, but Jess drew comfort knowing they sparkled brightly over her Amazon village. She hadn't believed she would live to see these campfires again.

Jess sighed and heard Kyla echo her softly from her place in Jess's arms.

Brenna felt the solid warmth of Jess's shoulder against her and leaned into it, sliding her arm around her waist. "Welcome home, Jesstin," she whispered.

Tears coursed down the angular planes of Jess's face. Brenna started to catch them, but she let them fall. *Tears shed in grief need comforting*, she thought, *but not these*. Brenna heard the words in her mind in Shann's voice and turned to see her smiling at them.

❖

"We'd best signal, Hakan."

They were nearing the outer periphery of Tristaine's patrol area. Jess was enforcing a deliberately sedate pace as their party neared the village, but it took all her will to sustain it. Home was tantalizingly close, and Jess hungered to feel Amazon ground beneath her feet again.

"They won't hear us for another half-league, Jesstin," Hakan said. "Theryn moved the outer watch closer to our gates."

"Did she now." Jess smiled sourly and felt Brenna press her hand. She met her inquiring look and shook her head slightly.

The music reached them long before Hakan finally paused to signal Tristaine's sentries with a complex series of whistled notes. They gathered in a close group and waited, and soft woodwind melodies trickled to them faintly through the trees.

"Hey. Hey!" Kyla sat up on her pallet, grinning hugely. "Cam, listen! It's the festival. We didn't miss it!"

"Ah, very cool!" Camryn brightened. She admitted to a killing headache, but otherwise seemed none the worse for the ridge. "Ky, you can still sing the Challenge at midnight!"

"Damn straight."

Shann winked at Jess and slid an arm around Brenna's shoulders. "I'm glad for you, Blades. You'll get to see us at our best, before our migration begins. It's the Festival of Thesmophoria. We celebrate it each fall to give thanks for our orchard's harvest."

"Partying Amazons." Brenna grinned at Jess and endless possibilities.

"Stand down, sisters." Shann was looking past them.

Jess saw Brenna whirl and brace for an army of ax-wielding warriors sneaking up behind them.

There were just two, and they carried bows.

"Sweet Gaia, it's good to see you safe, lady!" A dark-haired woman with a scarred face reached them first and went directly to Shann. She could have been twenty or fifty, and there was genuine affection in her brown eyes as she embraced her queen.

"I've missed you, Myrine." Shann released her and nodded at the other Amazon. "Hello, Patana."

"Lady," said the second sentry. She was young and heavily muscled and wore her hair clipped so short it was difficult to discern the color. She jutted a strong chin in Kyla's direction. "What's up with the young one?"

"Kyla's leg is injured, but she's healing well."

"Good." Patana's small eyes shifted and returned Brenna's gaze. "Who's this?"

Jess stepped up behind Brenna. "My adanin, Patana, and therefore yours. Her name is Brenna."

Brenna offered Patana a neutral smile, and Jess was aware of Patana's gaze on her breasts.

"Welcome, Brenna." Myrine clasped her hand, and then the dimple in her cheek deepened as she turned to Jess. "Demon's blood, Jesstin, who let you out? We send the City our ugliest Amazon, and they ship her back to us more dog-scarin' homely than ever."

"Still short, too," Vicar deadpanned from the rear of the group.

Jess felt her smile warm considerably as she drew Myrine into a backslapping embrace. "Thank you, Artemis," she intoned. "I'm truly home. Back to the daily abuse that is my birthright."

The hands of Jess's old friend were gentle on her back. Myrine kissed her shoulder before shrugging her off. She shouldered her bow again, a recurve hewn from cedar, beautiful in its simplicity.

"Your homecoming will brighten a sad Festival, sisters," Myrine said. "You can expect a grand welcome."

"My-rine, are you gonna come here and fawn over me, or what?" Kyla whined, levering herself upright on Camryn's arm. "Look. A pig bit me!"

Myrine's face lit again, and she jogged over to greet Kyla and Camryn.

"We'll see you in, Shann." Patana gestured toward a path into the trees.

"It's all right, Patana," Jess said. "We know the way. Wait here for the night watch to relieve you, and join us after—"

"Come on, Jesstin, the mountain's quiet." Patana slapped Jess's shoulder, and Shann winced. "The City's not going to ambush Tristaine in the hour before night watch gets here. Hey, I hear you've got some wicked wrestling holds! What say we try them out tonight when the matches begin?"

Jess turned back slowly and measured Patana's grinning face through a filter of memories that was less than kind. An intelligent woman and an able fighter, Patana had always struck her as a braggart and a bully. Dyan told her she'd been pressured to name Patana her second, an honor that had gone to Jess.

"A match sounds good," Jess replied. "Later. For now, Patana, stay here until you're relieved. This isn't the time to get lax on security."

It was quiet for a moment, except for the distant music from Tristaine.

"Guess you're the boss again, Jesstin." Still smiling, Patana rested her shoulder against a tree. "Theryn will be glad to have your support. Sure, 'Rine and I will hang here for a while. I'll look forward to those matches," she added.

"We'll save you some cider, Patana." Shann stepped smoothly between her two warriors and called back to Vicar and Hakan. "We ready back there?"

"Yes'm," Vicar called as they lifted Kyla's pallet.

Shann looked up sternly at Jess for a moment. Jess shrugged. Shann sighed and raised herself on her toes to kiss her cheek. "Let's go home."

The trees were thinning now. The full moon hung low over the valley, filling it with a ghostly blue glow. They began to see light through the trees, the warm flickering gold of torches and small bonfires, and the music grew louder.

Jess heard a murmuring beneath the melody, a subterranean rustle of many voices. An isolated bark of laughter rose, then the piping music drowned it out. It did seem a subdued Festival at best.

Shann touched Brenna's arm as she passed her. Vicar and Hakan followed, carrying Kyla, who reached out and grabbed Brenna's hand.

"C'mon, City girl." Kyla's wan cheeks were filling with color. "You're about to meet more hot women than you've ever seen in one place in your whole deprived life!"

Brenna laughed weakly and shook her fingers free before Kyla could pull her any farther.

Jess paused and had a private word with Camryn. Cam's eyes were stormy, but she nodded, then dipped Brenna a shy smile as she jogged after Kyla and her entourage.

Brenna studied Jess. "Everything okay?"

"Aye, it is. Just passing on some of Dyan's advice." She opened her arms, and Brenna stepped into them. "It's a cold night, adanin. You're shaking."

"Just stage fright." Brenna scrubbed her cold cheek against Jess's chest. "Are you sure we can't just camp here for the night?"

"We can." Jess regarded her seriously. "I'll stay here with you, Bren. If this would be easier in the morning—"

"Jesstin." Brenna lifted her head. "For a butch warrior, you can be flat-out kind sometimes, you know that?" She straightened in Jess's arms. "I'll be fine. Half of this is excitement, anyhow. I just hope the other half doesn't throw up on anyone."

"If it comes to that, aim for Vicar." Jess grinned, but then nestled Brenna's face in her rough palms. "I know you're scared, querida. I understand. And I wish I could promise you all will be well with Tristaine. Not just tonight, but forever. We can't know what these next days will bring. I'll promise you this, though."

"I'm listening."

Jess savored the fond light in Brenna's eyes. "You won't be alone, Bren. I'll be with you, whatever comes. And our adanin will watch over us both."

Their lips blended with a sweet, natural warmth, and they rested against each other for a moment to enjoy it.

Then Brenna stepped back. "All right, warrior. Take me to my in-laws."

Jess grinned, took Brenna's hand in her own, and led her home.

CHAPTER THREE

The murmuring buzz ahead gradually increased, then abruptly surged as shouting broke out, which swelled into cries of welcome. Shann and the others had reached Tristaine's village square.

Brenna was dazzled by the bright torchlight that marked the entry to the Festival, and she blinked, hesitating at the top of a small hill. Hand in hand, she and Jess stared down at the milling throng of Amazons below.

The sheer mass of bodies threw Brenna at first. Hundreds of women and a fair number of children, wearing an array of colorful wraps, were swarming around their sisters, and the noise was growing riotous. The baying of—wolves? dogs?—mixed with human voices, and the music was rising to reflect the joyous new energy in the square.

"Hoo," Brenna said softly, and Jess squeezed her hand.

She saw Shann surrounded by dozens of Amazons all trying to greet her at once. Unhurried, she addressed each of them for a private moment before moving on, bestowing a touch or an embrace. She knelt briefly to inspect one child's scraped knee, and Brenna lost sight of her. Kyla and Camryn were in the center of another welcoming throng, and several women ran back and forth between the two.

❖

Jess may have had to sling Brenna over her shoulder and tote her down the hill, because how they got there remained a blur. Brenna remembered being above the crowd and then in it, and after two months in a quiet mountain meadow, the racket alone all but flash-fried her nerves.

The square was lit with gold from bonfires and torches, and the scent of the pine boughs used in Festival decorations was everywhere. That's about all Brenna could take in before someone saw Jess and yelled her name, and then they were swamped.

Brenna never doubted Jess was well loved in Tristaine. She had found her irresistible in the City, under the worst conditions imaginable. But her lover had grown up with these women, and for almost a year, they didn't know if she was alive or dead. They couldn't stop touching Jess. A quiet part of Brenna realized she had never experienced anything like this, the kind of emotion that poured from these adanin. The intensity of that bond could power the City generators for a month.

No one paid any particular attention to Brenna at first, which was fine with her. She worried a little that Jess might be backslapped to death, but watching her, she couldn't stop grinning. Three of her old friends jumped her, a little too roughly for Brenna's taste, and Jess actually *bellowed* with delight. And that wonderful dark, rich, rolling laugh...Jess held her silence even under Caster's whip, but seeing these sisters again unlocked her throat.

Brenna's throat kept closing up. *I'm not sure I can live in this place if it makes you feel so bloody much all the time,* she thought. *Maybe Jess and I can live in a cave higher up. No, wait, lower down.*

"Walk with me!" Jess had to yell to be heard as she took Brenna's hand and began weaving through the rejoicing villagers.

Brenna was enjoying this, becoming light-headed with the buzz of euphoria in the women around her. Nothing much was demanded of her at the moment, and most of the Amazons greeted her with enough friendly interest to bolster her courage.

"Too many voices," Jess shouted cheerfully in Brenna's ear. They didn't make much headway at first, as it seemed every Tristainian they met was waiting to greet Jess with an ecstatic embrace. Gradually, they wended their way through the mob and reached the corner of the village square. Brenna paused, panting a little as Jess stopped at a handmade table bearing mugs of hot cider.

"Sip it," Jess instructed as she wrapped Brenna's cold fingers around the earthware mug. "It's strong."

The stronger the better, Brenna thought, and inhaled the tart fragrance that rose from the steaming brew. Its heady aroma seemed to expand her senses, and her gaze darted everywhere, taking in the village.

The blue moonlight revealed shadows of log buildings beyond the bonfires, spaced widely over the grassy plain. Tristaine was bisected by a fast-moving river about thirty yards wide, and Brenna could hear its muted roaring beneath the clamor of the Festival.

"That's our meeting house." Jess pointed at the stately lodge across the river, on Tristaine's highest ground. "It can seat six hundred Amazons for clan council. Those cabins are our homes. They extend farther up the mountain for those who want privacy. Those two long lodges over there," she indicated, "belong to our guilds, the artists and the tradeswomen. They made the cup you're drinking from, and our woodworkers built that bridge spanning the river."

Brenna heard the pride in Jess's voice and thought it was well justified. She had imagined this place for months and, at least by moonlight, it was truly beautiful. "Is that an orchard over there?"

"Aye, our orchard and gardens. And we house our animals in the field beyond them."

"Lions and pigs?" Brenna grinned.

"Sheep and goats," Jess corrected. "And the fastest mustangs ever bred in these hills."

"What's the little crater with the bonfire?" She nudged Jess. "Did you blow up a lodge when you were a stoned toddler?"

Jess laughed, a breeze lifting her hair from her brow. She looked fully healthy for the first time since Brenna met her. "That's our storyfire circle where we trade legends at night. It's the closest we come to mass entertainment, lass. We have great theater, though, and our chorus can invoke angels."

"Hey, is that a stadium?"

"Tristaine's arena." Now Jess was beaming. "Our warriors train there and hold tournaments. That's Shann's infirmary next to it. And north of the arena are the stables…" Jess looked down at her. "Ach, I'm going real fast, Bren. You'll not be tested on this stuff in the morning, I promise."

"I want a full tour in the morning." The cider was helping Brenna relax. "I'd love to see the infirmary, Jesstin."

Jess began to agree, but then they were swarmed again by a party of well-wishers. She kept Brenna's hand and introduced her, but gradually Brenna worked her way unobtrusively out of the group. She lifted another mug to warm her belly while she watched the festivities.

Brenna was entranced by the range of dogs of every shape and size, yapping and dancing freely throughout the village. The ownership of pets was carefully regulated in the City, and only the aristocracy could afford the few purebred species allowed.

Her eye fastened on a speeding projectile of white fur and traced the small yelping mutt as it raced through the square, launched itself fearlessly into the air, and crashed into Kyla's open arms.

"Max!" Kyla shrieked and laughed as the dog swiped her face with its tongue. Brenna worried briefly about germs, then chided herself for her City mentality.

"Maximillian." Camryn lifted the ecstatic mutt off Kyla's lap and held it squirming and kicking at arm's length. "Greetings, Max. How's the fiercest wee beastie in Tristaine? We missed you."

Brenna grinned as the somber warrior held off the wild gyrations of the thrashing ball of fur, determined to slurp her face.

"The clan's dogs belong to everyone," Jess's low voice rumbled at her side. "But like our horses, they choose their favorite allies."

"I can see that." Brenna felt Jess's arm around her shoulders. "Kyla looks wonderful, Jesstin. So does Cam."

"They do," Jess agreed. "Whoops. Look, lass, a royal summons."

Brenna followed Jess's gaze to a large canopy erected near the Amazons' storyfire pit. Shann beckoned to them from beneath its colorful fabric, and they picked their way down to her.

"You were looking a little overwhelmed, Blades." Shann pressed Brenna's shoulders. "I'm craving a moment of calm. Will you join me? You too, Jesstin. You have elders to greet."

"With pleasure, lady." Jess's eyes were shining, and Brenna turned to see three older women seated on padded benches around a small fire. They regarded Jess with unbridled delight as she bent to kiss their cheeks, her strong fingers gentle around hands gnarled and mottled with age.

"Jesstin, you've sprung up like a weed." The large woman seated in the middle beamed at them, and her two friends laughed, a sound like river water splashing over mossy rock.

"They've been telling me that since I was six," Jess explained to Brenna.

"These three elders sit on Tristaine's high council, Bren." Shann was pouring fermented cider into mugs from a ceramic jug. "They've guided me wisely for long seasons, and Jocelyn taught me everything I know of healing."

"I'm pleased to—Jocelyn?" Brenna's eyebrows arched. "Um, pardon me, are you Jode's mother?"

"That's me." Jocelyn smiled, and her smooth face wreathed in wrinkles. "Shanendra tells us Jodoch served his mother's line well in the City."

"He's my hero. Really." Brenna's shoulders were relaxing again. Jocelyn's maternal presence was as warming as the small fire at their feet. "We could never have escaped from the Clinic without him."

"Welp, at least this one has manners." The woman with a shaved head on Jocelyn's right grinned at Jess, her sun-weathered skin shining like mahogany in the firelight. The colorful glyph she wore on one side of her neck identified her as one of Tristaine's warriors. She waggled heavy eyebrows. "And she's better looking than most you've panted after, urchin."

"Sarah." Jocelyn tapped the bald Amazon's knee. "It would be nice if you'd let us greet just one new arrival with some courtesy, before your odd candor sends her screaming off into the night. Brenna? The serene angel on my left is Dorothea...and this old wretch is Sarah, our village banshee."

All three elders tittered again.

"Sit down, little sister." The sweet-faced Dorothea clasped Brenna's hand in her own and patted the small bench beside her. "We want to pick your brains a bit before we march off to our winter palace in the morning."

"You mean before we're banished with the rest of the crones." Sarah snorted into her cider. "Like the useless relics we are."

"Self-pity, adanin. Not attractive." Jocelyn plucked a corner of the other woman's shawl, but there was affection in her voice. "The migration is voluntary, and you know it. With that asthma, you can't take another winter up here. You wheeze like a bellows at night. Lady, you've told Brenna about our annual tradition?"

Shann nodded. "She knows Tristaine sends her infirm down to the southern meadows each fall to escape the mountain blizzards. A cadre of warriors goes with them for protection and hunting through the winter."

Jocelyn resettled her ample weight on the bench and directed her question to Brenna. "And you know that this year our queen will order the entire village emptied?"

"Yes. I guess that's necessary because Caster's getting ready to attack." Brenna eyed the pitcher of cider as it made its rounds. The focused attention of the three elders was a little unnerving. Even Shann was watching her with an odd intensity. "Everyone will leave except for a squad of Jesstin's handpicked warriors to make sure no one follows the clan." She sought out Jess, who stood in respectful silence behind Shann's bench.

Dorothea nodded. "It's a sad time for us, young Brenna. It's difficult to sever the bonds holding us to this land."

"Sever. As in forever?" Brenna looked at Shann, troubled. "You mean this migration is permanent? Everyone's leaving and never coming back?"

"I'm afraid so, Blades." Shann smoothed her hand over her arm as if to comfort herself. "We've always known that we can't match the firepower of the City's Military, not under full assault. If Amazons are to survive, we must move on."

"The high council who sat thirty years ago proposed this plan, Brenna, long before our lady's reign." Jocelyn's tone was gentle. "We've always known we would have to leave eventually. Shann and Dyan had the vision to prepare us for it."

Brenna didn't understand why her throat ached with tears. She had walked into Tristaine for the first time only an hour ago.

"The heart of Tristaine will endure." Shann looked up at Jess, who avoided her gaze. "Amazons are long accustomed to exile, Bren. We carry our heritage with us. And our culture. The City's grenade launchers can destroy our lodges, but as long as some of our sisters live to rebuild them, they can't touch the soul of our clan."

"But." Sarah leaned forward. "This Caster *puta* won't have grenade launchers, praise Anath." Her voice was low and firm in the quiet. "If we have to lose our village, lady, we should at least take out that craven bitch and her mercenaries first."

"Mercenaries?" Jess looked inquiringly at Shann.

"Yes, adanin." Shann quirked one eyebrow at her second. "Our elders bring us interesting tidings from Theryn's source in the City. Apparently, Caster has fallen badly out of favor with her superiors since your escape from the Clinic. She lost her Government funding and much of her reputation."

"But now the old hag has suckered money out of some private outfit down there." Sarah waved a gnarled hand. "Enough to hire a company of militia, anyway."

"How many? Do we know?" Jess's voice held new tension.

"Theryn's contact could only learn the size of Caster's private grant." Shann looked at Jocelyn, who nodded. "She has enough funding to pay and arm a small platoon at least."

"One platoon? Shann." Jesstin knelt next to her queen. "We can handle one scientist and a squad of thirty City soldiers."

"Soldiers far better armed than our warriors, Jess."

"But it's our terrain." Jess lifted Shann's hand. "We have the advantage there, lady, and we're better trained. We can drive Caster out."

"Perhaps." Shann brushed her fingers through Jess's hair. "But only perhaps. And if we did win that battle, Jesstin, what then? One small defeat would hardly stop the City."

"We could stop *Caster*." Jess pressed Shann's fingers. "Her vendetta against us is personal, lady. You've seen the venom that runs through her veins. The City's Military isn't going to bother to track down Amazons who've moved deeper into the mountains. That banshee might. We can end that threat."

"But at what price, adanin?" Shann's elegant features were pensive. "After tomorrow's migration, less than fifty warriors will remain to defend our village. We would risk shedding such dear blood—"

"Shanendra." Jocelyn's voice was compassionate. "You know as well as I that a queen of warrior women must find the courage to order her sisters to fight."

"Listen well to the counsel Jesstin offers, lady," Dorothea added. "Your own Dyan taught her, and she has your adonai's courage."

"Yes, Grandmother. She does." Shann kissed the back of Jess's hand. "All right, Jesstin. Instruct your cadre leaders to prepare for battle."

"Done, Shann."

"And this is where you come in, little sister." Jocelyn smiled at Brenna.

Brenna started. "Me?"

"Tell us about these dreams, Brenna." Dorothea patted her hand, her small eyes brightly studying her face.

"Oh, no." Brenna drew a breath. "Shann—"

"Brenna," Shann said quietly, "I'm sorry, adanin. I know this is hard for you. But things are moving quickly now. Even if you don't trust your own abilities, I'm asking you to trust me. These elders are leaving with the first party tomorrow. They need to hear this in your own words."

"Okay. I'll try." Brenna met Jess's gaze again and cleared her throat. "I dream about horses. Horses aren't allowed within City limits, and I don't have a travel permit, so I've never seen a horse, except on film. But I started dreaming about them when I met Jess, after she was transferred to the Clinic…"

Brenna recounted the series of nightmares that had plagued her for months. The night she first tended Jess, she had dreamed of riding a black stallion and falling with it when its heart was pierced by a spear. Then there was a milling herd of horses, trumpeting panic as two stallions fought to the death. And the most recent, a foal shrilling in terror, trying to escape a blazing fire hungrily consuming the forest.

Her throat was dry when she finished, and she gulped the cooling cider, feeling oddly depleted.

"Thank you, youngster." Dorothea patted Brenna's hand again. "You've done well. I'm sorry I won't get to know you better, Brenna."

"Maybe she could cough up something more specific tonight if we drugged her good?"

"Sarah." Jocelyn sighed and looked at Shann, her weathered face unreadable. "I agree, lady. Brenna follows Julia's star. But I don't know that she's helped us."

"We'll hold private council, Grandmother." Shann knelt beside Brenna and smiled into her dazed eyes. "Thank you, Blades. I'll see you and Jesstin later, after the Challenge." One blunt fingernail tapped the mug she held, and Shann whispered, "Slow down on these, little sister."

Brenna's face flushed with heat. She stood and found herself enveloped in Jocelyn's soft robes.

"Welcome to Tristaine, young Brenna." Jocelyn cupped her face in her hands. "Remember, we are an Amazon clan—not cabins in a mountain valley. Tristaine will rise again. We promise you that."

She released Brenna and winked at Jess. "Now go, widget, and show your adanin our Festival. We need to mutter wisely with our queen for a while."

Jess ushered Brenna out from under the canopy, and the happy chaos of the Festival descended again. Brenna filled her lungs with cold, pine-spiced air, overloaded with enough questions to keep Jess awake till dawn.

A laughing pack of children raced by, and she squeaked and dodged with relative deftness, she thought, given the amount of cider she'd imbibed. The Festival had transformed, with the return of Tristaine's queen, from a rather somber affair into the joyous celebration Kyla had described so lovingly. Everywhere Brenna looked, swarms of colorfully dressed Amazons gravitated to different gatherings.

Several circles of dancers had formed near the log meeting house, and the music was far more lilting and energized than the lonely woodwind notes they had heard outside the village.

Dozens of warriors decked in leather finery that weakened Brenna's knees were clapping and hooting around pairs of Amazons wrestling in an enclosed ring near the arena. The night was heady with music and noise and scented smoke.

"Brenna, I think it best you and Kyla leave with the first wave tomorrow."

"What? Say again?" Brenna straightened and blinked at Jess. "Are you drunk, too, widget?" She snorted laughter.

"I'm serious, Bren." There was a sadness in Jess's voice that aged her. "This battle will be bloody. Even when it's over, our last task here might prove just as dangerous."

"Wait a minute." Brenna tried not to slur her words. "What task, and what kind of dangerous?"

"We have to defeat Caster's soldiers, Bren, and then we must destroy the village."

"What?"

"Land is sacred to us." The tears glittering in Jess's eyes made them no less fierce. "Leaving this valley to the City would be the desecration of a shrine. We'll not allow whoever follows Caster to profit from Amazon lives, Brenna."

"Jesstin, slow down." Brenna frowned and waited for a wave of dizziness to pass. "First, with the Amazons gone, there's nothing here the City could want, and second, to repeat, what kind of dangerous?"

"Bren, it's nothing you can help with. There's no need for you to stay."

"Jesstin!" A cheerful voice hailed them from the small, sloping rise that led to the wrestling matches. "The ring awaits us, sister!"

Jess glanced over her shoulder. "A moment, Patana."

"Hey." Brenna's tone was ominously low. "You're awfully quick to dump me, Jess."

"You don't have much time to decide, lass. I'll abide by your wishes, but—"

"Damn straight you'll abide my *wishes*!" She slurred that time, but she didn't care. She was mad. "Damn it, Jesstin, you don't just stroll up to a person and suggest she leave you, possibly forever, because—"

"Ah, Jessie, come on!" Patana's merry shout turned several heads. "You can bring your City girl!"

Brenna saw the muscles in Jess's jaw clench. She fought off her fogginess and touched her arm. "Look, this isn't the time for a wrestling match, even if we weren't having our first fight. You're coming off a week-long hike with no sleep, and excuse me, but that Patana woman looks mean as a snake."

"She is. Don't worry about Patana." Jess's brogue was clipped, and she took Brenna's shoulders. "Adanin, no one expects you to risk yourself for a clan you've just seen. My warriors will join the rest of the clan in the southern meadows when it's over. It'll just be a few weeks."

"You're serious, aren't you?" Brenna stepped back, and Jess's hands fell from her shoulders. "You'd let me go, just like that."

"Bren—"

"Jess, you surprise me!" Patana taunted. "Dyan's finest, her right hand, surrenders without a fight?"

"I'll talk to you later, Jesstin. You better go. One of *your warriors* is calling you."

The crowd swallowed Brenna as she slipped between dancing Amazons and headed toward the river. The twisting figures moved around her in dizzying patterns. A few moments later, she heard a raucous cheer rise behind her as Patana's challenge was accepted.

❖

Brenna wandered aimlessly from one cheerful bonfire to the next.

She felt curious stares as she moved through Tristaine's village square, but she was long accustomed to shutting out appraising looks, and no one bothered her. The numbing warmth of the hard cider in her blood helped.

Cheers rose periodically from the direction of the stadium, and she heard one woman yell to two others that the wrestling matches had moved to the arena. Dozens were thronging toward it, but there were still seas of milling, laughing women to be lost in.

Brenna reached a smooth wooden bench at the base of a huge oak tree and lowered herself to it gratefully. She pressed the tight muscles at the base of her neck, whispering invectives against tall blue-eyed Amazon warriors. A cold nose poked her thigh, and she yelped. Max yelped back.

Never having held a dog, Brenna found the furry white creature with pointed ears and quizzical brown eyes as exotic as a miniature unicorn. After a few moments, the little dog's questing black nose and inquisitive sniffs convinced her that Max wasn't going to rip out her throat.

"You're Max?" Brenna smiled, a bit sentimentally. "Kyla's doggie."

She scratched the mutt under the chin, and his eyes closed blissfully. Max extended his neck and tipped his furry head to direct her fingers to the best itchy spots. The campfire glowed pink through his tufted ears. He growled softly in pleasure and Brenna laughed, delight breaking through her mild buzz.

"I'm glad to see you're making friends, Brenna." Myrine stood smiling at her from across the fire, and the little mutt yapped happily and trotted over to greet her.

An imposing woman with silver-streaked black hair followed Myrine. When Max saw her, he changed course and bounded cheerfully toward another gathering. Brenna watched him go, a little wistfully.

"I trust we're making you welcome, adanin." The second woman smiled, and the firelight glinted whitely off her sharp teeth. She wore a cloak of charisma not unlike the aura surrounding Shann, Brenna thought, but hers was bolder, more vibrant. "Introductions, please, Myrine?"

"Brenna, this is Theryn, Tristaine's liaison with the City." Myrine turned to Theryn with something like deference. "She's the reason we have any modern technology at all up here. Theryn makes an effort to welcome all new arrivals, and she especially wanted to meet you."

Brenna nodded. She could handle this. She was fine. Part of her registered the faint rumble of cheering coming from the stadium, but then she forced Jess out of her thoughts. She recognized this attractive woman's name. "You're on Tristaine's high council, is that right?"

"I have that honor." Theryn's shining cloak swirled as she sat on the bench close beside Brenna. "Myrine? Please go and find out who claims victory in the ring—Patana or young Jesstin." She winked at Brenna. "I have a fine jade dagger riding on the outcome of the match."

"Of course, Theryn." Myrine handed Brenna the cup of cider she held, winked at her, and moved off into the crowd.

"No offense, my new friend, but I bet against your beloved." Theryn's padded shoulder brushed Brenna's as she leaned into her confidingly. "Patana is one of Tristaine's best in hand-to-hand. Jesstin is good, but accepting Patana's challenge might have been a wee bit rash."

"Maybe." Brenna warmed her fingers around the mug. "But so is betting against Jess, so maybe you're a little rash, too, Theryn."

Theryn laughed softly, a melodic sound. "Your loyalty becomes you, Brenna! Please know I have nothing but affection for your brave warrior. I have great respect for Dyan's right hand. But Patana has become my own prodigy, and I have trained her well. I'm rather skilled in the martial arts."

"I see."

Theryn pursed her full lips. "But in all candor and truth, I can't claim to know either Patana or Jesstin well. Dyan and Shann were more my contemporaries, really, than Jess and her peers."

"Well, I guess Shann's still your contemporary then." Brenna drank deeply and shuddered. "She told me some Amazons here, mostly newer women from the City, believe Tristaine can make a deal with its Government."

"Loyal and direct." Theryn appraised Brenna. "Which is fortunate, because the migration begins tomorrow, and there's precious little time to prepare for a truce. I'm convinced we can negotiate with the City, Brenna, but I'll need your help."

Brenna blinked. Theryn's handsome face was blurring around the edges. "My help?"

"I know, from what little Myrine has told me, that Jesstin suffered a great deal in the City." Theryn's shoulder brushed hers again, a slower and more intimate caress. "Shann has always given Jesstin's counsel more…credence than mine. And Jess was stubborn before her arrest when it came to holding Dyan's word as gospel. Now I imagine she'll prove quite inflexible."

"Quite." Brenna concentrated on focusing on Theryn's intense gaze and speaking clearly. "Theryn, you've never met Caster. She's the Clinic's top scientist in Military Research. I know her really well. I worked with her. You have no chance of negotiating with her, I promise you."

"Ah, but you've just met me." Theryn lifted one of Brenna's cold hands and warmed it in her own. "Don't underestimate my persuasiveness, young Brenna. I'm no stranger to halls of power, and I carry considerable influence in Tristaine's council. With luck, I might find a workable alternative to the apocalypse Dyan had in mind for our village."

"Apoca? Lips?"

"If you'll trust me, Brenna, together we might be able to save Amazon lives. Perhaps even that stubborn warrior of yours." Theryn lifted one gloved hand and caressed Brenna's face. "You're truly not interested in hearing more?"

Brenna frowned again, flipping through her mental filing cabinet in search of Theryn's chart. This was one of the few Amazons Jess had spoken of without warmth, but her initial argument sounded pretty damn compelling. Besides, Brenna was ticked at Jess and didn't give her opinion much weight at the moment.

"But what could Tristaine offer Caster, Theryn? When she can just take anything she wants?"

"This Caster must be highly educated, of course, as am I. She's a woman of science, and I believe we can approach her on a purely logical basis."

"But spe…specifically—"

"Ah, Brenna. There is such beauty in this valley." Theryn's gaze moved from Brenna's eyes to her lips and back. She lifted her hand and pressed it to her breast earnestly. "Help me fight for our village, sister! Let your first contribution to Tristaine, to your new home, be its salvation!"

Brenna heard another distant cheer from the stadium.

"I see we're both right about Jesstin's obstinance." Theryn chuckled. Then her full lips parted, and she moved closer to Brenna. "All I'm asking of you is to keep an open mind in the days to come, young one, and an open heart."

"Jess's obstinance?" Brenna blinked, and Theryn came into focus again. "You mean that cheering's for *her*? That bloody stupid wrestling match is *still* going on?"

"Evidently." Theryn brushed two fingers down the side of Brenna's face again. "We badly need your fresh perspective, my lovely young friend. You have such wisdom and such—Brenna?"

Theryn's voice faded behind Brenna as she moved swiftly through the crowd. Irritation burned off some of her alcoholic haze, and she targeted the log stadium with swift certainty.

She crossed the footbridge over the river, not glancing at the women who walked with her in laughing groups of mixed races. Brenna kept her eyes fixed on the arched pines that marked the entrance to Tristaine's arena.

It seemed most of the village had crowded up on the log risers that surrounded the fighting field, a rectangle of hard-packed dirt.

Dozens of Amazons formed a large circle that marked the boundaries of the wrestling ring. Most held torches, flooding the fighters in gold light.

Brenna slipped quietly through the crowd, her annoyance increasing as she heard a thud of bodies and another raucous cheer split the chill night air. She spied two familiar forms, Vicar and Hakan, and tapped her way in between them to see into the ring. It was unfortunate timing.

The last cheer had come from this side of the circle, among Jess's friends. Now Brenna heard a burst of shouting from the far end, just as her lover flew bodily through the air to crash hard into a watching throng of warriors at ringside.

Jess was helped to her feet with an edge of urgency as well as revelry. The crowded stadium fell almost silent between bouts of cheering. There was a tension in the air that Brenna felt clearly, even through the dazing effects of the cider.

Jess grinned at the warriors who righted her and shrugged off their hands, her eyes still locked on the opponent waiting across the ring. Patana had her hands braced on her knees, head lowered, pulling for breath. In spite of the chill in the night air, her short-cropped skull gleamed with sweat in the torchlight.

Jess's face was just as damp, and Brenna saw a trembling fatigue in the long muscles of her legs. Her throat and shoulders were patched with angry red marks, and other harbingers of bruising stood out on her bare forearms. More alarming, Jess's slow walk to the center of the ring revealed the minute limp that surfaced only when her old back injury was flaring.

Patana finally straightened, and if anything she looked worse than Jess. But Patana was not Brenna's concern. Perhaps the cider fogged her reason, but not her bedrock resolve.

After the Clinic, Brenna would never stand by passively while Jess was hurt again.

She elbowed Hakan aside and would have stepped into the ring if Vicar hadn't snatched her arm and pulled her back.

"Wait, little sister." Hakan's broad hand touched Brenna's shoulder. "She knows what she's doing."

"Not even close," Brenna retorted. "Look at her, Hakan! She's been climbing mountains for days. She hasn't slept. She's exhausted!"

"Jess realizes all that." Hakan's tone was maddeningly patient. "Dyan trained her warriors to understand their limits and ration their reserves. Let Jess choose her moment."

Brenna fumed. "Dyan trained Patana too, I assume?"

"Not from birth, as she did Jesstin."

Brenna looked up at Vicar, who released her arm, her rugged face expressionless.

Then Vicar tensed, her gaze pinned on the fight. "There she goes!"

Brenna focused on the firelit center of the ring again, in time to see Jess's spinning kick. And then Patana went flying. Arms and legs flailing wildly, she crashed into her small group of supporters, toppling them like leathered bowling pins.

The cheer was instantaneous and deafening, as it seemed the vast majority of the Amazons crowding the stadium were backing Jess. The roar crested as Patana climbed stiffly to her feet and raised one sullen hand to Jess to cede the match. Beside Brenna, the hoarse shouts of Vicar and Hakan blared in her ears like twin klaxons.

As Jess walked out of the ring toward them, her limp diminished, and her shoulders straightened. She acknowledged the roars of approval around her with a brief lift of her hand, then ambled on with the relaxed gait of a tall woman at ease in her body.

It was pure bravado, and Brenna knew it. Jess was ready to collapse. She whispered brand-new invectives under her breath about macha Amazon stoicism and realized her own knees were trembling. She locked them.

Brenna was *not* going to be distracted, either by her own worry or by Jess's feral beauty, backlit by torchlight in a stadium resonating with cheers. There was romantic fixation, and then there was—

"*Stupidity*, Jesstin!" Brenna clenched Jess's arm. "You're going to be crippled tomorrow, you know that!"

"True," Jess muttered, flinching beneath the backslapping congratulations of her sister warriors. "It had to be done, though, Bren."

"I've been waitin' too long to see someone humble that blusterin' shrike, Stumpy!" Vicar's brogue ran rampant as she tousled Jess's hair. "Tristaine can go the way of bleedin' Brigadoon now, mate. Vicar dies happy!"

"Let her breathe, adanin." Hakan strong-armed the women who were starting to crowd in, and they pulled Jess to the side of the arena and the first tier of risers.

She sank down on the rough seat with a sigh, and Brenna sat beside her and lifted her hand to take her pulse. Vicar took off her own cape and tossed it around Jess's gleaming shoulders.

"Anything crucial?" Brenna asked.

Jess shook her head. "I'm just beat."

"Yes, slightly." The pulse beneath Brenna's fingers was rapid and rather faint.

Hakan rested her booted foot on a log riser. "The defeated party looks a bit played out too, Jesstin."

Brenna picked out Patana on the other side of the stadium, surrounded by a small cluster of women. She recognized Myrine and Theryn among them. Theryn was tipping the warrior's head back, checking her nose solicitously. She gave Patana's shoulder a comforting pat, and then, as if sensing Brenna's gaze, Theryn scanned the crowd and saw them.

Brenna felt Jess go still beside her. Theryn smiled and nodded graciously. Jess returned a courteous but formal gesture. Theryn's gaze lingered on Brenna for a moment before she turned back to her followers.

"Myrine and Patana?" Jess was speaking shorthand. Her breathing was returning to normal, but her color still wasn't good.

"They became adonai last spring." Vicar's tone was subdued. "Li and I have seen little of 'Rine since."

Jess nodded. "And Grythe?"

"Aye, Grythe is still with us, more's the pity. Just not around tonight." Vic sighed.

Then the shadows cleared from Jess's eyes as Camryn flopped down beside them.

"That was very, very pretty, Jesstin!" Camryn was grinning, and she looked more like the teenager she was than Brenna had ever seen her. "Ky and I saw the end of it. She's setting up to sing the Challenge. You were sincerely hot, Jess. You own Patana's smelly butt now!"

"Speak of your sisters with respect, Camryn." Jess sounded weary. "Have you seen our lady?"

"She's getting ready for the Queen's Council. Oh, hi." Camryn seemed to notice Brenna sitting next to her for the first time and smiled at her. "Ky says to tell you she's singing this Challenge right to you, Brenna."

"Yeah?" Brenna raised her brows. "Okay. Thanks. I'm honored, as long as she doesn't challenge me to sing back."

The mood of the open stadium was changing now. Amazons were flocking in, filling the rows of log bleachers, and there was still a sense of jubilant excitement among them. But the long match and its dramatic finish had bled some of the frenzy from the Festival, leaving a warmer and calmer essence.

The fighting arena was clearing. Brenna saw a stream of women wearing beautiful pastel-streaked robes, which shimmered like silk, move single file toward the center of the ring. Camryn pointed at Kyla in a light, ornate chair carried by two larger women.

Kyla's auburn hair fell in soft, shining waves to her shoulders. Her beautiful features were calm and alert, and she smiled thanks at her bearers after they set her down carefully in the center of the arena.

Jess nudged Brenna. "Lass, you're ice."

Brenna looked up at her and was lost for a pleasurable moment in her cerulean eyes. But when Jess lifted an arm to drape Vicar's cape over Brenna's shoulders as well as her own, Brenna leaned away.

"I'm still ticked at you for trying to kick me out of here, Jesstin." Brenna paused, frowning. "I'm also really cold. But that doesn't mean everything's okay."

"Understood, querida. We'll fight later." Jess's dimple appeared.

Brenna slipped down to the tier below them and leaned back between Jess's knees. She closed the thick cape around them both and rested her head against Jess's waist with a gusting sigh. The sudden warmth was blissful.

Brenna's gaze traveled the ebony sky overhead, picking out Tristaine's guardian stars easily. Jess's arms were solid around her, and she felt their hearts settle into their accustomed matching rhythm.

The buzz of noise in the stadium quieted, and Brenna returned her attention to the ring. Kyla had risen from her chair, and that simple movement had silenced six hundred Amazons.

After a moment of hushed expectation, Kyla began to sing. A complex melody flowed from her throat in a tone both darker and richer than her usual light soprano.

"This Festival celebrates the Amazons' harvest when we lived on the plains." Jess's breath stirred Brenna's hair. "It bids good-bye to the warmth and ease of summer. The Challenge Kyla sings is the call of Artemis to Her daughters, bidding them to have courage for the long winter ahead."

The hewn-log arena should have dispersed Kyla's lonely voice to the open sky, but the beauty and depth of her gift defied acoustics. Brenna felt gooseflesh that had nothing to do with the cold rise on her arms, as Kyla's melody soared and floated.

Her singing had been silenced in the City Prison, and her music had not returned immediately when she was freed. Weeks of fresh mountain air and the company of her family had finally restored her voice, and Brenna often woke, pleasantly, to Kyla's trilling song in the meadow near their camp. But the voice that emerged from their little sister now was fuller, more mature and resonant.

"What's she saying now?" Brenna whispered.

"The Challenge is given in Tristaine's mother tongue," Jess replied. "Our Lady charges Her Amazons to honor each other and to protect all women from any power that would enslave them."

Brenna felt a stillness take the crowd as they listened, a collective hush that connected them all to the girl in the center of the ring. There was sternness in Kyla's voice and a bleak note of adult desolation. Then such loving fierceness in the swelling climax of her chant that Brenna shivered in Jess's arms.

"Artemis ends Her Challenge by giving our clan Her blessing for the coming winter," Jess whispered.

Kyla's song ended in a fading note that echoed up the quiet bleachers. A sigh moved through the tiers of women, and then waves of applause swelled to embrace Kyla. She was radiant, her brown eyes large and still. Jess nudged Brenna and tipped her head toward Camryn, whose face glowed with love as she watched her adonai absorb the tribute. Brenna and Jess grinned at each other proudly.

Was life in Tristaine always so emotional, like being premenstrual, twenty-four seven? Brenna wondered. She had to smile even as tears threatened, and Kyla's tiny white-robed form blurred around the edges. She wasn't a sentimental person, at least she never had been. But she had dive-bombed through a dozen different feelings tonight, all of them stronger than anything she'd experienced in an entire year before she met Jess.

And Brenna was far from alone in this pleasant haze. The women around her were carrying on like the restored family they were. Just as the applause for Kyla's Challenge tapered, Shann walked into the circle of torchlight, and the thunderous ovation convinced Brenna that living among Amazons indeed awakened the heart.

It wasn't the mindless shrieking of City Youth Concerts, but a warm, welling wave of happiness given voice, and the applause and cheers bathed and soothed and invigorated Brenna in turns. Jess squeezed her, her eyes dancing as Shann reached Kyla.

The Amazon queen took Kyla's hand and kissed her cheek, then gestured for her to sit in the waiting chair. Kyla looked toward Camryn and rolled her eyes, then settled herself gingerly. Shann looked up at the tiers of women surrounding her, and Brenna remembered, again, that she was more than their wise elder sister and had always been more.

"The winter sun rises soon over Tristaine." Shann's silk voice reached them clearly, as if she stood within hand's reach. "And when

Selene's moon lights Her lodges again, the daughters of Artemis will have left for the southern meadows. Never to return to this valley."

Shann even seemed taller now, Brenna marveled, and she moved with a regal grace as unconscious as it was riveting. Unlike Caster, Shann bore the mantle of leadership lightly on her slender shoulders, but the aura of command she wielded was undeniable.

"We'll carry with us the ashes of our seven Mothers," Shann continued. "Their spirits will continue to guide us, as they have guided Amazons for generations. They have traveled with us to new continents—from seaside, to plain, to mountain. Tristaine has fallen and been born again a dozen times in our written history."

Shann bent gracefully and swept her hand across the packed dirt of the arena floor. She straightened, and black earth trickled from her fingers. Her voice was as intimate as warm wine.

"This land is not your mother, or your wife, or your adanin. This valley is not Tristaine. Tristaine sits beside you. She'll sleep in your lodge tonight. She'll walk at your side in the morning. She'll fight by your side at dusk. And with Her, you'll build our new home. Tristaine is our bond, sisters, the woman-spirit that connects us and makes us one clan."

Brenna sighed softly and heard that sound echoed around her. A light brand of exalted warmth was sweeping the arena. It was mirrored in Camryn's open face and in Vicar's softened features. This public address was the Queen's Council, Brenna remembered, but Shann could have been speaking to each of her women individually, in private trust.

"This land is precious to us because it nourishes and shelters our kindred. The daughters of Artemis have lived and died here for seven generations, so by our lights, this valley is holy ground. Our warriors are willing to die for this land."

Shann's lovely eyes hardened. "Our village will never fall into the hands of our enemies. You have your queen's word, adanin."

She brushed the black earth from her hands. "City-born or mountain-bred, the Amazons of Tristaine are sisters. We have thrived, while a hundred Cities crumbled to dust. The essence of Tristaine will flourish wherever Gaia leads us next. We follow Her path."

Someone shouted approval, and that call was echoed, at first by single voices, then dozens. Brenna felt Jess's arms tighten around her, and she was swept up in the rising applause, which crested in cheers and ringing war cries that shook the stadium.

CHAPTER FOUR

Theika, rise.

Brenna's head thudded in an unlovely rhythm, and her mouth felt coated with ash.

Wake up, little sister.

She tugged the fur over her shoulder and grasped at the fading remnants of sleep.

"Adanin."

Long fingers brushed through her hair, and Brenna snorted awake. "Here. Sorry? What?"

"Sleep a bit longer, Bren." Jess's lips touched her forehead. "I won't be gone long."

"Whoa?" Brenna sat up, then bit her lip to keep from groaning.

"We'll make that visit to Shann's infirmary as soon as I get back, lass." Jess's smile was sympathetic. "She's got an herbal concoction that might help your head."

Oh, lordy. The thought. Brenna had to swallow twice to keep her gorge down. "Where you—?"

"Just a quick errand with Vicar."

"I'm awake. I'm up." Brenna tried to look alert. Light had only begun to filter into Jess's lodge. She had a vague memory of coming to this small cabin after Shann's address and falling onto a luxurious pile of quilts. "Is it a private errand?"

"No." Jess hesitated for a moment. "Actually, you're invited, if you want to join us."

"I do." Brenna gave the fur a sluggish kick and accepted Jess's hand to help her up. She swayed once erect and felt strong arms encircle her waist. Her lover seemed to know this was not a romantic moment, and she supported Brenna quietly until she was steady.

"Good morning, lass." Jess's kiss on the top of her head was light and tender.

"Mrng." Brenna cleared her sandpapered throat. Jess had built up the fire in the stone hearth before waking her, and the light tang of cedar smoke filled the air. The small lodge was remarkably cozy. Tristaine's cabin-crafters must be wizards with natural sources of insulation.

She blinked through her spiked bangs at the neat interior of the cabin. Jess had earned her lodge with years of work with Tristaine's horses, and her sisters had kept it pristine during her long months of captivity.

It was simply furnished with pieces hewn from white oak. The chairs were padded with quilts. Art covered the walls— pictures drawn by adult hands and childish ones— scenes of battle, lovemaking, and Tristaine's river. Colorful masks of clay and plaster and wood adorned the support posts.

Brenna's own single unit in the City would have gone aesthetically barren if it hadn't been for Sammy's gifts. Politics were partially to blame. Once Homeland Security became more important than civil rights in the City, many forms of creative expression fell under Government regulation. There simply wasn't a lot of art around, especially not to hang on walls.

But Brenna had spent most of her City adulthood looking at her unit through the bottom of a wineglass, so she hadn't been too inclined toward interior decoration anyway. Now, the richness and diversity of the designs in Jess's lodge amazed her.

Brenna yawned against her shoulder. "Let me take a look at you before we go?"

"Nah. I'm creaky, but I'm all right."

Brenna looked up at her. "The migration's today."

"Aye." A sigh moved through Jess's long form. "The first wave leaves in a few hours."

"Ah, Jesstin," Brenna murmured.

"I know." Jess rested her lips in Brenna's hair again. Then she dropped her hand and slapped her butt. "Meet Vic and me outside. Five minutes."

❖

Sometimes the craving for it had been a raw ache in the back of her throat, especially when she was tense or scared. The temptation to seek out the sweet, sick haze liquor provided might always haunt Brenna, but she wouldn't give in to it again.

Brenna was breathing a little hard when she reached Vicar. The other woman had her shoulder braced against a pine, her arms folded, and her long legs crossed at the ankle. She didn't look up as Brenna reached her, but a muscle in her jaw flexed.

"Hey," Brenna panted, for lack of anything better to say.

"You'll feel easier with someone on your left." Vicar pushed off the pine and walked between Brenna and the sheer ledge. She strolled with an insolent ease that mortified Brenna all the more.

"Sorry about this." Brenna scowled at her feet. "Someday, I'd like to talk to you when I'm *not* expecting to fall off a cliff. I'm not always such a nit, Vicar, I promise."

Vicar said nothing, which Brenna found disconcerting. She let it pass. It was a beautiful morning. When she could force herself to look into the canyon, she saw striations of colors in the rock walls, colors she didn't even have names for.

"So, Brenna. You've met Theryn."

Brenna glanced at Vicar. "Last night, yeah."

"You two going to be friends, then?"

"I think Theryn's fooling herself if she believes she can bargain with the City. I told her as much." Brenna actually did feel safer having Vicar between her and the drop. And she preferred her questions to her silence.

"You worked with Caster? At this Clinic?"

"Right."

"And you made decent money in the City?"

"For a Medical Technician, yeah." Brenna was starting to pant again as the trail steepened. She waited.

"A Government Medical Technician. You helped with Jesstin's...experiment, then."

"Yes." She looked up at Vicar again. "Ask me whatever you need to. I understand. But get around to asking if I love her, okay?"

Vicar's eyes were measuring. "Do you?"

"With my whole heart."

They climbed silently for a while.

"Jesstin's my cousin," Vicar said. "Our mothers were blood sisters."

"No wonder you two are so—"

"I'd kill or die for her, Brenna. Our lady needs Jess, and so do Tristaine's warriors. You might prove to be our true adanin. I'll give ye every chance of that. And I'll protect you from any threat, because you're Jesstin's lady. But I'll be watchin' you too, lass."

They were nearing Jess, who waited for them at the top of the trail. Brenna simply nodded at Vicar, then surprised them both by resting her hand on her corded forearm for a moment.

"Were you able to counsel young Vicar on that regrettable bedwettin' problem, Bren?" Jess called.

Brenna didn't dare smile, but Vicar emitted an amused snort. "Does she look sound, Stumpy?"

"Aye, she does."

The "she" Jess and Vicar referred to, apparently, was the huge earthen dam, supported by both wooden beams and mortar, which walled off one end of a large mountain lake. The water lapped peacefully against it, confident of its solid support.

Brenna stopped short, astonished by the unexpected majesty of the lake. It stretched beyond sight, curving behind a protruding islet of conifers in the distance. The glassy surface reflected the brilliant blue of the sky overhead like an inverted bowl, and Brenna was struck speechless again.

Some part of her spirit mourned for the residents of the City, most of whom would grow old without ever crossing its electrified fences. She thought of the child Sammy carried, who would never see such a lake.

"Did Amazons build this?" Brenna was awestruck, and for a moment, Jess just looked at her, smiling a little. Then she nodded.

"Our grandmothers built it, generations ago. It was the work of the first thirty years we lived on this land."

"Where—?" Brenna kept looking from the dam to the ponderous lake it contained. "Where did they learn engineering?"

"Amazons helped design the pyramids," Vicar muttered. "We've never needed City men to build our beds. Or anything else."

The scorn in her tone was hard to ignore, and Jess threw her cousin a quizzical look. "Did the bairn keep you up last night? What's the matter with you?"

Vicar shrugged an apology at Brenna.

"Bren?" Jess held out her hand and she took it, gingerly stepping closer to the outcropping that became the walkway formed by the top of the structure. "We don't have to go far out. Look there."

She stopped in front of Jess and followed her long arm as she pointed over her shoulder. She spotted a particularly nasty bruise on Jess's wrist and frowned at her, then squinted at the dam.

"Not there. The hill next to the dam, near the base of that rock shelf."

"You mean that hole down there?" Brenna crouched, more to grip the walkway for balance than to see more clearly. "What is it? A cave?"

"A mine, lass," Jess corrected, steadying Brenna with one hand. "It leads to the richest vein of silver and lead ore our cavers have ever found."

"A silver mine." Brenna pivoted to stare up at Jess, the dizzying drop forgotten. "Tristaine has a silver mine? Does Caster know about this?"

Vicar smiled without mirth. "And you thought the City was after Tristaine because of our progressive politics."

"The allure Tristaine holds for an oppressed people does threaten the City, Vicar." Jess's tone was more formal as she helped

Brenna stand. "But the Government also wants Amazon silver to fill its coffers. Even if Artemis herself descended now and vanquished Caster's troops, the Federal Military would keep targeting this village."

Jess took Brenna's hands. "Do you understand why we couldn't tell you this, Bren, before you came to Tristaine?"

"Sure," Brenna responded, still trying to file this revelation in her head. "You don't owe me any explanations, Jess. I'm learning this stuff when I should. The mine is the reason we have to destroy the village, right?"

"Aye, we want to keep Tristaine's wealth from enriching City tyrants." Jess turned Brenna gently back toward the dam. "Take a look at the center section, about two-thirds of the way up."

"I see it, but what am I looking at?"

"We'll be building a small platform there tomorrow. Against the main support post."

"A platform to hold what?"

"Enough dynamite to take out the dam."

Brenna looked at Jess. "I'm sorry?"

"Several mountain streams drain into Ziwa, as we call this lake," Jess explained. "In turn, she feeds Terme Cay, the river that runs through our village. When the dam breaks, they will empty into the valley and fill it. Tristaine's mine and its lodges will vanish beneath their waters."

Brenna released a long breath. She could see it happening in her mind.

"Jocelyn safeguarded the box, Jess," Vicar said behind them. "She'll turn it over to Shann before the first wave leaves."

"The only piece of City high technology we've found a use for, Bren." Jess's smile was grim. "The explosives can be detonated by a remote transmitter. There are lots of safeguards. It would be hard to throw it without meaning to, but Shann can trigger the blast from Tristaine if necessary."

"It would move so fast." Brenna knelt and stared at the implacable lake, then at the dam, which seemed suddenly fragile to an extreme. "Just seconds to reach the—"

"The flood wouldn't hit Tristaine straight on," Vicar cut in. "The flow would follow the riverbed at first. It feeds east into the canyon, before curving down through the valley. Trees and other debris will slow it a bit, but not much. Dyan estimated it would reach us in about ten minutes."

"Or less," Jess added. "And anyone who can't get out of the valley in time would die. It wouldn't be like drowning in a City swimming pool, Brenna. Women would be crushed in the debris carried by the flood. They would suffocate among dead animals, logs, branches, mutilated bodies. Ugly deaths."

"Right. Got it, thanks." Brenna stood and brushed the dirt from her palms. She looked past Jess and smiled. "Vicar? Would you excuse us for a moment?"

Vicar arched one eyebrow, bringing home her familial resemblance to Jess again, in spite of her fair coloring. Then she nodded, offered a vague salute, and started back down the trail.

"Jesstin."

"Yes'm."

Brenna folded her arms. So did Jess, and somehow it looked more impressive when she did it.

"I'm not leaving with the migration today. I'm staying with you."

"I see."

"Want to hear why?"

"I can't wait."

"Are you listening, really?"

"I am, Bren."

She drew a deep breath. "Because I take this adonai stuff seriously. Because I'm in love for the first and last time in my life. And because the wife of an Amazon warrior watches her back. Is any part of that unclear at all?"

Jess swallowed.

Brenna smiled.

Tears filled Jess's eyes, and she dropped her arms in exasperation. "Well, *shit.*"

"Jesstin. Amazon obscenities are so much better than Cit—"

"What am I supposed to say to *that*?" Jess scrubbed her forearm across her eyes, then set her hands on her hips and studied the lake. "If Shann orders it, will you go?"

"No. Shann isn't my queen yet. I haven't taken the Amazon pledge of allegiance, or whatever."

"The *what*?"

"I'm staying with you, Jesstin."

Jess touched Brenna's face. "It rips me up, lass, thinking of you getting hurt."

"Hah," Brenna said. "Welcome to my world, warrior! That's the same fear I feel for you every time you fight." She pressed Jess's hand to her cheek. "Jess, you know this is my decision."

"Aye, I do. You know I had to try."

"Aye, I do, lassie." Brenna took Jess's arm and wound it through her own. "Walk on my right, please."

They started back down the trail leading to the village where the women, children, and warriors leaving in the first wave had already begun to assemble.

❖

Tristaine's square thronged with women again, but this morning the activity was as orderly as it had been clamorous the night before. Perhaps some Amazons struggled with the same alcoholic aftermath that plagued Brenna, or, more likely, the sadness of the coming parting weighted their hearts. No singing or friendly shouts were heard in the efficient assembly.

A long caravan of women and children was forming in the center of the village square. Brenna saw Patana, moving as stiffly as Jess, barking orders at the warriors preparing to escort the first party of refugees to the southern meadows. There was a new aroma in the air, strong but not unpleasant, and Brenna looked around for its source.

"Adanin, good morning!"

Brenna whirled and nearly fell into Jess, as Hakan rode up to them on a towering horse. Brenna gasped a curse that was certainly less creative than Amazon obscenities. "Don't you women *ever* get sick of sneaking up on people?"

"My apologies, Brenna." Hakan's teeth flashed in her ebony face, and the silver glyph webbing her high cheekbone shimmered. "Jesstin, you found the dam sound?"

"It's been ably tended, sister. Well done." Jess shaded her eyes against the rising sun and rested her hand on the horse's muscular neck. "And how is Val?"

"Valkyrie thrives, thanks very much." With the touch of one knee, Hakan sent the mare erect, her iron-shod hooves pawing the air once before clattering down again. Brenna nervously nudged Jess back. This looming beast looked like the horses in her dreams.

"These things are *huge*. And beautiful." Brenna gathered her courage and squinted up at Hakan. "May I?"

"Go ahead, Brenna. She's gentle as a half-ton lamb." Hakan moved her mount closer, and Brenna stroked the powerful jaw. Brenna grinned, surprised at its softness, like satin over steel.

During their climb to the dam, Jess had pointed out the pasture housing Tristaine's herd. The mustangs had looked mild and tame in the distance, cropping grass and puffing steam in the chill morning air. They all looked alike to Brenna, sturdy little beasts with flaxen manes and tails.

The huge horse before her was almost twice their size with a beautiful reddish gold coat and a white mane. The star on Valkyrie's forehead looked like a child had painted it, with white stripes dripping down from the lower points.

Jess nodded toward the caravan that gathered in the square. "They look about set."

"Yes. And the second wave will assemble at noon." Hakan patted her mount's neck. "I'm riding escort for the first, as far as the pass. I'll be back by dusk."

"Need one more, for escort?" Jess eyed the horse hungrily, and Brenna knew she was itching to ride again.

"Sorry, my friend." Hakan's grin flashed. "I'm afraid you've got warriors to command. You'd best get over there and muzzle Patana before she bullies someone into a fistfight."

"Me?" Jess hooted. "I spanked Patana last night. Let Shann muzzle her."

"Sorry, my friend. You were Dyan's second. Tristaine's warriors follow you, Jesstin." Hakan nodded to them both, then gave Valkyrie some unseen signal and trotted toward the caravan.

Brenna studied Jess's face. "You're in command of Tristaine's warriors?"

"Technically," Jess sighed.

"Hoo! Poor Caster."

Jess rolled her eyes, then leaned down and kissed her forehead and tousled her hair. Brenna combed her bangs with her fingers, muttering, and followed her into the crowded square.

Brenna blinked as little as possible, so as not to miss anything. Tristaine by day was a different world than the mystical realm of last night's festival, but it was no less intriguing. She was struck by the many shades of coloring among the Amazons, both in skin tone and clothing, and the proliferation of children, both male and female.

A beautiful, curvaceous young woman threw herself into Jess's arms, squealing, "It's *Jesstin*!"

"Hello, Monique." Jess grinned, patting the girl's back. "This is—"

"Oh, Jesstin, it's *you*!"

"Aye, it is," Jesstin agreed. She gently worked Monique's arms from around her neck and straightened, wincing. "Brenna, this is Kyla's friend, Moni—"

"Oh, *Jesstin*, we feared we'd never *see* you again!" Dark eyelashes fluttered up at Jess. "Thanks be to sweet Aphrodite you returned before we *left*!"

"Love that Ditey," Brenna said politely to Monique's back.

The young woman whirled. "Oh, you must be *Brenna*!"

Brenna found herself engulfed in her arms.

"Kyla just *adores* you, Brenna! Welcome to Tristaine!" Monique laid a smacking kiss on Brenna's cheek, then released her, beaming. "Ky needs me, so I gotta run, but I am just so, so *glad* we got to meet! Good-bye, Jesstin, you ravishing warrior! Gaia preserve you both!"

Brenna watched Monique scurry toward a cluster of young Amazons.

"Monique is in the guild of the artists," Jess explained.

Brenna spied Kyla and Camryn among Monique's friends, and she smiled with an unexpected blend of relief and pleasure. She and Jess had slept within arm's reach of these sisters for months, and she had missed them.

Cam stood over Kyla as she sat cradling a wriggling Max.

"Good-bye, my furry little burrito," Kyla crooned. "Be good. Behave yourself. Stay out from under the horses. Keep the mice out of the oat bins." Tearing up, Kyla kissed the small dog's black nose. "Here, Mon, take him, quick."

"C'mere, you adorable coconut." Monique scooped Max into her arms and giggled as he licked her nose. "Okay, we're *gone*! Bye, Kyla, and dear Camryn. Let me just say again you two are *so,* so great together. May Gaia preserve you both—"

"Thanks. Walk with Jade, Moni. Walk, walk." Camryn waved her on urgently, patting Kyla's shoulder.

Kyla watched her friend carry little Max to the wide column of women forming in the square, and her shoulders lifted with another deep sigh. She smiled weakly at Brenna and Jess. "Hey. Morning, you guys."

"I'm glad you got to see wee Max before the migration, adanin." Jess bent and kissed Kyla's cheek. "You know our sisters love him too. They'll keep him fed and happy."

"Yeah. I wouldn't want him here. It's too dangerous." Kyla swallowed, then looked past them. "We all have hard good-byes to say."

Brenna turned and saw Vicar standing close to a lovely woman with oriental features. She wore a beautiful red and silver glyph on her forehead, and she carried a small bundle wrapped warmly in a quilt. Vicar lifted a corner of the blanket and rested her large palm lightly on the baby's dark, fuzzy head. Her lips moved in prayer.

"That's Vicar's adonai, Wai Li," Jess murmured behind her. "She's taking their son to the meadows."

Brenna felt sadness drape her shoulders. The expression on

the women's faces was indescribable. She turned so she wouldn't see the mother and child walk away, or Vicar's eyes as she watched them go. She laid a cold hand on Jess's arm, suddenly needing to feel its solid warmth.

"Go on," she whispered to Jess.

Jess nodded and walked over to Vicar. Her broad shoulder brushed that of her cousin, and they stood together for a while in silence.

Brenna pressed her hand to her waist. It was rising all around them, the grief of parting, permeating the air as visibly as smog clouded the skies above the City. Everywhere she looked now she saw families sharing a last embrace, and her eyes filled with tears.

Kyla took Brenna's hand and cradled it in her own cold ones. "I don't see how they stand it. Saying good-bye to this place forever. And the wives of the warriors, they might never see their adonai again…"

Camryn looked pale beneath her tan. "They can sleep well, though, Ky, knowing we'll never surrender Tristaine to the City."

"Oh, fat bloody lot of comfort *that* would be for me today, Cam, if I was leaving you here!" Kyla swiped the back of her hand across her eyes. "I can't believe you asked Shann to make me go, Camryn. I'm still pissed at you for that."

"*Thank* you," Brenna said to Kyla, vindicated. "Jess tried to kick me out, too."

"Figures."

"But you've been injured, Ky," Cam protested. "You're not going to be able to fight with us. If Dyan were here, she'd make you go, with that pig bite on your—"

"Oh, Titan's tits she would, Camryn!" Kyla sighed gustily and looked at Brenna. "Warriors."

Brenna nodded.

"Pardon me, little sisters." Dorothea was making her way toward them through the crowd, clutching a beautiful shawl of pure blue silk around her shoulders. She lifted her gnarled hand when Kyla rose from her stool. "Sit down, sit down, little one. Rest your leg! I've just come to give you your elders' blessing before we go."

"We're honored, Grandmother." Kyla hugged Dorothea with a gentleness that was almost maternal. "Please kiss Jocelyn and Sarah good-bye for us, okay?"

"I'll kiss Jocelyn. Sarah, I will shake by her warty old paw." Dorothea motioned Camryn's head down so she could kiss her cheek. "Now. Young Brenna? Help me find our lady."

"Okay," Brenna said. Dorothea was already winding her shawled arm through hers and starting into the throng. The sturdy maple cane she carried served her well, and Brenna didn't have to slow her step to walk beside her.

"Watch over Kyla and Camryn, my little sister. Guard them well." Dorothea studied Brenna as they walked. "Remember, all Amazons are mothers to the young of our clan."

"I will. We all will." Brenna led Dorothea around a horse and cart being loaded for the journey. "What's going to happen to Tristaine's mothers, if we can't come back to this valley? Aren't most of the men who sire our children City dwellers?"

"Most," Dorothea confirmed, striding sturdily along. She waved her cane at two women who called greetings. "Most fathers of Amazon children are sons of Amazons themselves. But all our brothers don't reside in the City. There are smaller towns on the other side of this range that house several of our male kin. And other nomad tribes, of both men and women, wander these hills." Dorothea winked at her. "Amazons have never wanted for quality seed, Brenna. Our Nation may indeed perish one day, through war or other calamity, but never through lack of reproductive opportunity."

"That's good to know." Brenna smiled, then eyed Dorothea with concern. "Will you be comfortable on this migration? You've got a strong gait and great balance, but I worry about your arth—"

"Oh, weeping Cyrene." Dorothea's lilting laugh cut her off. "I'll be fine, little one, riding in a lavishly cushioned wagon. Now, you have five more minutes with an elder of Tristaine, Brenna, before her august wisdom vanishes forever into the mists of the southern meadows! Do you really want to spend them fretting over sources of semen and my creaky joints?"

Brenna grinned, liking the warmth of the other woman's arm

in her own. Liking *her*. "I wish you could stay, Dorothea. I bet you could tell me some wonderful clan stories."

"I could tell you some wonderful clan gossip." Dorothea chuckled. "But as our time is short, daughter, I'll try to hold myself to two brief sermons."

"I'm all ears."

"First, I speak for Tristaine's elders in blessing the bond you've made with Jesstin. She's very dear to us, Brenna, and we know she's chosen well."

"Thank you." That cavalcade of emotions was swamping Brenna again, and she hadn't even had her morning coffee yet. "I'm really—thank you."

"And last, listen to Shanendra, and trust your instincts, girl." The spotted hand patted her again. "You don't have the luxury of self-doubt, young Brenna, or foolish modesty. Banish them both and embrace your legacy if you're to serve Tristaine."

Brenna's head was starting to pound again. This was getting a little heavy. "Dorothea, I know Shann thinks I've got some kind of psychic ability, but honestly, what I have is bad dreams."

"If that's all they are, this sad world may finally have seen the last of the Amazons."

Brenna stopped short.

Dorothea's voice was still mild. She stood gazing at the crowd around them, as if memorizing faces. "The greatest Amazon queens have always come to power in times of our greatest need, Brenna. We're in one of those times now. If our queen can't rely on your guidance—the guidance of the first seer Tristaine has bred in generations—our clan might well die out at last."

"Sweet Gaia," Brenna murmured, the first time those words passed her lips. "Dorothea, hey, please, don't put that on me. I'm not a seer. I'm really not. I'm a medic, and a good one, and I want to serve Tristaine and Shann with everything I have, but—"

"Poor little sister." Dorothea cupped Brenna's cheek. "I've thrown you for quite a loop. Here, take this. You look cold." She swept the colorful shawl off her shoulders and reached up to wrap it around Brenna's.

"Oh, Dorothea, thank you, but you need—"

"You can only offer your clan what is yours to give, little sister. All I have to give you is this." She smiled. "If Artemis is kind, all we can give will be enough. Ah, here's our lady!"

Shann, a walking emblem of grace under pressure, was moving smoothly through the continuous volley of summons and questions that flew at her from all sides. Her step was unhurried, and she answered each call with a single, calm instruction before nodding to hear the next. Shann spotted them, gave a quick wave to ask for a moment's peace, and then took Dorothea's hands.

"Good morning, Grandmother! Brenna, how did you sleep?"

"We both slept better than Tristaine's queen did, Shanendra." The small lines etching Dorothea's mouth deepened with her frown. "You're going to ruin that nice, clear complexion if you don't get enough roughage, lady, and at least eight hours' rest every night."

"Then I shall pass a law mandating two-hour naps and adequate roughage for everyone." Shann did look like she hadn't slept since addressing the village last night, but she was still cloaked in an aura that Brenna could only call regal. "Brenna, I've called a meeting of our high council tonight after the migration. I'd like you to join us."

"Me?" She felt Dorothea's gaze on her. "Sure, Shann, of course."

"How can I serve you, adanin?" Shann stepped closer to Dorothea, and her expression softened. "I know we have to say good-bye soon."

"That's why I've come, lady. To ask for the Queen's Blessing."

"Oh, Dorothea," Shann exclaimed, stricken. "Are you sure?"

"Very." The old woman nodded. "I haven't told Jocelyn yet, but I will soon. The timing is rotten, but my loom is packed. I'm ready. I'll miss you, little one."

"And I you, Grandmother." Tears rose in Shann's eyes, and she laid the palm of her right hand gently at the base of Dorothea's throat. Brenna watched quietly as a subtle curtain of privacy lowered around the queen and her elder.

"The Queen's Blessing on your journey, Dorothea. You've served your clan well, and you leave Tristaine much richer for your wisdom. Your daughters will remember you around storyfires for generations to come. You'll find our Mothers waiting to welcome you with a warm fire in the hearth." Tears spilled down Shann's cheek, but her smile carried a profound tenderness. "Dorothea, daughter of Marthe, walk with Beatrice. She'll lead you home. We'll see you again there."

"Thank you, sweetheart. That was just lovely." Dorothea beamed up at Shann, then touched her lips to her cheek. "Walk with Killian, Shanendra. Brenna? Walk with Julia."

Brenna watched Dorothea move purposely through the crowd, and she turned to Shann, at a loss. "What just happened?"

Shann cradled Brenna's hand in her own. "Dorothea senses she's going to die soon, Brenna. The Queen's Blessing is given to Amazons who are certain they're facing death."

Brenna felt a sinking in her gut. "Dying? Shann, she seems so healthy—"

"Dorothea is almost a hundred years old, little sister."

Brenna's mouth fell open. Then she closed it. Explanations about Amazons and their bizarre metabolisms and elongated lifespans would have to wait. She realized she was still wearing the blue silk shawl that Dorothea had given her. She moved her shoulders beneath its softness, a hollow ache of loss in her chest.

"Shann, I'm so sorry. You're close to Dorothea."

"Yes, I am." Shann slipped her arm around Brenna and led her toward the caravan forming in the square. "Tristaine has given birth to some extraordinary women, Brenna, and it's been my blessing to know many of them."

"I've already met a few of those." Brenna put her arm around Shann's waist. "Extraordinary women."

"Shann, a moment?" An Amazon draped in soft doeskin loped toward them. "The first wave is set, lady, but now there's some row among the warriors."

"Mercy, imagine that," Shann muttered to Brenna. "We're coming, Siirah, thank you."

It seemed most of the population of Tristaine had gathered in the village square, either to join the caravan or see it off. Brenna followed Shann around the end of the column and saw several women in leather leggings poised on the brink of an all-out clash.

Brenna wasn't sure how she knew that, because no one was waving weapons. But the menacing quiet that gripped the circle of warriors seemed more ominous than shouted curses. She looked around quickly for Jess.

Two warriors faced each other in the middle of the loosely formed ring.

"You sure about this, little girl?" The brawny woman on the left smiled.

"I'm right here, *pendeja*." The second Amazon, a young Latina, balanced lightly on the soles of her feet and made small beckoning motions with two fingers. "Bring your City-spawned ass to Elodia."

"Perry, Elodia, stand down!" To Brenna's relief, Myrine hustled between the two women, her face flushed. "Dyan would throttle you both! Theryn and Shann will settle this tonight—"

"We can settle it here and now, 'Rine." Perry's smile carried a grimness that worried Brenna. "Let's keep it between us warriors. If this young half-breed really thinks she can claim that title."

Shann was already moving when Jess walked into the circle, and at the same moment, the two women charged each other.

Myrine grappled with them for a moment, and then Jess grabbed Perry's collar and yanked her free of the struggle. She tossed the larger woman to the ground, where she fell to all fours, her muddy eyes glittering.

The young Latina shook off Myrine's restraint and charged again. Jess tripped her neatly, then stepped between the two sprawled combatants.

"Jesstin, this *bruja* sneers at Dyan's memory!" Tears sparkled in Elodia's dark eyes as she sat up.

"Raise your hand in anger to another Amazon again, either of you, and you'll clean the stables alone for a week." Jess's voice silenced the circle. "Any warrior who makes another reference to half-breeds, or mongrels, or City spawn will face me in the arena, one on one."

Brenna swallowed. Neither of the prone Amazons seemed inclined to challenge Jess. The brawny woman glared at the ground, and the girl held her tongue. Camryn shouldered her way between two of the onlookers and helped Elodia up.

Jess rested her hands on her hips and looked toward Shann. The cobalt coolness in her eyes couldn't be more distant from the warmth they carried when she and Brenna were alone. Jess lifted her chin, and Shann nodded slightly.

"No need to make anything heavy out of this, Jesstin." Patana pushed into the circle, and she and Myrine helped Perry to her feet. "It's just a disagreement among sisters. Shann and Theryn can discuss it at the high council meeting."

"Shann has better things to do than settle personal clashes, Patana," Jess said. "This ends today."

The activity in the square had quieted, and several women drifted closer to the confrontation. Brenna felt the tension like a mild current, lifting the fine hairs on her forearms.

Jess addressed the circle of warriors. "Shann's high council meets tonight, so I want a double watch around our perimeter. We muster tomorrow at dawn. Clear?"

"Clear, Jesstin," Camryn called, and she was echoed by several others.

Jess ticked off points on her fingers. "Now, we check the gear of the packhorses of the first wave and make certain our sisters are well armed for their journey. We see them safely to the pass. And we patrol the expanded borders. Questions?"

"Can't ye order us to warm the blankets of our women, Stumpy, between watches?" Vicar called. "To stoke our battle lust?"

"So ordered." Jess grinned at her cousin, and only then did a gust of relieved snickering move through the warriors. "Make a last check of weapons in the packs, adanin. Hakan, prepare to escort the first wave."

Hakan lifted a hand in acknowledgement, and Valkyrie backed up a few steps to put her in position at the head of the column. Noise began to rise around them again, and Brenna willed her shoulders to relax.

Myrine went to Jess and laid her hand on her arm, but before she could speak, Patana called a gruff summons.

"'Rine, Theryn wants us. Now."

Jess spoke to Myrine, who shook her head. Her hand slid off Jess's arm, and she followed Patana to the caravan.

"Jesstin's grown, Brenna." Shann's voice held a note of pride. "Grown, and deepened. Sweet Mothers, how I wish Dyan could see her. Do what you can to protect her from bitterness, little sister."

Jess reached them before Brenna could form a reply, and Camryn and the Latina warrior were close behind her.

"Shann, Jesstin, may Elodia have a word?"

"Of course, Camryn." Shann took Elodia's hand. "Sister, tell me your thoughts."

"Shann, lady, you don't know what's gone on since you left." Tears were coursing freely down Elodia's thin face. "Our warriors drew lots to see who would stay here and who would escort those leaving with the migration. The drawing was fixed, lady. It had to be. Half the warriors staying are loyal to Theryn!"

"Tristaine's warriors' guild has a hundred and fifty Amazons, Shann." Camryn looked to Jess for confirmation. "Theryn's got twenty or thirty in her party, tops, right? What are the chances that *all* of them made the cut?"

"Slim." Shann's eyes found Jess.

"The draw was fixed to favor Theryn's cult." Elodia scowled at Brenna. "And most of them came up from the City in the last five years, Shann."

"Your queen was born in the City too, adanin," Shann reminded her. "Most of our mothers were. Now listen well." She paused, but they were already attentive. "We can't win this fight divided, sisters. Internal strife has wiped out more Amazon clans than ever rode the forests. It can't happen here, not again. We must be unified if our clan is to survive. Am I clear?"

"Clear, Shann," Jess answered.

"Elodia, thank you for bringing this to our notice." Shann

took her shoulders in her hands. "I'll ask for your trust in letting me deal with it."

"You have that, lady." Elodia nodded to Camryn before trotting back to her sisters.

A piercing whistle sliced the chill morning air. Hakan wheeled her mount and addressed the milling column of women and children. "Amazons, ready the line!"

Two warriors jogged to the high fence encircling the village square. They unlashed the catch of the tall central gates and pushed them open. Behind them, the column was forming: Amazons gathering children, picking up litters, mounting horses, and climbing onto wagons.

Dozens of Tristaine's hardy mountain mustangs milled in the square now, most laden with provisions. Others carried oak trunks containing Tristaine's artifacts, its scrolls and history. These chests would be protected as carefully as human life.

"Lady?" Hakan called.

"This part always makes me feel like holy Moses on the mount," Shann murmured to Brenna.

Jess escorted Shann to a raised platform at one side of the gates, and Shann ascended the stairs. She turned and looked out over the long caravan as Hakan's whistle sounded again.

Brenna heard music, the chorus of Jade's guild, singing as the column began to move. Their song was wordless, and it contained a solemn note of ritual. *Jess was right*, she thought. *This is a chorus capable of invoking angels*. They sang a dirge of farewell, sad enough to inspire tears, but it also rang with hope. It was an anthem of migration, a song of passage for an Amazon clan long accustomed to exile.

Shann looked less a queen right now than a mother, watching her children leave home. Her expression was the anthem made human. But her stance was relaxed, and so were the encouraging calls she made to the women who hailed her as they filed past. Laughter began to break out in small pockets in the procession.

Brenna glanced up into Jess's face and wound both arms around her waist. Her gaze moved over the neat log structures on the perimeter of the square, including the large lodge that served as the village's meeting house.

She saw Theryn there, a striking figure, leaning against the rail of the lodge's upper balcony. A beautiful woman stood beside her, her glittering gaze searching the crowd below. Her pale and exotic features were set off by the lavender glyph covering half of one cheek. The woman's eyes met Brenna's, and a cold shiver coursed down Brenna's back.

Her clinical training hadn't included a psychiatric rotation. In the City, most chronic mental patients were not housed in richly funded Government Clinics, so she had only limited clinical contact with psychosis. But something in Brenna recognized real madness when she saw it, and her arms tightened around Jess until the woman looked away.

Save for forty warriors and members of Shann's high council, Tristaine's lodges were deserted by dusk.

CHAPTER FIVE

Brenna walked through a ghost town. She had worked in the infirmary most of the day. Shann was needed everywhere, so Brenna was entrusted with tending a small series of mishaps and minor ailments. She avoided the casks of dried herbs on the shelves in favor of the conventional medicines she knew well.

There had been nothing major, just the kind of injuries that accompany distraction and stress in large groups. The most serious was a broken wrist suffered by a young boy who held on to a wagon's wheel a moment too long. Brenna had splinted his arm and given him aspirin for pain, which was in plentiful supply, as well as herbal analgesics. She was surprised to see the sophistication of Tristaine's small hospital, in both equipment and medications. According to Jess, these supplies were bartered through Theryn's City contacts.

Now Brenna made her way carefully across the footbridge arching over the river, the echo of her feet on the planks hollow and lonely. She remembered that the Amazons called this rippling stream Terme Cay. *A pleasant name for a river that might become a raging flood,* Brenna thought, *in under ten minutes.*

The village seemed all but deserted, though at least fifty Amazons still lived within its gates. She saw a lone sentry lighting the torches that marked the perimeter of the outer wall. Then other forms emerged, almost invisible in the dusk, standing watch at regular intervals on the catwalk on top of the fence. Night was falling earlier with each day's passing, and the full moon was already edging up behind the tree line.

"Hey, hi." Camryn met her at the foot of the bridge. With the automatic courtesy of Tristaine's warriors, she took Brenna's hand to help her step down. "Shann sent me after you, Brenna. The council's gathering in the firepit instead of the meeting lodge."

"That sounds ominous."

"The storyfire pit," Camryn amended. "I think it's a bad call, but Shann wants an informal setting. To defuse tensions, she says."

Brenna nodded, folding her arms against the cold as they walked through the deserted square. "Why do you think it's a bad call, Camryn?"

"The pit's round. Seating is too equal." Camryn scowled at the moon. "The table in the lodge is a big rectangle. Shann always sits at the head at high council, and that's where Theryn and her crowd should see her tonight. Visibly in charge."

This was easily the longest conversation Brenna had had with Camryn in weeks. She murmured something that might have been agreement, then decided to speak her mind.

"Maybe Shann's really making a stronger statement by meeting in the pit. She's showing she doesn't need physical position to enforce her authority as queen, so equal seating doesn't threaten her."

"Hey, that's what Shann said!" Camryn's shy grin made her look as young as her years. "You healer types are ganging up on me with your weird logic. Oh, look. Great, dinner's ready!"

As she and Camryn crested the edge of the storyfire pit, Brenna saw a dozen Amazons seated around the cooking fire in its center, passing platters of fragrant bread.

The crackling flames, ordinarily a bonfire, burned only high enough now to heat the big pot suspended over them. Shann stood next to it, spooning deep wooden bowls full of something that smelled so heavenly, Brenna's toes curled where she stood.

"That's Rae's mutton stew." Camryn's tone was reverent. "Rae's mutton stew and Jocelyn's bread."

"I am *so* glad Amazons aren't vegetarians," Brenna said to no one. Impulsively she took Camryn's hand, and she let her keep it as they moved down the risers.

"Brenna," Theryn called in greeting, "I'm delighted Shann asked you to join us." She waited for them and smiled charmingly as she took Brenna's other hand. "Hello, Camryn! Can I get you both some victuals?"

"Thanks, we can grab our own." Camryn stood still when Theryn patted her shoulder.

"Fine, sister, but first, I'd like to introduce Tristaine's newest Amazon to her high council." Theryn offered Brenna her arm before turning to the gathering. "Sisters, adanin! Forgive my interruption of our feast!"

The conversation around the cooking fire faded, and Brenna felt all eyes turn toward them. She sought out Jess and saw her next to Shann, who had paused in the midst of filling her bowl.

"I'm proud to introduce Brenna, rescued from Caster's clutches by our own stalwart warrior hero, Jesstin." Theryn's deep voice resonated around the circle. "Brenna is not only a superb healer and a fine fighter, but she also possesses a rare and specialized talent. She follows Julia, who guides Tristaine's seers."

Brenna had told Theryn nothing about herself, and she wasn't sure how these details had come out. She felt Jess's quizzical gaze. She obviously wondered about Theryn's prescience, too.

"This is DeLorea, leader of Tristaine's tradeswomen." Theryn indicated a small black woman, who nodded a greeting at Brenna. "And Teresias, who guides the guild of mothers. This lovely flower is Opal, who rules over our orchards and gardens. And this is Constance, head of the guild of weavers, and Kas, mistress of our artists."

"Welcome, Brenna." Constance lifted her cup, which steamed with a heavenly aroma of chocolate, mixed with Tristaine's excellent coffee.

"Brenna is well acquainted with Shann, our honored queen and high guardian," Theryn continued. "And with Camryn, our council's youth representative. And soon, I hope, her circle of close friends will include the humble Theryn, who uses her skills as a negotiator to serve Tristaine as liaison with the City."

"Let the kid eat, Theryn." Teresias's tone was teasing. "She needs a little more meat on her. She'll starve by the time you run out of words."

"Teresias is Sarah's cousin, Blades," Shann called, and Brenna was pleased to understand why the remark brought laughter. "Sit down, little sister. Taste this."

Amazons had asbestos tongues, Brenna decided, watching the other women savor the steaming stew. But when she chanced a mouthful, the tender meat, the fresh vegetables, and rich broth filled her eyes with the same prayerful awe as Camryn's. She'd never dreamed of such flavors.

"That's how vegetables taste, Brenna, when they're not poisoned by City pesticides." Opal's smile was friendly as she passed her a fragrant platter of sliced bread. She didn't look much older than Jess, while the other Amazons were closer to Shann's age.

"You'll find Tristaine's Amazons more robust than City-dwellers too, girl." Teresias spooned a creamy slab of butter onto Brenna's bread and topped it with fresh honey. "Mothers raised on this food give the best milk under Gaia's sun and nurse a strong immunity into their young. Or both mother and babe answer to me," she added, to more snickering.

"We've harvested enough fresh produce to last through our own migration to the south meadows," Opal finished, "so you'll get a chance to sample the best Amazon agriculture can offer, Brenna. A few weeks on this stuff, and we'll have you more fit than you've ever been."

"Well, I've noticed your warriors do heal fast." Brenna winked at Jess between bites. "A pretty handy talent." Some part of her floated above the firepit, amazed at the ease she felt among the governing body of an Amazon clan.

"Adanin." The woman named Kas, who headed the guild of artists, stood and brushed the breadcrumbs from her hands. "Before our lady opens this council, raise flagons, please."

There was a rustling of skins and leathers as the assembled women lifted cups of the flavorful tea.

"In praise to our Mothers, for the safe return of our clan's high guardian." Kas's eyes crinkled as she smiled at Shann. "Tristaine thrives tonight, lady, even scattered to the winds, knowing our queen sleeps safe among her sisters. And Gaia's blessings, too, on Jesstin, and Camryn, and Kyla, and on our newest member, Brenna. *Tervetuloa kotin,* adanin."

Welcome home. Jess mouthed a translation to Brenna through the approving murmurs that followed Kas's toast.

"Our thanks, sweet Kasling." Shann cupped the back of the smaller woman's neck and rested her forehead against hers for a moment. "I'm blessed to have the wisdom of this council for guidance."

She addressed the others sitting around the storyfire. "Please know how grateful I am to all of you for tending Tristaine with such care while I was gone."

"Some with more care than others." DeLorea filled a pipe carved of hickory and scowled openly at Theryn.

Brenna clicked into listening mode, which wasn't unlike the heightened senses and concentration Jess utilized when following a trail. Across the storyfire, Theryn's handsome face remained pleasant, her voluptuous body relaxed against the earthen risers.

"My heartfelt thanks, too, for preserving the sweet harmony that has long enlivened our council debate," Shann added, and even DeLorea snorted laughter. Jess smiled down at her folded arms.

"We'll address the division among us presently." As Brenna watched, Shann pulled that effortless transformation again, changing in seconds from a smiling friend to an Amazon queen. "First, let me recite what I've learned from you and our elders last night and today. I'll want your counsel in anything I've missed."

"Gladly given, lady." Constance fanned away DeLorea's pipe smoke, frowning.

"The City kept Tristaine under constant scrutiny after Jesstin and our sisters escaped from the Clinic," Shann began. "Caster's soldiers patrolled the two paths leading to our village throughout the summer."

Shann walked slowly around the fire circle, making eye contact with each Amazon in turn. "As we've learned, Caster is relentless, and her motivation is highly personal now. Public disgrace has to be anathema for a City scientist of her stature. She wants to redeem herself by capturing Tristaine, and our warriors stand ready to meet her attack."

Brenna folded her arms against a chill. Jess stepped quietly across the circle and sat beside her, then lifted one long arm around her shoulders.

"The City wants to make Tristaine's Amazons compliant Citizens," Shann continued. "The Government wants our silver, our taxes, and an end to the constant trickle of City women escaping from the beds of their men to seek new homes with us. Caster wants professional salvation and private vengeance. Have I summarized our quandary?"

"Well enough, Shann." Teresias studied the flames, her expression dark with worry.

"Jesstin, I want our warriors brought to full alert, beginning tonight."

Jess nodded. "I'll double the watch, lady."

"As you order, Shann, of course." Across the pit, Theryn looked grave in the red light of the fire. "But according to my sources, we have several days before Caster could possibly launch an assault, perhaps even weeks."

"Possibly," Shann repeated. "But tomorrow marks the end of Tristaine's grace period, according to Brenna."

"Oh," Brenna said in a small voice, as several faces turned toward her. She could feel a flush moving from her collar to her hairline.

Theryn responded as though Shann's sentence made sense, which both relieved and disturbed her. "But, Shann, doesn't it make sense that if young Brenna foretold any immediate danger to our clan, it's more likely to threaten our traveling adanin, rather than the fortified village they left behind?"

"Our sisters who migrate toward the southern meadows will be in our prayers." Shann returned Theryn's gaze evenly. "The majority of our warriors who ride with them are already on highest alert. Bringing our own vigilance to full strength costs us nothing. Jesstin, are we prepared?"

"We are, lady," Jess rose, and her low voice poured over

Brenna's tight nerves like liquid balm. "Vicar and Hakan have done well keeping our warriors fit. We're as battle-ready as we can be, given the advantage our enemy has in arms."

"Thank Anath you're back, Jess." DeLorea's eyes gleamed through the smoke of her pipe. "Short of Dyan herself, there's no warrior better able to guide Tristaine's defense. Will Vicar or Hakan stand as your second?"

"I've chosen Camryn."

Camryn looked from Jess to Shann, clearly astonished.

It was obviously an honor. Brenna beamed, almost as happy for Camryn as she'd been for Sammy when she graduated from high school. Then her smile faded, even as Camryn finally blushed with pleasure. Her younger sister's diploma hadn't brought her closer to the front lines of a battlefield.

"Good choice, adanin!" Teresias slapped Camryn's thigh. "Dyan handpicked this one for our council, Brenna, and we've never regretted it. She's the sharpest of the young arrows in the guild of warriors, I promise you that."

Shann's smile held nothing of maternal indulgence, only approval and respect. "Do you accept the office, Camryn?"

"Sure." Cam swallowed, and Brenna heard a dry click in her throat. "I do, lady, yeah."

"Jesstin." Theryn stood. "I have every faith in your capable protégé, honestly. But given Camryn's youth, I believe you'll want a proven lieutenant. No insult to—"

"Camryn will work closely with Hakan and Vicar, Theryn," Jess said. "They're both well versed in combat."

"And I intend no insult to Hakan, or to your blood-cousin, Jess, but I must mention that Patana has more actual fighting experience than either of—"

"Aye, but only because Patana picks fights with every warrior in the guild. I've made my appointments, Theryn, thank you." Jess nodded at Shann and sat down again beside Brenna.

"Shann." Theryn's handsome face was filling with color. "Will the time come this evening when I'm allowed to complete a thought without interruption?"

Shann nodded and gestured gracefully. "The council is yours, sister." She sat down on one of the earthen risers.

This abrupt acquiescence startled Brenna. She felt a new intensity in the energy of the women around the fire. Theryn seemed mildly surprised as well, but she rallied quickly.

"Thank you, lady." Theryn's eyes met Brenna's and held them for a moment. "Sisters, my agenda is no secret to anyone here. I call for a truce with the City."

DeLorea made a rude noise. "You proposed this same truce the last three times this council met, Theryn. I can only thank Gaia that Shann and our sisters are back. Lady, this *Amazon* hoped to force her pact down our gullets before our messenger falcon even found you!"

"Lorea," Opal reproved.

"It's all right, little sister. DeLorea speaks truly." Theryn looked both grave and serene, if such a combination were possible. "We all know I had no luck in persuading Dyan to hear me in this matter last year. We all know our queen is opposed to negotiation with the City, as are Jesstin and Camryn. Yes, I hoped to sway the rest of you to consider it before they returned, for one simple reason."

Theryn strode into the firelight and turned quickly, so her cloak swirled around her. "I'm trying to force Tristaine's survival down your gullets, sisters! I am desperate to avoid bloodshed! And frankly, it appalls me that none of you—"

"You're desperate for a power base, Theryn," DeLorea spat.

"Peace, adanin." Shann touched DeLorea's arm, and the uneasy murmuring that started to rise in the group faded.

Brenna tried to catch every nuance of expression in those seated around the fire. Various shades of emotion were reflected in the faces there, ranging from worry to foreboding to banked anger.

"Higher education and personal prosperity do not make me a villain, DeLorea." Theryn looked at Brenna again, as if for support. "Amazons, hear me! This *can* be done. I've worked with City contacts for years. I can deal with one Government scientist!"

"But to what end, Theryn?" Shann asked. "The concessions required for any pact with the City are unthinkable."

"With all respect, lady, the destruction of our home should be as well." Theryn's eyes flashed in the firelight. "Washing Tristaine from the face of the mountain can hardly be a suitable alternative to compromise!"

Jess shook her head. "Death is preferable to enslavement, Theryn."

"Enslavement? Jesstin…" Theryn filled her lungs slowly. "The City wants to incorporate our village. Period. Yes, our goods would be taxed. We would be subject to *some* Government laws. But our clan would survive, adanin. We could even thrive!"

Theryn knelt beside Constance. "Sister, the garments turned out by your weavers are sturdy and warm, but think of the glorious tapestries your women could produce if we had access to City textiles! Kas, imagine the creative output of Tristaine's artisans, stocked with real oil paint supplies and decent—"

"The City couldn't possibly offer lovelier colors than our painters mix themselves, Theryn, from plants nurtured in Opal's gardens." Kas threw Brenna a friendly look. "Tell me, little sister, is Theryn correct? Do the finer arts flourish in the City?"

"Well, there's the Federal Youth Symphony…" Brenna bit her lip, thinking.

"You miss the point, Kas."

"No, Theryn, our gentle artist is right on target." Jess stood. Brenna's nerves stretched another notch. "The City has nothing Tristaine truly needs. And under its law, if they chose to enforce it, we would have no queen. We could be forcibly segregated by race and class, as the City's Boroughs are."

"That's ridiculous, Jesstin. Of course they won't expect us to emulate—"

"We'd be denied free worship." Constance folded her arms. "That alone leaves nothing to discuss."

"I'm afraid I agree, Theryn." Opal's tone was compassionate. "I still can't see any mix of Amazons and a Federal Government ever working."

"Shann…" Theryn turned to her. "I appeal to you, lady. Reconsider, for all our sakes! I am confident that if I'm allowed to negotiate with Caster, I'll be able to secure an agreement we can all live with."

"You have outstanding skills in diplomacy and commerce, sister." Shann rose, forming a triangle with Jess and Theryn that spanned the storyfire. "But I fear your personal ambitions might be shading your judgment."

Theryn's face flushed, and for a moment she couldn't speak. "Lady…Tristaine needs a queen with vision now, capable of seeing beyond the immediate crisis. Please, be that queen!"

"I've looked into Caster's eyes, Theryn. I must guide Tristaine by what I saw there," Shann answered.

Brenna saw a ripple of unease move through the others as Theryn pressed on.

"Shann, all my sisters, you must listen to simple reason! Amazons have always demonized anyone outside our all-holy clan, isn't that true? Just as today, Tristaine's old guard demonizes the City." Theryn lifted her hands again. "We're not waging war with ancient barbarians anymore, adanin! Citizens are not monsters or enemies! We're dealing with an educated, advanced people who can offer Tristaine endless bounty. Technologies undreamed of in our—"

"The City imprisons its rebels, Theryn." Jess's voice was dangerously mild. "It outlaws free expression. It restricts travel, marriage, reproduction. Citizens are arrested for owning the wrong books, for violating midnight curfew—"

"Jesstin," Theryn snapped. "Tristaine would hardly be subject to cur—"

"Their Government executes hundreds of political prisoners every year." Jess stepped closer to Theryn. Brenna saw the set of her wide shoulders, and her internal alarm rose higher. "They fill slave camps with dissidents. They assassinated our queen's adonai and my best friend."

"Jesstin," Brenna whispered. She'd seen that odd light in Jess's eyes only once, in the Clinic, before she attacked Caster. She felt Camryn's hand brush her leg.

"I still stink of the City's Prison," Jess continued, "and its Clinic. I would shed my blood, and that of every warrior left to us, to keep Tristaine free of that stench. And at our lady's bidding, this council will raze our village to the ground, Theryn, before letting Caster set one foot on Amazon land."

"Enough, sisters. I've reached my decision." Shann waited until Theryn and Jess returned to the risers and sat down.

"There will be no truce with the City. We will defend Tristaine against Caster's attack, whether it comes in one week or three. Then, before we rejoin our clan, we'll burn the village, to keep its spiritual legacy intact." Shann spoke with quiet strength.

She smiled at the silent circle of Amazons. "Our council is closed, adanin. Sleep well."

Brenna stared at the pitched ceiling of the dark lodge and played with Jess's fingers. Her head rested on her muscular arm. She found batting Jess's fingers around helped her think. She knew Jess was awake, because her breathing hadn't deepened yet to the slow rhythm that usually lulled Brenna as well.

But sleep was far from her mind at the moment. She was filled with an energy that hummed with anxiety and something else as well—remnants of the muted exaltation first inspired by Shann's address to the village. It would be a while before Brenna recognized this feeling as a sense of belonging.

"Hey," she whispered.

"Yes'm."

"Why did both you and Shann say we'd burn Tristaine down before letting Caster have it? I thought we're all doomed to die horribly in a big flood."

Jess yawned. "Not everyone needs to know about that dynamite, lass."

"Ah." Brenna played with Jess's fingers some more. "Camryn's really young, Jesstin."

"She's seventeen." Jess stretched her stiff back, following Brenna's thinking without effort. "Older than I was when Dyan named me her second."

"Yeah? Dyan saw your potential way back when you were a stoned toddler?"

The moonlight filling the small cabin glinted off Jess's teeth when she smiled. "If I named Hakan or Vicar my second, it would be like choosing myself, Bren. Cam has the grit to make a great warrior, but she's of a different weave than us. Not as strong as Vic, but faster. She's smarter than any warrior I've known, save Dyan. And her courage...the kid's got the heart of a damn lion."

"She does. You're right." Brenna smiled too, remembering the first time she ever saw Camryn and Kyla in the City. They stood behind a barred window in the Prison, defiantly hailing Jess with a shimmying dance, risking blows from the guards if they were caught. "You look after her, Jesstin, if it comes to a fight."

"*When* it comes. I will, lass." Jess's fingers drifted lazily up and down Brenna's arm. "And how much of a fight would you give me, querida, if I ordered you to sit out Caster's attack?"

"Sit out?"

"Stay in the main lodge with Shann and Kyla and the council instead of fighting."

"You won't order me to do that." Brenna yawned too. She was finally getting sleepy.

"I could," Jess countered. "I've both the clout to do it and the reason."

"You might have clout, but no good reason," Brenna snorted, "not unless everything you and everyone else around here ever said about Tristaine is a flat-out lie."

Jess was silent long enough that Brenna lifted her head and looked down at her. "You still insist on seeing me as fragile, don't you? Is it because I froze on the ridge?"

"No. That was a simple phobia, Bren, and you're working on that. You're able enough in drills, adanin, but you've not trained long in the Amazon way of fighting. And Shann's going to need your help with the wounded—"

"Whoa." Brenna kicked off the heavy furs covering them and in one lithe movement, swung her leg over Jess's waist and straddled her. She let her weight drop abruptly. Jess whoofed.

"I plan to help Shann with our injured after the battle. But when Caster attacks, Jess, I'm going to fight as well as I can. I'll follow your orders to the letter, and I'll be fine, because I'm a lot stronger than you think."

Brenna clasped Jess's wrists and lunged forward, pinning them to the quilt on either side of her head. "Which I will prove to you now."

"Fierce Artemis," Jess entreated the ceiling, "look down on yer poor sufferin' servant, in this her time of true tree-vai—"

"Funny, warrior." Brenna dropped full-length on the tall body beneath her to make Jess whoof again. She sought Jess's mouth and drew her into an intense, sucking kiss.

The kiss went on for quite some time.

Jess's bare left foot rose off the bed, hovered for a moment, then dropped back with a thud.

"Sheesh!" Jess gasped, when Brenna finally let her breathe. Brenna knew Jess could have flipped her easily to the floor, and she found it interesting that she chose not to. From her grin, it seemed Jess thought it was interesting too.

"All right, I'll explain," Brenna said. "You're going to let me fight with the rest of your warriors, Jesstin, because Caster is my enemy as much as anyone's. And also because Amazons are allowed to make their own choices."

Jess scowled.

"So. You'll let me watch your back in battle." Brenna still had Jess's wrists pinned on either side of her head. "Just like you're going to let me love you tonight. Because I need it and so do you. Keep your hands there. Please," she added.

Brenna lowered herself again and touched her lips to Jess's taut throat. She released her lover's wrists and let her hands roam hungrily down the lean body. Her palms found Jess's firm breasts beneath her tunic.

"You have to start letting me be a part of this clan, Jess, if

I'm ever going to be." Brenna's low voice matched the rhythmic kneading of her fingers. "I'm only taking on the risk faced by any Amazon who's capable of fighting, right?"

Jess seemed uninterested in answering, much less debating. Her long body was beginning to move beneath Brenna's hands, arching to answer her touch. Her breathing deepened.

"Brenna," she whispered, "I can't lose you."

"Hush, Jesstin. Let me love you."

And Brenna did, for the first time, in that most intimate of ways women cherish each other. She had often been the sated recipient of the warm caress of Jess's tongue and lips, but her lover had never before allowed her to reciprocate.

Outside their lodge, Selene's moon bathed the silent valley in blue light, and the cold waters of Ziwa lapped gently against the dam. In Tristaine's private cabins, women made love with the same blend of intensity and tenderness that swept Brenna and Jesstin.

Brenna lay on her side, curled against Jess, who was starting to breathe evenly again. She stroked one of her arms lightly with a feather-soft brush of her fingers.

"*Hoo*," Jess whispered.

Brenna grinned.

"Th-thanks," Jess added.

"Thank you." Brenna lifted Jess's hand to her lips and kissed it. "Go to sleep, Jesstin. It's been a rough day. Tomorrow's got to be better."

❖

Brenna knelt on the walkway formed by the top of the dam and focused on Jess's form below. Her task didn't call for much strength, as the lines the climbers used were separately anchored by ground ties.

Vigilance was required, however, to keep the ropes from snarling, and Brenna would rather hurtle headfirst off the dam herself than fail another phobia test, as self-imposed as it might be.

Her gaze didn't waver, not even when sweat beaded on her forehead despite the brisk morning air. She knew Jess was in no immediate peril, and neither were the four other Amazons working with her, all supported by rope harnesses. Brenna was doing fairly well convincing her mind to disregard the drop looming before her, but her stomach was fixated on it.

"Take up your slack, Brenna," Vicar reminded her. "She's steady. Just sing out if she gets snagged."

"Oh, I'll sing," Brenna muttered. She divided her attention between Jess and DeLorea, who was supervising the placement of the dynamite. Working with explosives was never routine, even for modern-day Amazons, but Tristaine's trust in their diminutive chief tradeswoman was well founded.

Camryn, Hakan, and Elodia had helped Jess secure the platform to the dam's main support post and now waited for DeLorea to finish wiring the detonator to the wrapped bundle.

Cam shaded her eyes and called up to the women waiting on the walkway. "Looks like Fugiera and Venore are ready below, Vicar!"

"Aye, youngster, I see."

Brenna threw a glance at the two Amazons assigned to secure sticks of dynamite to the rock shelf above the opening to the silver mine far below. One small figure was waving some signal, which Vicar returned.

Jess tossed her hair out of her eyes to look up at Brenna and sent her an encouraging wink. She smiled back, carefully playing out line as Jess shifted to the far side of the platform.

The waves of vertigo that had plagued Brenna when she first knelt on the walkway had largely subsided, but she'd feel better when the five dangling women were safely topside again.

Besides her and Vicar, four Amazons stood on the narrow ribbon that comprised the top of the dam, anchoring the climbers. Brenna had met them all at least once, but Amazon names were beginning to blur in her mind. They were Jess's warriors, her adanin, and those titles would serve for now.

"We're set!" DeLorea called as she snugged the canvas wrap gently around the explosives. "The leads are fixed. Shann should consider the remote armed as of now."

"She does," Vicar answered matter-of-factly. "Let's bring 'em up!"

Vicar checked the lines of the five climbers as their anchors took up slack, then patted Brenna gruffly on the shoulder in passing. Apparently her efforts to battle her demons hadn't gone unnoticed.

But Brenna barely registered Vicar's touch. The cold air on her face faded, and the rich trilling of birdsong that had formed a constant backdrop to the pleasant morning suddenly dwindled.

"You're about to snarl Elodia, Hakan. Space yourself," Vicar called.

"Aye, space yourself." Jess grinned at the warrior who climbed beside her. "Move yer buttocks, Hakan!"

"Bite my macha black butt, Jessica," Hakan said, panting.

Camryn chortled at both of them, but Brenna heard little of it.

J'heika, rise.

Jess peered upward, winding excess line around one forearm. Brenna was looking beyond the dam toward the village. Jess whistled softly to gain her attention, but Brenna's intense gaze held on Tristaine.

The sound alerted Vicar, who turned back to Brenna, eyebrows arched. "Brenna? What's up?"

Brenna stood up. "Take Jess's line, Vicar."

Vicar moved at once, lifting the coils of rope from Brenna's extended arm.

The other Amazons anchoring the lines exchanged glances, clearly surprised to see Vicar obey anyone other than Shann or Jess without question. Brenna stood with her hands at her sides, balanced on the narrow walkway. "Caster's here."

"Vic?" Jess called.

"Just keep climbing, Jesstin!" Vicar took up the slack in Jess's line.

Hissing tension in the men's voices, small branches snapping in the wake of their swift advance. Vehicles were useless past the foothills, so the last league up the mountain was covered on foot. The tall gates of the Amazon village were in sight.

Brenna watched Jess clamber over the railing of the catwalk. "Tristaine is under attack, Jess. Right now."

"What?"

"Trust me, Jesstin."

Jess looked into Brenna's oddly serene eyes and then whirled, looking for her second. "Camryn!"

"Here!" Cam answered at once, shaking off the rope halter.

"Take Grady and Briggs and meet Venore and Fugiera at the trail to the mine. Approach the village from the west and expect attack."

Cam's eyes widened; then she moved quickly down the walkway toward the descending path without asking questions. The rest of the warriors gathered closer, watching Jess.

"Vicar, Hakan," she glanced at each in turn, "take two warriors each and approach from the north and east." Jess's hand wrapped around Brenna's arm. "Elodia, DeLorea, you're with us. The top priority is protecting Shann."

"Right, Jess." Hakan nodded at two of the warriors. "We'll listen for your signal."

They were moving fast when they first heard enemy fire.

❖

Reaching Shann was never an option.

She refused to stay hidden. Tristaine had virtually no warning of the attack, but Shann managed to launch a swift reactive defense. At least until the canisters of gas exploded in the village square.

The vision that riveted Brenna had vanished. She remembered what she saw, though, and she still felt the certainty behind her words. Figuring out the rest would have to wait. She focused on gripping Jess's hand and racing down a mountain path that had terrified her to walk only the day before.

One moment Brenna could breathe and the next there was no air, just a cloying mist coating her face; then her throat caught fire. She coughed spasmodically and stumbled.

Jess staggered when the gas hit her lungs but kept her grasp on Brenna's hand, and they kept running. Behind them, Elodia clenched DeLorea's sleeve and hauled her bodily along, both of them gasping and coughing.

Rapid volleys of gunfire splintered the air. Brenna heard cries of shock and men's voices shouting commands. Jess flattened her against a broad pine, then looked around it. She sent a piercing whistle through two fingers, loud enough to make Brenna flinch.

"Stay beside me!" Jess ordered, her voice ragged from the fumes. She gestured to Elodia, who nodded. She pulled a retching DeLorea toward a nearby bank of trees.

Another burst of gunfire pressed them back against the pine. When it stopped, Jess squeezed Brenna's hand, and they ran for Tristaine's southern gates.

Clouds of the noxious gas were billowing through the village square. Through streaming eyes, Brenna saw green-clad soldiers wearing heavy masks that gave them a malignant and insectile appearance. They shoved staggering Amazons toward the stadium. Other women—unconscious—were being dragged along the ground.

Brenna's throat constricted with a rage she had never known, and when Jess bolted for the square, she matched her pace. When the heaviest concentration of the gas hit them, the scene grew surreal in her blurring vision, grainy and shadowed.

She saw Jess duck under a swinging rifle, then dropkick one soldier where he stood. As another spate of bullets tore into the lower branches of nearby trees, Brenna realized that the soldiers were firing into the air. The world grayed out, and she lunged toward Jess, groping for her as her senses faded.

❖

There were things Brenna hated more than throwing up, and as soon as she could stop doing it, she would try to remember them.

She felt Jess's arms around her and she sat up, snarling her hands in the soft fabric of Jess's vest.

"Easy." Jess's voice was reduced to a croak. "Water's coming, Bren."

The mention of water made her aware of a raging thirst, and Brenna blinked hard, trying to clear the tears from her eyes. A sudden and sharp series of hacking coughs bent her double, and she joined the rasping chorus all around her.

Black-booted soldiers moved among the Amazons sprawled in the center of the arena. There were easily seventy mercenaries— of mixed gender and age—encircling the stadium floor. All of them carried rifles, which they used to push the women aside if they fell into their path.

Soldiers had removed the protective masks that had shielded them from the gas, and Brenna saw that the smoke and fumes had cleared. She realized with a queasy start that she'd been unconscious for hours. The weak sun overhead was already coasting down toward the western peaks.

"Here, Brenna. Sip it."

Brenna felt Jess's cold fingers brush her brow, and she accepted the canteen. She held herself to the few swallows Jess would allow, but it took restraint. Her throat was coated with a nasty chemical slime.

"What happened?" she managed.

"The village is taken, Bren." Jess took the canteen and lifted it to her lips.

"What about K-Kyla and Shann?" Brenna asked anxiously.

"Stay here," Jess croaked calmly. She brushed Brenna's hair off her forehead and checked her red eyes. "I'll find out what I can."

Brenna knew an order when she heard one, and she didn't try to stop Jess as she climbed to her feet. Her fierce eyes streamed tears that had nothing to do with sentiment and everything with chemicals, but she seemed to be recovering quickly.

"Hey!" A soldier at the periphery of the group raised his rifle. "Get down, over there!"

Jess ignored him

"Hey!"

"Hold your water, boy." Jess coughed and spat on the ground. "You've taken our weapons. You're safe enough."

Not necessarily true, Brenna thought, but now that she could see, she realized how badly Tristaine's warriors were outnumbered. Three dozen Amazons were scattered separately and in small groups on the hard-packed ground of the arena. Brenna didn't see Shann or Kyla, or any of Tristaine's high council. The retching sounds around her were starting to fade.

Jess walked stiffly over to three of her warriors and crouched to speak to them. Then she rose, her hand on the shoulder of the youngest in the group, and scanned the open stadium.

"Sit down, you big *pendeja* bitch!" the soldier barked.

Brenna saw several rifles rising toward Jess.

"If you were allowed to fire on us, *cabron*, I'd see wounded." Jess scrubbed her forearm across her face. She surveyed her troops. "My sisters look whole enough."

"I said sit *down*!" The man's voice cracked, which scared Brenna.

"Go find your witch doctor, mercenary." Jess spied Camryn and gave her a hand up. She looked her over, brushing off her leggings. "Tell her we want to see our queen."

The soldier tossed his rifle to the woman next to him. "Dana, this is *your* fucking squad. Speak the fuck *up*!" He stalked toward Jess.

Brenna threw herself far enough to wrap her arms around one khaki-clad leg as he strode past. He yelled in alarm, flailing, and the Amazons immediately cheered.

Brenna ground her teeth at the embarrassment of being dragged across the dusty arena by the kicking, staggering soldier, but it gave her enough time to crawl up his leg. Her well-placed fist, midstride, brought both his cursing and his momentum to an abrupt halt. The mercenary toppled like a sack of laundry and lay curled on his side, cupping his testicles.

"Two," Camryn crowed, and the Amazons' laughter, choked and sputtering as it was, heartened Brenna. But more soldiers were moving now, and rifles were coming up fast.

"Stand down, militia!" Theryn's command rang across the open stadium.

Brenna swiveled on her hands and knees, shock sluicing through her.

Theryn's handsome features were congested with anger. She stalked over to the woman the soldier had called Dana and snatched her firearm from her hands. "I just ordered your squad to lower their weapons, you young idiot!"

Waves of disbelief coursed through the Amazons around Brenna as palpably as ocean surf. She stared, aghast, at the small group of familiar faces entering the arena in Theryn's wake. There were about twenty warriors, including Patana, Perry—the warrior who had clashed with Elodia—and the hauntingly lovely woman Brenna had seen on the balcony with Theryn.

And Myrine. Brenna's heart fell when she saw Jess's old friend hand in hand with Patana in the small assembly that gathered around their angry leader.

Camryn saw Myrine at the same moment, and Brenna heard her muffle an anguished curse. Jess's eyes were expressionless.

"Where's Shann, Theryn?"

"Jesstin, Shann is safe. She's right here." Theryn was calming now, and she injected authority into her voice. "Just tell your warriors not to resist, and I promise you, Amazon blood won't stain this—"

"Sow's daughter." At the far edge of the group, Vicar stood. She spoke quietly, but the venom in her tone carried her curse. "Your liver, Theryn, my fist."

An angry murmur went through the women surrounding Theryn, but she quieted them with a wide gesture. Theryn's chin lifted, and she clasped her hands behind her.

"I expected your enmity, sisters. I knew I would pay a heavy personal price for living by my ethics." She paused a moment, then continued. "But I prefer the hatred of Tristaine's old guard to the death of our village. I would have done anything…" Theryn looked directly at Brenna, "*anything* to avoid this. Your high council chose this fate, adanin, when they chose to silence me."

Brenna considered throwing up again, but her need to reach Jess and Camryn overrode the impulse. Hearing a scuffling noise high in the risers of the arena at the door to the review stand, she took advantage of the distraction and scrambled to her feet. Cam took Brenna's arm and drew her in protectively when she reached them.

She heard hissing rise from the Amazons, and as she focused on the review stand, she saw Shann accompanied by two guards who still wore the bulky gas masks. They pushed her roughly to the railing.

Shann straightened, her patrician features composed. Her arms were tied behind her, and the soft fabric of her robes was mud-spattered and torn. A bleeding bruise capped one high cheek. Her bloodshot eyes sought out Jess and held a moment, then swept across the other warriors below.

Theryn gasped, and even the women with her looked shaken. "Shann, I ordered that you not be harmed! Lady, I swear to you—"

"Really, Theryn. Still your heaving breasts." One of the soldiers holding Shann tittered and released her. "Our barbarian queen here is far thicker of skin than you imagine."

She pulled off her black gas mask and shook out silver hair, ruffling it with long, tapered fingers. The distinguished woman turned to the sea of faces watching her.

"Amazons of Tristaine, good morning!" she called, and gave them a dazzling smile. "My name is Caster."

CHAPTER SIX

Jess's arm braced Brenna, and she felt Camryn's shoulder brush her own, a small gesture of support that warmed her, even through the sick pounding in her head.

Caster's bright gaze coasted over the Amazons until she saw Brenna, and her ebony eyes sparked with pleasure.

"Brenna, Jesstin! And young Camrie, isn't it?" She pressed a well-manicured hand to her heart. "I've worried about you all through this long, tedious summer! Little Kyla is safe and well, you'll be pleased to hear. She's been taken to one of your—bunkhouse things, along with your noble tribal chieftains."

A harsh cry rose. "Release our queen, banshee!"

Jess kept her eyes on Caster. "Stand down, Sage," Jess ordered.

"Why, thank you, Jesstin. Standing down would indeed be a sage decision." Caster's gaze caressed Jess's face. "My, my. And wowza. What a dashing hunk of leathered Amazon you've landed, Miss Brenna! It's quite a thrill to see our brazen warrior here at last, isn't it? In her natural habitat, among others of her primitive ilk! I have literally dreamed of this day."

So have I, Brenna thought.

"And I'm just as pleased to see *you*, young Brenna." Caster's sharp teeth glinted as she smiled at the Amazons. "Ladies, please know my former med tech has a special place in my heart. And I've brought both Brenna and Jesstin souvenirs from the City."

Brenna didn't have to look up at Jess to know that her tears had dried the moment Caster revealed herself. Faced with an enemy, Jess had a warrior's discipline, even over her rebellious tear ducts.

As she studied the scientist she had once respected, Brenna realized she was trembling, but not with fear. It was fury, a fury that heated her blood and put steel in her spine.

A slipstream of images swam through her mind of the Festival of Thesmophoria: Kyla singing the Challenge of Artemis, Shann's address, and the grieving pride of the Amazons as they left their village. Brenna would later describe this moment of rage in her second journal as the beginning of her life as an Amazon.

"I realize how anxious you all must be to hear from Tristaine's attractive lead dominatrix." Caster smiled at Shann. "And I will indulge that desire straight away! We have a great deal of important work ahead of us, Jesstin, and I don't want your warriors distracted with worry."

Shann glanced at the soldier that still kept a tight grasp on her right arm. At Caster's nod, he released her. She looked out over her women and her shoulders relaxed, despite the cruel ropes that bound her.

"I'm not badly hurt, adanin. And last I saw them, neither was Kyla, or Terme, or Cay, or Ziwa, or anyone else on our high council. I can assure you that Tristaine's greatest treasures, the wise women who guide her queen, are all safe and whole."

Shann's voice rasped with the after-effects of the gas, but her remote calm helped ease Brenna's concern for her. She made vague note that Shann was talking in code and hoped Jess would be able to translate it for her sometime soon.

"Our village has been taken without real bloodshed. That tells us Caster needs something from us." Shann's red eyes fell on Jess again as she went on. "For now, sisters, we will not resist."

There was a murmur of disquiet among the Amazons, and the cords stood out in Jess's jaw, but she nodded.

"Shann." Theryn stepped forward and tried to catch Shann's eye. "Lady, I give you my bond that your warriors will not be injured. All Caster wants to do is film a documentary about her—"

"Cooperate as Gaia allows, sisters, and keep fast to the path of our Mothers," Shann continued. "I ask for your patience and your trust."

The same small, detached part of Brenna's mind that was thinking clearly noted that this was the first time she had ever heard Shann interrupt anyone.

"Our trust is yours, lady." Hakan's voice was heard from the back, and Brenna looked around for her in relief.

Caster let the silence linger after Shann finished speaking. Then she gestured to the female soldier who stood next to Theryn. "Miss Dana! Please escort our pagan queen back to her barracks."

The girl grimaced in reply and shouldered her weapon. Brenna caught her eye as she stalked past, and the young woman scowled and looked away. Fascinated, Brenna watched her until she was out of sight.

"Brenna?" Jess's rough hand touched her arm. "You know her?"

"Never seen her before in my life." Brenna hadn't. There were several women soldiers among Caster's mercenaries. She had no idea why this one stood out for her.

The breeze that felt pleasantly cool on the dam chilled Brenna now as she watched Shann being escorted out of the stadium. Jess's arm pressed her shoulders, and she leaned into her, both offering comfort and accepting it.

None of the Amazons around them moved, but it seemed the group gathered closer to them in spirit. Brenna could feel the breath of twenty warriors warming their backs.

"Sit down, Bren," Jess said.

Brenna folded her legs gratefully and let the cold, hard-packed ground support her. She drew in deep draughts of mountain air and watched the remaining soldiers space themselves around their circle. Then she saw Theryn, walking slowly to the front of their gathering.

Theryn's padded shoulders were slumped at first but lifted as she turned to address Tristaine's warriors again. Her stentorian voice rang in the quiet arena.

"Whatever your anger toward me, sisters, listen well! I entreat you to heed our lady's command. Cooperation is your only hope for survival." Theryn paused with a showman's timing, making sure every eye was on her. "Caster holds your queen and several members of Tristaine's high council. Because of young Kyla's injured leg, I've arranged to have her stay at Shann's side. I warn you, any deviation from Caster's agenda will put *their* lives at risk, as well as your own!"

Brenna was distracted by movement from Theryn's cluster of followers. The woman she had seen on the balcony broke free of them and ran to Theryn, who lifted her arm to embrace her.

"Who *is* that?" Brenna whispered to Camryn.

"Grythe." Camryn grimaced. "She's Theryn's adonai."

Flaxen curls billowed around Grythe's lovely face, and her posture next to her taller mate was fiercely protective. She lifted one arm, adorned with thin silver bracelets from wrist to elbow, and tickled the base of Theryn's throat with long, ragged nails. Her glittering eyes fell on Brenna.

Theryn raised one arm. "I have succeeded in securing a pact with Caster!" Theryn's followers gave a supportive cheer, and she waved a benediction over the crowd.

"Caster is a practical woman, and she will convince her Military funders to honor our agreement. Never fear. Now, this is what Tristaine offers the City." Theryn enumerated the terms of the truce on her gloved hand. "Amazons will become legal Citizens. We will accept a City delegate on our high council. Our silver will be taxed. And that's it! That is all Caster demands."

Utter silence in the arena.

"In return," Theryn continued, "the migration will be recalled! Our sisters will be permitted to return from their exile in the southern meadows. A new high council will rule. And we will be allowed to live out our lives here in Tristaine!"

Celebratory war cries erupted from Theryn's group, in vivid contrast to the bleak silence of Jess's warriors. Patana pumped her fist in the air, her hawkish features elated. Brenna saw Myrine close her eyes, looking more relieved than elated. She never glanced their way.

Theryn waited for the cheering to fade, stroking Grythe's slender arm, which was draped seductively across the base of her throat. "Now, sisters, let me explain the logic behind our truce. Caster's capture of Tristaine will validate the project she began in the City Clinic. She will prove to the Government that her techniques *can* turn their enemies against each other."

"The City doesn't need Caster for that, Theryn. They have you." Jesstin's brogue was clipped. She looked up at the scientist in the review stand. "My clinical study had nothing to do with turning Amazons against Tristaine, Caster."

"Of course it did, Jesstin." Caster sipped delicately from a canteen. "Or at least it will, with proper film editing and a few payments—a few *silver* coins—in the right pockets."

"Our strategy is this," Theryn continued. "Caster will film our two companies in mock battle." She moved until she was in Jess's line of sight. "*Sham* combat, Jesstin. No one will be hurt."

"Or what, Theryn? Your truce will be null and void?" Jess smiled without mirth. "Caster will pack her expensive toy soldiers and march them back down the mountain?"

Grythe looked at Jess as though she were tasty carrion.

Theryn bent as Grythe whispered to her, then shook her head and straightened. "You and your warriors, Jesstin, and our lady and her high council, will be banished from Tristaine. Forever. You'll be given your freedom to move deeper into the mountains to form that new commune Shann spoke of so movingly in the Queen's Address."

"Our freedom isn't yours to give, Amazon." Jess's voice was low and ominously quiet. "You've struck a deal with a demon. Caster has no intention of letting anyone loyal to Shann leave Tristaine. Not alive."

"Fine with me, bitch!" Patana elbowed Myrine aside and grinned at the warriors sprawled on the ground. "I don't care if we skewer each and every one of you *sisters* and hang your pelts from our lodge poles. I figure it's worth a little carnage if we finally win Tristaine a queen worthy of the name."

"Fucking *pendeja!*" Elodia exploded to her feet. "We *knew* you wanted Shann's throne, Theryn, you bloody *traidora!*"

"We will continue to honor all of Tristaine's Grandmothers."

Theryn raised her voice, obviously trying to tamp down the ire rumbling through the warriors. "And I will maintain our sacred ceremonies—"

"You betrayed your clan for power, *puta!*" Elodia hurtled toward Theryn, but Jess swiveled and caught her attempted rush.

"You want to rule Tristaine, and you want City medicine for your crazy wife!" Elodia could still yell under Jess's restraint. "That sick *bruja*, Grythe—"

Jess's hold on Elodia moved smoothly from a simple hold to punishment, and the girl gasped. Jess lowered her with a distinct lack of gentleness to a seated position beside Camryn. Jess's eyes on Elodia were as cold as Brenna had ever seen them.

"You don't mock an Amazon's affliction, girl. *Any* Amazon. Now stand down and tame your temper." Jess straightened. "You believe you can convince our clan to accept your rule, Theryn?"

"I do." Theryn smiled directly at Jess for the first time. "I'm confident, Jesstin, that the prosperity I bring Tristaine through this truce will soothe any ruffled feelings eventually."

"Let's wrap this up, ladies, shall we?" Caster snugged her parka around her. "We've lost the light for filming today, at any rate. Get these primitives sorted out, Theryn, and lead me to a decent dinner."

"Happily, Caster." Theryn gently freed herself from her wife's clinging grip. She clapped her hands. "All right! On your feet, Amazons!"

No one moved, which seemed to surprise no one but Theryn. Brenna couldn't read Grythe's expression. The woman's face rarely betrayed any emotion other than hate. After a moment, Jess glanced down at Camryn. Cam whistled, and the group of warriors grumbled to their feet.

"I'm not foolish enough to let all your warriors in the ring at once, Jesstin." Theryn braced her gloved hands on her hips. "Pick ten of your best for the war games. Patana and Myrine will have fourteen in their cadre. I'm sure you won't begrudge us the extra bodies. Your fighters trained longer with Dyan."

Hakan frowned, brushing the dust of the arena from her broad hands. "What about the rest of the warriors, Amazon?"

"Don't worry, my violent sister. I'm sure Jesstin won't pass *you* up!" Theryn's face was flushed, either with cold or with relief that this assembly was ending. "The warriors she doesn't select will go into lockdown in the barracks of their guild until filming is complete."

"Oh, Brenna?" Caster trilled.

Brenna was examining Elodia's elbow, badly scraped in their mad dash through the woods. Jess and Camryn both turned when Caster called her.

"I do hope you've picked up some dazzling Amazon combat tricks, my former colleague, because I must insist that Jesstin include you among her warriors." Caster leaned on the railing of the review stand looking at Brenna fondly. "As you might remember, you were rather alluringly displayed in our Clinic films of Jesstin's study. I watch them nightly, like home movies. And I'll want our funders to see you and Jesstin battling together, side by side, for Tristaine's mining rights."

"Caster, I'm not sure that's entirely fair." Theryn measured Brenna with her eyes, while Grythe pierced her with hers. "As you know, this girl is new to our village. And Brenna is a healer, not a warrior. Judging by—"

"Judging by the way she bagged your soldier, Theryn," Hakan called, "she's worth any three of your fighters."

There were a few defiant snorts of agreement among the warriors, and Camryn grinned at Brenna.

"Save your worry, Theryn. Brenna doesn't need anyone's permission to watch my back." Jess's gaze flickered over the twenty warriors around her. Finally, she pointed several times, then snapped her fingers.

The milling women separated into two groups, shivering as twilight fell over the village. Brenna spied the mercenary named Dana coming back into the stadium. One of the soldiers jogged to her, carrying a clipboard. Dana nodded and began rapping out orders.

"Rodriguez, take that group to the barracks east of the stadium. I'll settle this lot in here." Dana raised her voice, which sounded painfully young. "Theryn? We've got five guarding the queen's council, five on watch, and ten each on both Amazon buildings."

"Thank you, Dana." Theryn settled Grythe's thin hand in the crook of her arm. "Lock Jesstin's warriors down with care, please."

"Good night, ladies!" Caster called brightly and waved from the review stand. "Perhaps I should interview your queen this evening about the reported joys of all this inverted Sapphic activity! See you bright and early tomorrow."

Jess gripped Camryn's arm and kept her walking steadily toward the gate where Dana herded them. "She's trying to goad us, Cam. Don't bite."

Jess turned and whistled a complex series of notes between her fingers at the other group of warriors who were being led out of the stadium. One of them raised a hand in acknowledgment.

"Keep moving!" Dana pushed Brenna's shoulder as they passed.

Jess's warriors were being confined in the small stable at the south end of the arena used to shelter Tristaine's horses during tournaments and drills. Brenna squinted, trying to make out familiar faces in the gloom. She saw Hakan and Vicar and Elodia, eyeing the soldiers standing guard at the railing surrounding the stable. Camryn was already directing four other warriors in clearing an area on the wood-plank floor.

As always when needing reassurance, Brenna sought out Jess. The nightmare progression of this day finally seemed to be winding down toward some kind of quiet, and she craved Jess's solid presence. She saw her ducking through the door into the stable. Dana was standing behind her.

"You're Jesstin, right?"

Jess turned back to her. "That's right."

Dana grimaced. "Here's Caster's souvenir from the City." She lifted her sidearm and shot Jess in the stomach.

There was immediate chaos in the stable, but Brenna heard little of it.

The impact knocked Jess off her feet, and she crashed bodily into the three Amazons behind her before falling to the hay-strewn floor, out of Brenna's sight.

"You crazy *cunt*." The soldier named Rodriguez joined the other rattled men at the stable railing. His rifle snapped up to join the line of muzzles targeting the stunned Amazons. "Dana, what the fuck were you thinking?"

"It wasn't my idea, Rodriguez. Caster's direct order."

"You could have given us some fucking warning!" Rodriguez barked.

"Tell the lunatic paying for all this, gonad! She wrote the script, not me!"

"Let me see her," Brenna said.

Dana looked into the stable, startled by the commanding voice.

The hot blonde who had kept staring at her in the arena had just silenced the entire group of Amazons. Caster's notes said the dark woman named Jesstin was commander of the warriors, but there was nothing in her report about this girl—Brenna, was it?—being some kind of leader. One by one, the warriors stepped away from the fallen prisoner and cleared a path.

The tall Amazon with the white hair and bitter eyes eased Jesstin into a seated position against a support post. "She's breathing, Brenna," she said quietly.

Brenna knelt beside her patient. "Camryn, call them down."

Dana watched one of the younger warriors, her face the color of ash, climb to her feet, then look at the rifles and the Amazons beginning to turn their new anger on their captors.

"Amazons, stand down!" Camryn's voice cracked painfully.

To Dana's astonishment, the brutish warriors heeded the girl. A few still lingered close to the railing, staring silent hatred at the line of soldiers, but most turned back to the circle of women surrounding Jesstin.

Dana frowned, rising up on her toes to try to see the unconscious woman. "It was just a taser," she called to the anxious throng, "a strong one, but she's not badly injured."

Brenna had indeed been able to learn that much, and the wave of relief made black sparks flare behind her eyes. She had Jess's denim shirt open and saw the plastic projectile clamped to her pale skin a hand span below her breasts. Four distinct, thin lines of blood wended from its corners, trickling down her lean sides.

Jess's eyes were fluttering. The cold air held the bitter smell of cordite, and Brenna hesitated, her hand hovering over the taser bolt.

"What in bloody hell *is* that?" Vicar was gripping Jess's shoulders with white-knuckled hands.

"Pull it out, Brenna," Camryn told her quietly, her voice having not yet regained its strength. Hakan took her arm and pulled her closer so she could kneel beside Brenna. "It won't hurt you, but it's still shocking her, so hurry."

Brenna steeled herself and gripped the small square of vibrating plastic. She pulled up in one smooth motion and Jess gasped, her back arching as four thin metal prongs slid out of her skin. Vicar stared at the device in revulsion, but Brenna didn't spare it a glance. She handed it to Camryn and cupped Jess's face in her cold hands.

"Jesstin?" Brenna demanded. "Do you hear me?"

"She was woozy for a while the last time this happened." Camryn lifted Jess's limp hand onto her knee. "She'll be okay, Brenna, just weak and sore for a few days."

"They use *that* on prisoners at the Clinic, Camryn?" Hakan asked, shock in her voice.

"There's nothing like this at the Clinic." Brenna raised Jess's eyelid to check her pupil in the dim light. "I've never seen this before."

"They use stunners in the Clinic, not tasers." Camryn smoothed one thumb over Jess's wrist. "Tasers are for the Prison."

"Hey, tasers hurt, but they don't kill, for god's sake!" Dana called. "She'll even be able to fight tomorrow, honestly." After a moment, Dana whirled and stalked toward the arena door. "Rodriquez, as you were, you idiot!"

The soldiers lowered their rifles, grumbling.

Jess's awakening was abrupt. "Brenna!"

"I'm right here, Jess," Brenna said, her voice both warm and stern. "Look at me."

The long muscles of Jess's body trembled, but she relaxed against her cousin, and her dazed eyes found Brenna.

"*Sheesh!*" Jess gasped.

Brenna nodded. "Tell me how you are."

Jess winced, then looked up at her second. "I'll be next to useless tomorrow, Cam."

"Jesstin. Answer me." Brenna's firmness had won out over her warmth, but Jess just shuddered and rested her head back on Vicar's shoulder.

"It'll hurt for a while." Cam nodded thanks to Elodia, who brought a clean dipper filled with water for Jess. "I think we have to just let her rest. There's not a lot we can do. Except make her keep still. Ha ha."

Brenna gauged Jess's breathing. The frightening rapid-fire of her pulse was calming slightly. The voltage of the taser was powerful enough to contract muscle in strong spasms, and the effect was obviously painful. Sweat still beaded her forehead.

Jess filled her lungs with a deep breath. She frowned up at Vicar, still supporting her against the post. "What, Bigfoot, you waiting for a kiss?"

"Hardly, Stumpy," Vicar snorted. "Not unless your healer here packed some fierce antibiotics." Her hands were gentle as she helped Jess sit up against the post.

"Freya, Elodia, Jaye, Shasa." Jess swallowed, and Brenna helped her sip from the dipper of water. Find some bedding, adanin. We'll hold council in the morning."

"So you're all right, Jesstin?" Elodia's arms were folded, but concern softened her voice.

"I'll live." Jess smiled at Elodia grimly. "Have Brenna check that scraped arm again before you turn in, youngster."

Jess's listless wave signaled a general dismissal, and the warriors turned to setting up something resembling bedding. A sullen soldier offered them a medical kit, which they accepted. They were also offered armloads of scratchy Army blankets, which they declined. The stable held enough hay to warm them through an early winter night.

As twilight gave way to full dark and Selene's moon began her slow climb over the mountain valley, the Amazons were served shrink-wrapped bags of rations, which Brenna informed them were tasteless but harmless.

The captives formed a tight circle in the center of the wood floor. Vicar and Camryn stacked enough hay to provide Jess relative comfort.

The Amazons rotated guard throughout the night, keeping watch while their sisters slept. Hakan finished her stint just as the small generator the soldiers carried clicked on, providing a solitary light. It cast macabre shadows over the cramped space, adding to the stable's aura of bleakness.

Hakan sat beside Jess and studied her pale features, pursing her full lips in thought. She balanced one elbow on her meaty thigh and flexed her fingers, inviting an arm-wrestling match. Jess smiled at her friend and, with effort, raised an extended middle finger and waved it at her. Vicar and Camryn laughed, but the sound was quickly subdued.

Hakan's deep voice was pitched low. "There's no lasting paralysis then, Brenna?"

"No, just a lot of residual stiffness." Brenna's tension tightened her own shoulders. "Your pulse is steady, Jess, and I don't see any sign of shock."

"There's no real damage, lass. I'll be peachy in three days." Jess frowned and shifted against the hay bale. "But in the morning, I'll fight like a bloody crone."

"You mean an older one?" Vicar's rejoinder was automatic, but her expressive features were grave.

"Yeah, we'll need to protect you, Jess." Camryn looked worried as well. "We don't even know what kind of fight we're facing tomorrow. We're supposed to 'sham' fight for some stupid documentary?"

"Shann was right, Cam," Jess said, "This is all about Caster's redemption. I think Theryn's warriors are supposed to beat us in this film and then pretend to surrender to Caster."

"Is that what this was about? Caster's souvenir?" Brenna laid her hand lightly on Jess's bandaged side. "Do you think that taser bolt was just stupid revenge, or do she and Theryn want you physically rocky for some reason?"

"Good question, Bren. Hey," Jess's brows rose, "we have company."

Brenna heard it too, a muffled cursing in the arena coming closer.

"...and Caster can take *you* with her, fuck you very much, you *pinche* excuse for a City warrior, *get* your sorry hand off me, I've been walking upright for..."

Jess groaned, but she was grinning. Camryn's face lit up, and incredible as it seemed after this day, Brenna found she could smile too.

Kyla ragged the hapless Dana, loudly and obscenely, through the door, down the short hallway, through another door, down six stairs, and up to the penned stable, but then Kyla saw Camryn and her sisters, and she stopped short.

"What's she doing here?" Rodriguez asked, still morose. "Caster's orders again?"

Dana just looked glad to be rid of Kyla. "This one's not on Tristaine's governing board, so I want her here where we can watch her."

She lifted a section of the wooden railing to let Kyla duck into the stable, then trudged wearily to a hay bale in the corner and sat down. "Go back to sleep, Rodriguez."

Kyla's bandaged thigh gave her a pronounced limp, but there was nothing wrong with her sharp eyes. Her gaze zeroed in on Camryn, who rose to meet her. The two adonai met with a passionate embrace.

"Sheesh," Jess sighed. She nudged Brenna. "Remember the good old days when Camryn avoided public displays of lewdness?"

"Oh, hush," Brenna chided Jess gently. She enjoyed watching

the kiss that melded the two young Amazons together from nose to pelvis. A few of the warriors hooted softly in encouragement.

"You're okay, good!" Kyla finally broke the embrace. "And Brenna, you're okay." She limped over to Jess and plunked down hard on the hay-strewn floor beside her. "Well?" she snapped. "What happened to *you*?"

Camryn lowered herself beside her young wife. "Taser, Ky."

Kyla blanched, and some of the starch drained out of her. She lifted Jess's hand to her knee. "Oh, Jesstin. I'm sorry. Are you hurting a lot?"

"It's not as bad as the first time, adanin." Jess used a gentle tone she seemed to reserve only for Dyan's blood sister.

"Uh, hello, it *better* not be as bad as the first time." Kyla looked at Brenna. "Jess got tasered when she was in the City Prison. The night Cam and I tried to break her out."

"We were almost over the wall." Camryn looked at Vicar remorsefully. "We came really close, Vic. Jess hadn't had any decent food in weeks, so she was kind of weak, but she would have made it over. The one lousy guard we couldn't find to bribe had to play hero, and he tasered her. The bolt got her in the butt that time, though," she added, "on the left."

"Your plan butt-fired," Vicar said sadly, and Brenna smiled again.

The warmth of women sitting in close formation comforted Brenna, and she consciously relaxed her tense back. Jess's hand moved in hers, and she looked down and lost herself, as she often did, in her lover's fond gaze.

"How do you feel?" Brenna whispered.

The corner of Jess's mouth lifted, and she shrugged carefully.

"The City must have had a special on mercenaries this week." Hakan jutted her chin toward the five guards slung in various phases of boredom against the railing. "Looks like poor Dr. Caster got shortchanged."

"They're a pretty motley lot." Vicar helped Cam cover Kyla

with enough clean straw to keep her warm. "I'll sleep no easier picturing these oafs pawing at that dynamite tomorrow."

Brenna's back cramped again. She'd forgotten about the dam and the huge lake it held at bay. She imagined the implacable black surface of the water, glinting beneath an impassive moon, less than a mile from where they lay.

These mercenaries might be oafs, Brenna thought, *but surely they could handle removing a few sticks of dynamite safely. Which would also remove the risk of a flood. Which could reach us in ten minutes, if even one of the soldiers fouls up.*

J'heika, rise.

"Shann still has the detonator." Jess kept her voice low. "Or she knows where it is."

"She does?" Vicar glanced over her shoulder at their guards and lowered her voice. "When Shann said 'Terme and Cay and Ziwa' were safe with our high council, is that what she meant? That we can still blow the dam ourselves if we have to?"

"I think so." Jess nodded at her second. "Make sense to you?"

"Oh, yeah. Wait." Camryn's smile faded. "Won't Caster suspect that Shann has it, the detonator?"

"Not if she doesn't know about the dynamite." Brenna watched dust motes coast down a slow waterfall through a weak beam of light. She felt Jess's hand on her wrist and realized the circle of Amazons was staring at her. "What?"

"Hey, are you doing it again, Brenna?" Kyla craned forward to see Brenna's face. "That spooky oracle thing Cam said you pulled up on the dam?"

Vicar frowned as she spoke. "Why wouldn't Caster know the dam's rigged? Theryn filled her in, the traitorous shrike."

"Not on this." Brenna blinked and looked at Jess. "Don't ask me how I know that, but I'm sure. Theryn didn't tell Caster about the dynamite."

"But the mercs will find it come sunrise." Hakan seemed to accept Brenna's statement as fact. "Those tarped bundles are hardly hidden. They'll see them the first time they scout the area."

"Which they should have done today, the moment the captives were secured." Jess's eyes glinted, cat-like, and Brenna realized she was starting to enjoy herself. She nodded slightly toward their lounging sentries. "This is a City squad, adanin. If Brenna's right, Theryn reserved an escape route. I don't know why, and tonight I don't care. Just remember it's possible the explosives are securely in place."

"Jesstin?" Elodia's tone was respectful as she approached the group. "What's our strategy here? We need a plan."

"We do," Jess agreed, sitting up with effort, "and I'd like to hear ideas before the morning's council."

"Well, we can't know what Shann and the council would order." Hakan spun a wisp of straw across her smooth cheek. "But our guild's priority is always the safety of our queen, our council, and the vulnerable among us. I say our goal is to get our adanin out of here whole, Jess."

"Aye, and then blow the dam." Vicar's eyes were as cold as her voice.

There was a bleak silence in their circle that Brenna recognized as agreement.

"What about Theryn's followers?" Jess's tone was neutral.

Another moment of silence, this one ticking with tension.

"Take as many as will come," Camryn said, finally. "We'll sort it out with them later."

"But we won't let them stop us," Vicar added, and agreement murmured again through the circle of Amazons.

"Great! We have a plan." Jess smiled like a rogue, which heartened Brenna. "And no bloody idea how to carry it out. We're going to have to play it very much by ear tomorrow. Therefore, it's important that you barbarian ladies follow my lead, yes?"

It was a perfect pitch imitation of Caster's affected speech, and it earned the laughter Jess obviously wanted.

"Brenna." Jess pressed her hand. "It's happening more often now, these flashes of yours."

"I guess. Yeah." Brenna closed her eyes for a moment. "But please, Jess, please don't act blindly on anything I spout off like that. We still don't have any idea where this stuff comes from. For all we know, I'm a raving psychotic."

"Given," Jess agreed, which coaxed another smile out of her. "But you're proving a damn accurate lunatic, lass."

"No kidding, Brenna, absolutely." Kyla, avidly eavesdropping as usual, chimed in. "You told Shann that Tristaine only had a week of safety, when Theryn claimed Caster would hold off for months."

"And you knew when the attack came today." Camryn was looking at Brenna as if she were a fascinating new breed of horse. "And when it hits you, Brenna, you should see yourself. You do this butch thing, you become this uber blonde."

"Oh, please," Brenna sputtered.

"That's true." Vicar's eyes measured Brenna.

"So, can you tell us anything, Brenna?" Hakan's rich voice was friendly. "I think you'll find our minds open."

Brenna looked around their circle and found attentive faces, but she saw Jess eyeing Vicar as they waited for her reply.

"You guys, I don't have a clue." Brenna slumped her shoulders. "Right now, I don't know any more about what's going on than any of you."

"Good enough for tonight." Jess's voice was still rough from the taser effects. "Get some sleep, adanin. The sun rises early. Keep your eyes on me and Cam tomorrow. Never forget, our primary goal is to find a way to get Shann and the council out of here alive. And as many of the rest of us as we can manage."

A sigh of agreement moved through them, a settling in that signaled an end to this surreal and harrowing day. *Only one day*, Brenna thought. *Yesterday they were free, and tonight Tristaine's daughters chased sleep as captives on their own land.*

Brenna nestled into Jess, feeling her long arm wrap around her waist. She felt them both relax almost at once, which surprised her a little. Well, she reasoned, prophecy, betrayal, mortal terror, rabid rage. All of it was tiring stuff.

"Hey, Jesstin?" Kyla's stage whisper roused them, and Camryn groaned. "Which one of those hairy creeps tasered you?"

"The young hairy creep. The girl." Brenna felt Jess wince as she adjusted her weight. "Her name's Dana."

"I thought so. She's the one who brought me back here. Sweet Gaia," Kyla grumbled, burrowing closer to Camryn under the straw. "I hate butch women who don't even know what side they should be on. I think her bringing me down here was her apology for zapping you, Jess."

"What?" Camryn yawned into Kyla's luxuriant red curls. "Show me the City merc that has that much heart, Ky."

Jess was quiet, and Brenna rubbed her forearm gently. "Hey. Hurting a lot?"

"Not too much." Jess's breath warmed her ear. "Brenna, I want you to be on your guard tomorrow, lass. You heard what Caster said."

Brenna's mind filtered through Caster's file of venomous statements of the day and remembered she had her own souvenir coming. "Caster doesn't scare me anymore, Jess. Try to rest, okay? And you wake me up if you need anything."

"Yes'm," Jess mumbled.

Brenna heard the breathing of the Amazons around them grow slow and deep. She had lied about having no fear of Caster, and doubtless Jess knew it. The City scientist held a wickedly sharp blade to her throat and would as long as she loved the woman warming her back.

Brenna turned her head on the scratchy straw. Wrapped in Camryn's arms, Kyla smiled and blinked at her sleepily. She slid her hand across the space separating them and clasped Brenna's hand.

"I miss Max," Brenna whispered. "I wish he were here."

"I do, too," Kyla answered. "Go to sleep, adanin. We'll all be here when you wake up. That's what Shann says, when she wishes the little ones good night."

Brenna slept.

CHAPTER SEVEN

A glowering shiner capped Caster's high cheek the next morning. It would soon be as glorious as a sunset. The Amazons brayed with laughter when they saw it.

Rodriguez frowned and nudged Dana. "What are they cackling about?"

"How should I know?" She rubbed her face. She hadn't slept well. "Just stay alert."

Dana examined the two portable camcorders mounted on tripods at opposite ends of the arena, and a third, braced on the railing of the review stand. They were inexpertly operated by three soldiers who were too clumsy to be trusted to carry carbines.

"How did last night's seduction go, Caster?"

It was Jesstin's voice, and Dana gaped at her. She stood at the head of her small troop of warriors regarding Caster with a brazen smile. Except for the pallor beneath her tan, she looked like a taser had never touched her in her life.

The Amazons were snickering again, and Dana finally got the joke. Caster had made some stupid parting shot yesterday about bedding Tristaine's queen. The woman named Shann hadn't looked like a warrior on the review stand, but apparently Caster's attempt to seduce her had been forcefully rebuffed. Dana smiled sourly at the toe of her boot.

"My, you look fit, Jesstin." Caster's tone was ominously mild. Dana figured she too must have noticed her souvenir from the City had little lasting effect on its intended target.

Caster feigned oblivion to any change in her appearance. She rose from the padded bench in the review stand and smiled down at Jess. "Actually, I'm pleased to see you so robust, dear. In truth, I really didn't want your fighting prowess in any way compromised today. You know, it's very nearly a sexual experience, Jess, watching you fight."

"Voyeurism might be your safest bet, darlin'," Jess agreed, and the warriors behind her emitted another bark of laughter.

"Careful, Jesstin. I only bend so far."

The note of compassion in Caster's voice made Brenna uneasy. She hated that sound. It heralded the woman's worst instincts. The immediate threat seemed to fade as the door to the review stand opened, and Shann and Kyla were escorted in.

"Shann's fine," Kyla called down to them at once. A frowning mercenary hushed her with a poke of his rifle. Having delivered her message, Kyla offered him a withering smile.

Shann looked better than she had the previous day, Brenna noted with relief. Her robes were clean and mended, and the few marks on her face were countered by the alertness in her eyes. Her gaze found Jess, who made a subtle twirling motion with her fingers. Shann nodded.

She and Kyla were seated roughly at the other end of the long bench, and Caster regarded them with interest. She waited until Shann looked at her, then smiled brightly, winked, and stood up.

"All right, Miss Dana, cameras rolling!" Caster clapped her hands together, an unnecessary bid for attention in the silent arena. "Theryn, we're ready for you!"

A sharp command sounded near the main entrance to the stadium, and Brenna saw a cloaked figure standing by a large gate. It was Myrine, pulling swiftly on the rigging that opened the entrance to the fighting ground. Over the whine of the cameras, she could hear the clopping of a single horse.

Theryn rode into the arena with the kind of solemn grandeur reserved for affairs of state. Swatches of purple silk brought out the intense lavender light in her eyes. The towering bay she rode moved at a regal pace across the hard-pack of the arena.

Behind horse and rider, Theryn's cadre of warriors followed on foot, led by Patana and Myrine. Like Jess's fighters, they wore a generic blend of Tristainian attire—furs and skins that were warm and supple, along with the modern denim that somehow never seemed incongruous on Amazons. The cameras pivoted obediently as the procession came to a halt at the base of the review stand.

Brenna heard Vicar's dry brogue. "No slave girls tossing rose petals?"

The warriors around her snickered, but Brenna felt another odd wave of disquiet.

Theryn's Amazons, versus those who follow Shann. Evil sisters against good.

That was how Vicar saw it, and Jesstin, and every other woman who followed Shann. But good and evil were never that simple, and only Shann truly understood that. These women were all Amazons. They were all Clan.

Nothing else followed that rather mundane insight, and Brenna was surprised to feel brief disappointment. *Thanks heaps,* she thought to the elusive Grandmothers. *Platitudes are a big help.* It was her first spontaneous prayer to her Guides.

Her hands were freezing, which had little to do with the biting cold of the mountain morning. Brenna had won all-City in the Youth Division in kickboxing, but she'd only been in a real fight once, and that had been last spring, in the foothills, when she'd thrown herself at Caster and brought her down, just before she fired the bullet that hit Camryn's leg.

Please don't let me mess up. Her second prayer. *Don't let me get anyone hurt. Including me.* She kept her eyes pinned on Jess's broad shoulders in front of her, suddenly aware of the warmth of the blue shawl Dorothea had given her, seemingly years ago. Brenna had tied it around her waist as a kind of a belt—a shawl not being ideal battle attire—and now she was glad she had. Its warmth felt protective.

Theryn had assembled her troops in a half circle in front of the review stand. Sitting the elegant bay as if born to the saddle, she graciously inclined her head. "Whenever you're ready, Caster."

"Close-up on me, Miss Dana. Tight frame and keep it that way until I tell you to pan back." Caster cleared her throat and adjusted the collar of her parka.

Brenna caught Kyla's eye as she jutted her chin at Caster and twirled one finger rudely around her ear. Brenna glared at her with an older sister's fierceness. The soldier guarding Kyla and Shann could have caught that insolence, but beside her, Camryn snickered.

Dana was peering into the eyepiece of one of the cameras, correcting its focus. "Sound check!" she called.

"Good morning." Caster's voice was full and warm, but not especially loud. Brenna saw her adjust a small clip near her collar and realized she was wearing some kind of mike.

Dana lifted a hand. "You're set, Caster."

"Jesstin?" Caster peered down at her. "You and your bloodthirsty horde are to remain absolutely silent while I speak, yes? Or your queen will have cause to regret it."

From her vantage point at the edge of Jess's group, Brenna saw Theryn frown, but she said nothing. Brenna noticed her wife, Grythe, was not in attendance this morning.

Caster folded her hands on the railing and looked into the camera on her left.

"Good morning." Caster smiled as if addressing old friends, then became somber. "I reference Clinic Study T-714, ladies and gentlemen. Contracted to the Clinic's Military Research Unit, the so-called Tristaine Project involved developing techniques for nonchemical, noncoercive behavioral control. At first, we feared that our efforts had failed." She paused, then smiled again. "They have not."

Caster turned to address the other camera. "The gentle layfolk on our distinguished panel must forgive me for my deceit. I realize you were all told that our Clinic study ended in disaster. That our Amazon subject, Jesstin of Tristaine, miraculously pulled off a daring escape from our top-secret, heavily guarded Clinic facility."

Caster's ebony eyes flickered to Brenna, then returned to the camera.

"As you can see in Attachment 1-C of our prospectus, this so-called escape was very much part of my original protocol! Jesstin 'escaped' at my direction. She was always under the direct monitoring of my assistant, a Government-certified Medical Technician. Jesstin and my assistant returned to Tristaine in order to lead City forces against these so-called Amazons—per *my* programming."

There was an angry stirring among Jess's warriors, and Dana shifted uneasily as rifles rose around the arena. Jess lifted a hand, and the rustling immediately subsided.

"The film you are about to see records the battles that occurred just as I arrived in this remote mountain village." Caster turned to the last camera, and her expression grew solemn. "The conquest of Tristaine is a harrowing and, in many ways, tragic story. Both our test subject, Jesstin, and my assistant were lost in the gruesome fighting. But, in the name of decency, I have edited out the sordid scene containing their deaths, and I'm pleased to tell you that our documentary *will* offer a happy ending."

Caster raised her voice. "Pan back cameras, please."

Dana scowled, watching the soldier next to her jerkily widen the image appearing in his viewfinder. Theryn appeared in the frame, along with the semicircle of Amazons surrounding her.

"Ladies and gentlemen, I give you the new high council of Tristaine!" Caster's voice rang with pride. She paused as if to accommodate the imagined gasps of surprise in her audience. "All eager to sign Citizenship papers! All willing to abide by City laws! Now…would you like to hear more?" Her voice was almost girlish in its coyness. "Then sit back. I have quite a story to tell!" Caster smiled sweetly at the camera, then nodded at Dana. "All right, cut! Lord, Theryn!" She fanned her face. "How do you stand the horrid stink wafting from that beast you're riding?"

Jess's shoulders were stiff. Brenna looked up at Shann, whose features were an eloquent expression of sorrow.

"I believe we're about ready to begin the filming of the first battle." Caster glanced down at Brenna. "Oh, stop glaring at me like that, my ex-colleague. No one's *really* going to die! But my Military funders will be none the wiser, *and* you needn't worry about your younger sister Samantha learning of your supposed death, Miss Brenna!"

Brenna felt her body tremble. She kept her gaze on Caster, trying to emulate Jess's calm.

"Fortunately, little Samantha won't have to grieve for you, as she was killed six weeks ago in quite a horrific traffic accident. She burned, I believe, along with her husband and the baby she was carrying. I'm terribly sorry, Brenna. I meant to tell you earlier." Caster smiled down at her. "Cameras ready? Remember, this is supposed to be a spontaneous battle! Oh dear, we did forget to talk about those darn rules, but ah, well. Theryn?"

Theryn wheeled her mount. "Amazons, attack!"

The fourteen women led by Patana and Myrine unleashed a chilling war cry and flew straight at Jess's warriors. Brenna was stunned, both by Caster's statement and the abruptness of the attack, and she almost let the small Amazon who raced toward her knock her flat.

Jess shoved Brenna aside, then kicked her attacker away with one powerful sideswipe of her booted foot. "Brenna!" She gripped her upper arms, hard. "Samantha is *not* dead! Now *fight!*"

Then Jess spun, her hair lashing Brenna's face as two of Theryn's best jumped her.

Hand-to-hand combat, Brenna learned long ago, meant different things in the City than in Tristaine. In the City it was a game; among Amazons it could be deadly. But when her opponent picked herself up out of the dirt and lunged for her again, Brenna still wasn't prepared for the ferocity of the attack, and a knee punched into her stomach.

After that she had no rational thought; she just fought.

War cries filled the air from both sides, chilling Brenna's blood. This was no drill, no tournament. She didn't know the young Amazon she faced. While the girl wasn't a warrior, she still had the fighting prowess expected of every able-bodied woman in Tristaine. Her second blow was a fast slice with the side of her hand.

But Brenna had learned much in a summer of tutelage by Dyan's best. She dodged the strike with a deft twist, and it whickered past her. Then she countered with a neat back kick. Breath exploded out of her opponent as she bent double.

At least Theryn's women aren't armed, Brenna thought, catching her breath. If the Amazons commanded by Patana and

Myrine had the advantages of numbers and surprise, at least they weren't allowed weapons.

It was to be a long battle. Small groups of fighters, in twos and threes, had spaced themselves around the field. The strongest warriors in Jess's group, like Vicar and Hakan, fought one-on-one with the best fighters in Theryn's. Here and there two pairs of smaller warriors squared off against each other.

Dana was more unnerved by the war cries and the viciousness of the fighting than she allowed her face to reveal. The mercenaries under her command paced the perimeter of the field tensely, their rifles ready. She frowned. This was not the time for men with guns to get dicey nerves.

Dana was distracted by the sight of Theryn's bay horse, loping riderless through the stadium gates toward the stables. Through the unbelievable racket of the battle, she watched Theryn emerge from the door to the review stand and seat herself next to Caster. The beautiful Amazon with the strange eyes named Grythe was with her.

Watching the expressions of the other two women in the stand, Tristaine's queen and that profane young redhead, Kyla, Dana felt an unexpected twinge of sympathy through her chest.

Brenna finished off her opponent with a well-placed punch that left her gasping in the dirt, then looked around wildly for Jess. She found her grappling skillfully with Patana. To her great relief, despite the lingering effects of the taser, Jess was holding her own.

Brenna scanned the chaotic field. Myrine fought Vicar, and Hakan battled Perry, the big Amazon who had clashed with Elodia. Hakan executed a dazzling flip, kicking the other warrior off her feet. A scattering of lesser-skilled women from Theryn's group ran from pairing to pairing.

Up in the review stand, Caster was watching the action avidly, her chin resting on her folded hands. The bruise beneath her eye was more evident against the excitement that tinged her cheeks.

Brenna gasped as two more of Theryn's fighters headed for Jess. She knew her lover was fully engaged countering Patana's brutal strikes and couldn't possibly see them. Hitting low and hard in a flying tackle, Camryn cut one of Jess's attackers short. With effort, Brenna took out the other.

The battle seemed to go on for hours. Brenna fought carefully, helping Camryn keep a series of random assailants off Jess. Ordinarily a miracle of stamina, Jess was tiring, her body running with sweat despite the morning chill. Brenna reacted instantly to Cam's every shouted instruction, and, finally, bouts began to stumble to a halt across the arena.

"And that's a *cut*!" Caster gave the railing an exuberant slap. "Ladies, that was utterly magnificent!"

Patana straightened, glaring at Jess with muddy hate. "Stand down," she gasped to her warriors.

"S-stand down," Myrine echoed her. Vicar eased out of her fighting stance and stepped back.

Brenna went immediately to Jess. When Camryn joined them, Jess put a hand on Cam's shoulder and leaned hard.

"Check," Jess ordered, panting.

"No serious injuries, Jesstin." Cam steadied her.

"Tell Shann."

Camryn lifted a hand toward the review stand and twirled her fingers in a complex motion Brenna couldn't follow.

Theryn's voice rang commandingly from the review stand. "Amazons, rest!"

"What she said," Jess managed, and then her legs folded abruptly. They guided her to the ground.

"Hey! Cam, is she all right?"

Brenna saw Myrine across the field. The long scar on her face was livid, and she was still breathing hard.

Vicar intercepted Myrine as she started to walk toward Jess and jammed her muscular forearm against her chest. "Go back to your new *queen*, Amazon." The venom in her old friend's voice froze Myrine where she stood. She turned and went back to join Theryn's warriors.

Jess was fully conscious, but more spent than Brenna had ever seen her. She sat with her head lowered, her soaked sides heaving as she pulled in breath. Brenna knelt beside her and went through the motions of checking her pulse and respiration.

"There will be a two-hour truce between battles!" Theryn raised her voice to be heard over the harsh breathing of the Amazons below. "Jesstin, your warriors will all be fed. Sisters, if any among you are injured, just signal Dana and you'll receive aid!"

"I stopped listening after she mentioned food," Jess muttered, her eyes still closed.

"It's all right. I'll catch you up when you've rested." Brenna didn't like how long it was taking Jess to catch her breath. "Just sit still for a while, Jesstin. Camryn's getting everyone sorted out."

"Yes'm."

Dana felt as tired as the Amazons looked. Just watching such acrobatic fighting had exhausted her. She ducked quickly into the small stable beneath the arena and brought out as many Army blankets as she could carry.

She tossed a few to one of the soldiers who had been filming the fight, and he frowned. "What am I supposed to do with these?"

"They've been sweating for hours in this cold, you cretin," Dana snapped at him. "Pass these out. Then we need to get some coffee and decent chow in here. Move!"

"Miss Dana?" Caster called from the stand. "Your immediate responsibility is to bring me the footage of this morning's efforts! I plan to keep my new films warm and safe in my quaint little cabin unit. Then you can escort Her Highness, here, back to her tribal chieftains."

Dana ground her teeth and handed off her armload of blankets to another female soldier. "Pass these out."

"Hey, Dane?" The uniformed woman grinned at her. "That was the most beautiful damn fighting I've ever seen. Can we learn that?"

Dana stared at her, incredulous. "Sure, Landolt, I'll set up weekly drills, us against them." She grumbled on toward the next camera, picking her way cautiously between the Amazons sprawled on the field.

Jess had recovered enough to speak, and Brenna brushed her hair back so she could see her eyes.

"Brenna." Jess took her hand and held it tightly. "Caster has all the reason in the world to lie about Samantha."

"She's right," said Camryn, handing Brenna a canteen. "That bitch would lie about anything, Brenna, and she told you right before Theryn's goons—" She glanced quickly at Jess. "Before Theryn's warriors jumped us," she amended, "just to shake you up."

"That's true, she did." Brenna bathed Jess's face with a wet cloth. She was quiet for a moment. "I guess I don't have any choice but to assume Caster's lying, for now. Because if Sammy's dead, I'll go nuts, and I simply don't have time today."

"Bren—"

"It's all right, Jesstin." Brenna kept her gaze on her hands, washing the dirt from Jess's face. "There's no way I can find out if Samantha's alive, at least not right now. Maybe I'll never know. That's the way it is. But I can help us fight Caster today. I can do that much for Sammy, so that's what I'm going to do."

Brenna wrung out the cloth and poured fresh water from the canteen over it again. She looked at Camryn and frowned. "Come here. Is that a broken nose or a bump?"

"It's probably a zit." Camryn felt her nose glumly and shrugged. "Not broken."

Quiet settled over the cold arena as the weak sun centered itself overhead. The review stand was empty, and Theryn's warriors had all limped out of the stadium. Brenna looked for Dana, but she wasn't among the soldiers guarding Jess's Amazons.

"You fought well today, Cam." Jess appraised her. "You're faster than I was at your age."

"When boars fly," Camryn snorted.

"It's only the truth." Jess lifted her arm, wincing, and laid it across Brenna's slumped shoulders. "How's my lady?"

"Tired, scared, worried." Brenna considered a moment. "Hungry."

"I will go make you a tasty pig sandwich."

Brenna smiled in spite of her fatigue and allowed herself to rest against Jess.

❖

Dana was fascinated by the fine carpentry of the footbridge that spanned Tristaine's swift river. She bounced experimentally to test the wood, and the red-haired Amazon turned back and threw her another evil scowl. The girl was gorgeous, but she seemed to carry an endless supply of frowns, for Dana at least.

The woman named Shann walked on, and Dana skipped a step to catch up to her prisoners, cursing herself for the lapse.

Tantalizing smells beckoned from the mess hall. Dana wasn't sure what Amazons called the lodge where they prepared meals. The women of Tristaine's council were cooking for their captive warriors. Dana's mouth watered. City food offered nothing like these alluring aromas.

She almost walked smack into the queen of the Amazons. Shann stood regarding her with curious gray eyes, and she seemed unimpressed by the swift rise of Dana's rifle. She gave a slow, mannered blink, as if too polite to comment.

"She's the one who tasered Jesstin, lady." Kyla waited at the base of the stairs leading up to the mess hall. "Her name is Dung."

"The name is Dana," Dana corrected sharply. She gestured toward the mess with her rifle. "Move on, Amazon."

"The name is Shann," Shann corrected. "Kyla? Wait for me inside."

To Dana's surprise, the insolent redhead turned and started up the stairs. She wouldn't have thought Kyla capable of simple obedience. Dana flushed. Prisoners should not be giving orders. She glared at Shann.

"Let's move on, ma'am."

"No, I need to speak with you a moment. Shoot me, if you feel you must." Shann began rummaging in the soft folds of her patched robes, a task made awkward by her tied hands. She withdrew a small, tattered spiral notebook. "Take this, and give it to the blond healer called Brenna." She held it out to Dana, who looked at it warily.

"I'm not taking that anywhere." Dana swallowed and brought her voice down out of its highest register. "You shouldn't even have it, whatever it is. Weren't you searched?"

"Dana, take this to Brenna. It's important. Tell her she must bring her entries up to date."

Dana was unable to describe the tone of Shann's voice, because she'd never heard anything like it. Her authority felt nothing like Caster's sinister coercion or Theryn's grandiosity. This woman wore a cloak of calm command as natural as a second skin.

"You should give that thing to the redhead to give to Brenna. You know she'll be returned to the stable tonight." Dana stared at Shann, curious in spite of herself. "What makes you think I wouldn't take that notebook and your message straight to Theryn? Or Caster herself?"

"Well…" Shann studied her with those adroit eyes. "I knew within five minutes of meeting Theryn that she was highly intelligent and highly ambitious. Within three minutes, I knew your Caster had no soul. I've watched you for six hours today. And it's important that *you* take this to Brenna, Dana. I'm asking you to trust me."

So Dana took the notebook.

"Thank you." Shann turned and went into the mess hall, and Dana watched her go. Then she looked around and slid the notebook deep into the pocket of her jacket.

❖

"It's a lovely day for a battle!" Caster stepped to the railing and beamed down at Theryn's warriors. "We're ready for round two, Amazons!"

Jess's gaze locked on Myrine as she helped Patana pass out a variety of hand weapons to their line of fighters. Brenna heard an angry rumbling in their ranks, and Jess turned and signaled. Her warriors moved in closer.

"We see what's happening." Jess's alto was calm. We'll be fighting open-handed against armed opponents. We may not get a choice of targets, but you all know your strengths. If you can, match yourself against the weapon you know best."

"Wait a minute." Brenna touched Jess's arm. "They have weapons, we don't?"

"Right." Jess nodded.

"There's nothing in Tristaine's laws about not bullying other Amazons by killing them?" Brenna folded her arms against both cold and fear. "Shouldn't we protest this?"

"No, Bren. You're right, this is unfair, and it's dangerous as hell. But it would weaken our stance to complain, and it would be futile." Jess searched Brenna's face. "This is how Caster wants it. Theryn's willing to go along with it. Clear?"

"Unfortunately." Brenna swallowed.

"Patana's fighters aren't as skilled as we are." Jess raised her voice and addressed them all. "That might make them damned deadly, even if they don't mean to hurt us. Understood?"

"We hear, Jess," Hakan said from the rear of the pack.

Jess nodded. "Camryn, instructions?"

"Uh, watch me and Jess. Remember our purpose. Don't take foolish chances. Take any weapon you can and use it to restrain and confine your opponent. And fight without harm. Brenna, that means defend yourself and try to disarm your target, but don't injure—"

"She knows," Jess said. It was how Jess had fought in the Clinic. "They're not using anything lethal. No crossbows or daggers. Mostly clubs. If we're careful, we can fight without harm."

"Artemis, shield your daughters," Camryn finished, and Brenna heard the phrase repeated softly in at least three different languages.

Jess signaled again, that subtle twirling of fingers that Brenna kept forgetting to ask about. Shann's warriors turned to face Theryn's line.

"Miss Dana, check our cameras, please." Caster primped before opening the afternoon session. She cleared her throat and carefully patted her styled coif in place.

Shann and Kyla, seated again at the other end of the review stand, knew well enough the increased dangers of this second battle. Kyla looked pale, and Shann's remote features couldn't conceal her tension.

"Amazons!" Theryn rose, and Brenna realized for the first time that Grythe was seated beside her in the stand, clothed in finery.

Theryn patted Grythe's shoulder, then joined Caster at the railing.

"The terms of our truce with the City are almost fulfilled. We have two more battles to film. One begins now, and the last will be staged tomorrow. Then our guests will return to the City, and our adanin can return from the southern meadows!"

A cheer rose from Theryn's followers, but a ragged one. Brenna noted that most of the women facing them still looked weary from the morning's strenuous bout. But the weak afternoon sun glinted off their weapons, and Brenna found her sympathy for them was limited.

Theryn extended her hand over those assembled on the fighting field. "Amazons! Fight with no harm!"

"Roll 'em!" Caster snapped her fingers at Dana.

"Space yourselves," Jess called.

A hissing breath escaped Brenna as they moved apart and the battle began, and any sense of time fled along with it. The afternoon became a frightening series of slides that flickered through her mind in rapid succession.

The Amazon named Perry whirled long strips of a rawhide sling over her head and released a stone from its leather cup that flew halfway across the arena where it clipped Vicar's thigh. She staggered, and Brenna ran for her.

Vicar kept her footing, but her handsome face contorted with pain. She recovered quickly, whirled, and raced toward Perry, so Brenna veered off. And promptly dropped flat on her butt. A staff whizzed through the space formerly occupied by Brenna's head, fast and hard enough to do real damage.

She dodged the warrior wielding it by crawling between her spread legs, then rolled free. She didn't mind clownish acrobatics if it saved her a concussion. She took out her clumsy opponent with one neat flip.

After an hour of constant battle, Brenna began to tire, and from the sound of the grunts of effort that rose around her, she wasn't alone. She scanned the chaotic arena for Jess and found her. Brenna scuttled like a crab across the fighting field. It wasn't dignified, but it got her to her lover's side in one piece.

Jess was finishing a match against a woman who swung escrima sticks—two trim hardwood clubs. Jess swept her feet out from under her with a spinning kick; then she almost collapsed herself. Brenna darted to her feet and steadied her quickly.

"How are—?" It was all Brenna could get out, before pulling for lungfuls of thin mountain air. She didn't see how Jess stayed erect. The high planes of her face were the color of old linen.

"Pace yourself, Bren." Jess straightened with effort. "Stay close to me."

"Oh, yeah."

J'heika, rise.

Brenna went still and scanned the dusty field of battling Amazons. Their hoarse war cries faded for a moment and then returned at full eerie volume.

She saw that the lenses of the three cameras filming the war game moved continuously in and out, as close-ups gave way to panned shots. The thirty women who fought in the arena had settled into grim matches that were bound to end more quickly than they had this morning. Weapons and fatigue shortened fights—and increased risk—but kept the action going.

Camryn battled with the small warrior who had attacked Brenna earlier, an uneven match. Cam fought close beside Jess, listening to her instructions and helping watch her back. Jess had just kicked a longknife out of the hand of her new opponent.

At the other end of the arena, Vicar grappled with Perry, both of them snarling, a sound that chilled Brenna. She saw Hakan take a nasty clout to the temple from Myrine's staff, but made herself focus on fighting.

The war cries grew more discordant in Brenna's mind, and for the first time since the battle began, she felt real fear. A swirl of white caught the corner of her vision, and she turned to the review stand. Shann stood at the railing.

Shann's tied hands were clasped on the rail, her eyes narrowed and intent on Brenna's face. She lifted one hand and made a twirling motion with her fingers.

What's happening, Blades?

The words reached Brenna clearly, and for a moment, she was so stunned at hearing the question she didn't immediately realize she didn't know the answer. She knew that her heart was racing, that she was afraid, and that was it. She lifted her hands to Shann in confusion and appeal.

Then Brenna looked across the arena and saw Patana raise a crossbow to her shoulder. The bald warrior took careful aim and smiled. Brenna saw the crossbow bolt and then tracked its intended path. She started to run.

"Jesstin!" A voice rang out across the arena.

It was Shann who called Jess's name, not Brenna. She, too, had finally seen Patana's forbidden crossbow. Out of the corner of her eye, Brenna saw a skirmish in the review stand as the guards there reacted to Shann's unexpected agitation. She ran on.

The twang of the bolt's release reached Brenna above the war cries, as keen and isolated as a note plucked on the string of a terrible harp.

Jess was just turning in response to Shann's cry. Brenna forced an extra burst of speed out of her exhausted legs and threw herself at Jess. She tackled her hard and took her down.

Patana's crossbow bolt whizzed harmlessly past them both and struck Camryn full in the chest.

CHAPTER EIGHT

"Take me to Theryn."

Dana let out a long breath. "I can't do it, Brenna."

"Tell me how to make you do it."

Brenna was shorter than Dana by at least two inches, but in the tense air of the stable she seemed to be growing, in formidability if not stature.

"Look, keep your voice down." Dana glared at Rodriguez, who watched them from his post a few yards down the railing. "I'm sorry your friend got hurt, but like I said, there's nothing I can do for you. You can use the contents of that medical kit to help her, but that's it. *Caster's* orders," she said for the third time.

"We need to get this woman to Tristaine's infirmary, under sterile conditions, with the right supplies, or she's going to bleed to death." Brenna's lips trembled, but her voice was steady as a rock. "If you can't authorize that, then take me to Theryn."

Dana had heard this girl described as one of the finest Med Techs the City had ever educated, and she also remembered the way Brenna had fought during the war games. If Dana were honest with herself, she wasn't sure she could take her in a fair fight.

But this was not a fair fight, and there was nothing she could do for the wounded Amazon. Dana had to accept that reality, and so did her prisoners. She clenched her rifle in both hands and met Brenna's flashing eyes.

"Okay," Dana said, "come with me."

Dang it! Dana fumed. What is it with these Amazon witches, some kind of damn feminist mind control? She gestured to Rodriguez, who lifted the wooden railing that separated the stable from the soldiers.

Brenna ducked beneath it, then glanced back toward the Amazons gathered around Camryn. Kyla lifted her head and caught her gaze. Brenna had to grit her teeth against the desolation in her eyes.

"You taking this one up to Theryn's lodge?" Rodriguez said. Brenna could smell liquor on his breath as she passed him. The smell nauseated her.

"That's right," Dana answered dismissively. "As you were."

Brenna preceded Dana up the stairs that led out into the deserted arena. Her hands were tacky with blood, her arms streaked red from wrist to elbow. Now that she wasn't tending Camryn, Brenna could feel herself start to shake. When the mercenary named Dana took her arm as they crossed the rough ground of the fighting field, Brenna dimly registered that her hold was supportive rather than cruel.

"Just what do you imagine Theryn's going to do about this?" Dana knew her voice sounded angry, which was fine; she was. She never should have read that fucking journal; she was risking her entire fucking career. "Theryn's no doctor. Caster's the one calling the shots!"

"Shann's a doctor. A good one."

Brenna was walking fast, and Dana lengthened her stride to stay with her. "Theryn is *not* going to let you take that wounded prisoner to the infirmary, and she's *not* going to let that Shann woman come back with us. Didn't you hear me? Caster was real specific tonight."

"I heard you. I have to try." Brenna folded her arms and waited as Dana keyed open the padlock of the outer gate, then went through it and out into the moonlit Amazon village.

Brenna was terrified. She wasn't sure they could save Camryn, even if she and Shann had her in the infirmary now and they had a double line of cross-matched blood donors waiting. But the reminders Jess had whispered to her in the stable rang true. Camryn came from strong Amazon stock. She was young and healthy going into this, and she had a warrior's heart.

Their quick steps sounded over the footbridge that spanned

Tristaine's river, Terme Cay. Brenna glanced down at the black water that swirled beneath the bridge. It looked cold, fast, and merciless.

The silent village was flooded with the blue light of the full moon. If there were soldiers posted as sentries, Brenna didn't see them. She kept her eyes pinned on the lodge Theryn shared with Grythe, one of the larger, more luxurious cabins nestled in the trees.

Adrenaline fueled her up the four split-log steps to the cabin's ornate door. The mixture of fear and dread that gripped Brenna didn't eclipse her professional instincts, and she was grateful for that. Her practical goal kept her focused.

She was on a mission to secure the best medical care possible for an injured patient. The fact that the patient was Camryn, Kyla's adonai and Jess's second, her own adanin…

Brenna knocked, hard.

Dana's stomach hurt, and the ache didn't improve when her prisoner struck the door again, harder. They heard the neat click of a well-made latch, then blinked in the sudden light of the lamps and candles that filled the cabin. Dana was unpleasantly surprised. She hadn't expected to see Caster.

"Well, Miss Dana, I am less than pleased." Caster was dressed in a flowing robe of silver silk, but her stylish hair was as carefully coiffed as ever. Her black eyes glittered as they crawled over Brenna.

"I'm here to see Theryn, Caster," Brenna said.

"Well, that leaves you standing on this quaint little porch all alone, then." Caster turned and strolled back into the cabin. "Theryn and that pretty little lunatic she beds have gone to fetch me a long-delayed dinner. They'll be back presently. Bring her in, Dana."

Brenna hesitated, and Dana had to nudge her gently. They followed Caster into the sumptuous lodge.

Dana closed the door and leaned back against it. She studied Theryn's ornate decor and fine furniture, and let out a low whistle. This was by far the most luxurious cabin she'd yet seen in Tristaine. She wondered if Shann's private unit was this grand. Somehow she doubted it.

Caster left Brenna standing on a fringed rug in the middle of the hardwood floor and reclined heavily on the loveseat. She lifted the jeweled eyeglasses from the delicate chain around her neck and fit them in place. Then she picked up a folded document from the neat stack on the table before her.

"Tristaine's mine yields a much higher quality ore than even City geologists suspected, Brenna." Caster smiled at her over her glasses. "The samples I'm taking back to the City along with my film will please my funders a great deal."

"Camryn has a collapsed lung, Caster. I've stopped the external bleeding and bandaged the wound, but she needs surgery."

"Well, clinical medicine is hardly my first field, but if a chest wound isn't sucking any longer, you've patched any leak, yes?" Caster went back to her review of the mine schematics. "Just treat her for shock, Brenna. The girl will be excused from the filming of the final battle tomorrow, of course."

"She's hemorrhaging internally, and that bolt needs to come out. We need Shann, Caster. She's had years of experience with battle wounds."

"I'm sorry, dear. You know how I hate to lose anyone. But better this young Amazon, than your own dear Jesstin, yes?" Caster tossed the paper on the table and removed the reading glasses to examine her former assistant carefully.

"By the way, I underestimated you, Miss Brenna. You saved the life of your warrior-mate quite handily today. It's regrettable that you can't help poor Camrie now, though. Especially since she'd be fine and dandy tonight, had you not interfered. Does little Kyla blame you, too?"

"Listen to me, you spiteful City shrike." Brenna had stopped shaking, and her voice was low and hard. "I don't care how much you hate me or Jess. I don't care how long we've festered in your corrupt little mind. You're going to get your reputation back, and the City is going to get its silver. That's enough. Our friends don't have to die."

"Oh, sure they do." Caster lifted her eyeglasses. "My killing your loved ones is entirely in keeping with the spirit of the Tristaine project, Brenna. Isn't that how the Amazons of old avenged themselves, dear? By slaughtering not only their enemies, but their families as well?"

Dana had studied history on the sly even though it was illegal, and she could have told Caster she was thinking of the Mongols, not the Amazons. But she wasn't about to correct her. The air between the two women fairly crackled with danger.

"We must take Camryn to the infirmary," Brenna repeated. "And Shann must do the surgery."

"No," Caster answered simply.

J'heika, rise.

Great, Brenna thought. *If I ever needed coaching from spirits, now's the time.*

But no instructions came, just a slow flood of sadness.

"Theryn realizes she must concede to my wishes in this, Brenna." Caster smiled at her. "She's smart enough and ambitious enough to know when to be flexible with our terms."

Camryn.

"But you're welcome to stay until Theryn returns and try to work your feminine wiles on her." Caster tittered. "I'd love to watch that, Bren! Miss Psychotica Grythe would tear out your heart with her small, misshapen teeth."

Brenna turned. "Take me back," she snapped, and Dana scrambled after her.

The same inner pull that had alerted Brenna weeks ago in the glade, when the boar attacked, drew her to the stable now. But unlike the first time, there was no urgency in this summons. Somehow she found that much more ominous than comforting.

They stepped down the cabin's log stairs and almost walked into Theryn and Grythe.

"Brenna!" Theryn steadied her glowering wife who was, as usual, draped over her arm. Both were laden with covered plates that emitted a heavenly aroma. "Dana, what's she doing here?"

Brenna pushed past the finely dressed couple, upsetting a platter intended for Caster. "Get out of my way, Theryn."

"Wait! Tell me about Camryn."

Brenna wheeled. "Just tell me. Did you order Patana to try to kill Jess, or was that her own bright idea?"

Theryn regarded Brenna with sorrow. "I had no knowledge of Patana's move against Jesstin, little sister. I promise you."

"Crossbows were banned from the field, Theryn. Where did Patana get one?"

"I honestly don't know. She acted without my—"

"Is Patana fighting tomorrow?"

"I have no control over that." Theryn scrubbed one hand across her face, the first natural gesture Brenna had ever seen the pretentious Amazon make. "I stood before the entire clan this morning, Brenna, and ordered a battle without harm. You saw me, you were there! Now, how is Camryn?"

"Camryn is dying, Theryn. She took a bolt to the chest today. You saw her, you were there."

Brenna continued toward the arena, and Dana scrambled after her.

"Will you hang on, for crying out…" Dana fumbled with the keys to the padlock on the stadium gate.

Brenna waited until the hasp of the lock lifted, then pushed open the gate.

Dana caught her arm. "Here, take this."

She was holding out the small spiral notebook Brenna used for a journal. Brenna stared at her.

"Shann says to bring it up to date."

Brenna grabbed the notebook, shoved it into her pocket, and ran for the stable.

❖

Everything was so quiet, Brenna thought she was too late.

The soldiers were seated in their part of the room playing cards without much spirit.

In the stable, the bloodied straw had been cleared away. Camryn lay cushioned on two blankets and covered by three more. Her head rested in Kyla's lap, and she was conscious.

Most of the other Amazons weren't clustered around her any

longer. They stood or sat, in groups of twos and threes, and stared at nothing. The stable was silent. No sobbing, or even anger, and Brenna could sense a feeling of peace and acceptance in the stable. She refused to share it.

Only Elodia, Vicar, Hakan, and Jess still surrounded Kyla and Camryn. These were the faces Camryn wanted to see at the end. When Brenna knelt in their circle, Cam waved her fingers in welcome.

Brenna had seen death. Not a lot of it. She hadn't been working that long, but she'd seen it. She'd even seen violent deaths during her internships, and the death of children. This was unlike any other deathwatch she had ever attended.

It was peaceful, for one thing. There were no life-sustaining measures underway, no alarms, no intercoms that screamed protocols. Camryn was dying in a quiet space, surrounded by women she loved. She wasn't free from pain. Even as Brenna watched, she stiffened for a moment in Kyla's arms. But those moments didn't happen often. Camryn was almost ready to die, and her pain was ebbing along with her strength.

Brenna saw that Vicar, Hakan, and Jesstin all wore similar expressions, a kind of restrained grief. She recognized it as the stoic mask Amazon warriors always wore when their sisters died in battle.

Elodia was the only woman in the circle who cried. Her tears were soundless, but she clasped Camryn's hand and prayed—a soft, subterranean flow of musical Spanish.

Kyla's ashen face was a study in control. She held Camryn with gentle strength, stroking her hair and murmuring to her occasionally. Brenna gazed at her, remembering that Kyla had lost her innocence when her blood sister Dyan was murdered. Tonight, she would leave the last of her youth behind.

Finally, Jess cleared her throat. "Anything else, Cam?"

There was a pause before Camryn answered, and the weakness of her voice told Brenna how very close she stood to the doorway.

"I'm sorry to leave." Cam's unfocused eyes found Kyla's brown ones above her. They filled her sky now. "Bye, Kyla. You be good."

"I love you." Kyla sobbed once, but only once. She wanted to be able to see and hear Camryn while she still lived.

"Me you back, adonai." Camryn rested for a moment. Then she focused on Brenna and grinned. "Thanks."

"Thanks?" Brenna lifted Camryn's cold hand to her knee. "For what, Camryn?"

"You can call me Cam. For saving Jess like you did. You were great, Bren."

"Okay," Brenna whispered.

J'heika, rise.

"Give me the Queen's Blessing?" Cam asked Brenna.

"What?" Brenna didn't know who she was asking for information, Cam, or that spectral voice in her head.

Camryn spoke again, with effort. "Give me the Queen's Blessing, *j'heika.*"

Camryn closed her eyes, and Kyla stroked her brow.

"Who is *J'heika*?" Vicar asked Jess, but Jess shook her head, puzzled.

"None of us can give the Queen's Blessing, mi amiga." Elodia's callused hand lay on Camryn's blanketed leg. "But you know Shann will send you a Blessing from the new Tristaine. We'll get our lady out of this, hija, and we'll avenge you. You have Elodia's promise."

"Elodia." Across their circle, Hakan stirred. "Never speak of vengeance at a warrior's deathbed, little sister. You'll be cursed."

"But she should know—"

"The Queen's Blessing on your journey, Camryn," Brenna said softly. Jess and the other Amazons all stared at her. She ignored them and laid the palm of her right hand lightly at the base of Camryn's throat.

"You leave us too early, little sister. The few seasons we had with you were much too brief. Our hearts are breaking, Cam."

All the energy in the stable, possibly all the energy in Tristaine, condensed and spiraled down to illuminate a small space, occupied only by Brenna, Kyla, and the dying warrior they comforted. No one could see this energy, but Brenna's deepest instinct recognized it as the granting of the Queen's Blessing.

"But along with grieving for you, Camryn, we'll honor you." Brenna smiled, and her eyes overflowed with tears. "You gave your life in defense of your clan. You're a warrior worthy of Kimba's mantle, and you'll be remembered around our storyfires for generations. Now, close your eyes, honey. Let your adanin tell you good-bye."

Brenna's spirit glowed with a gratitude that was almost sacred, and she suddenly realized that was how an Amazon queen bid farewell to her fallen warriors. The gaze of the Amazons around her felt like warm beams touching her skin. Gradually, the women focused on Cam again and started saying their own silent and final farewells.

"You'll find our mothers waiting to welcome you," Brenna promised Camryn, "with a warm fire in the hearth, a platter of venison on the table, a flagon of cold mead in your hand, and the embrace of lost sisters to warm your heart. Camryn, daughter of Louisa, walk with Kimba. She'll lead you home to the real Tristaine. We'll see you again there."

"Thanks," Camryn murmured. Her eyes opened wide a last time. "Samantha's alive, Brenna."

Brenna felt as if she were waking from a long nap. She couldn't speak.

Jess leaned forward. "Are you sure, Cam?"

"Yeah. Brenna's sister is alive."

"But how do you know, adanin?" Jess asked gently.

"I'd see Samantha here, if she was dead." Camryn smiled at them and closed her eyes. "Because I can see Lauren now…"

Camryn relaxed in Kyla's arms. Brenna's palm measured the fading of her valiant heart as it faltered and stopped.

❖

Dana stood against the wall and shivered with a weariness that was tinged by nausea. She tried to stifle the latest in a series of jaw-cracking yawns.

The Amazons had been quiet since they covered the warrior's body with a blanket and carried it to lie in state beneath one of the stable's barred windows. Maybe some of the prisoners slept, because no one had stirred for hours.

Kyla sat beside the blanketed body of her life-mate, her face in her hands. She seemed to be praying, though Dana couldn't hear any words, just soft snatches of song. She had offered to bring the girl some hot tea, but Jesstin had politely turned her down.

Now Jesstin sat in the shadows and watched over Kyla. She got up every hour or so and made a slow circuit of the stable, checked with the Amazon on watch, and made sure the others slept. Then she would fade into the shadows again.

Brenna was the only other prisoner who sat apart from the others. She sat on the woodplank floor, in the one meager pool of light offered by their portable generator. She'd written in that spiral notebook nonstop for the past three hours.

Dana pushed herself off the wall and went over to a stack of Army blankets. She unfolded one, then went to the railing and draped it over Brenna's shoulders.

It wasn't that Brenna didn't notice Dana's gesture. She did feel and appreciate the blanket's sudden warmth, but she hardly glanced up.

❖

It's almost dawn.

I've caught up on everything that's happened since my last entry. From freezing on the ridge—that had to be months ago, but it was only days—to tonight, Camryn's death.

I don't know why Shann wanted me to write all this. If she was hoping I'd vent some pent-up emotion, it's not happening. I can't let myself think about Cam right now, or even about helping Kyla survive this loss.

Jess can't focus on anything but what comes with morning, either. In a few hours, she's got to get everyone through this last fight alive.

Then, somehow, we have to get Shann and the rest of us the hell out of this valley.

Then—please, Gaia, only then—we have to use the remote detonator to set off the dynamite, destroy the dam, and flood the village.

And we thought yesterday sucked.

I'm sorry, whoever is reading this, I'm not being flip. I'm just scared and a little sleep-drunk. I don't know about Theryn's fighters, but we haven't had decent rest in days. Jess isn't sleeping now, I can tell, and she was already running on a long sleep deficit.

I've got to talk to Shann. Who is this "Jaheeka"? No one here knows. This goes on my list of questions to ask Shann, unless we both drown. It will come right after, "Was Cam's death my fault?"

I don't know why I believe Theryn when she says she didn't know Patana was going to attack Jess. For that matter, I'm not sure why I believe Theryn never told Caster about the dynamite on the dam. Theryn's done nothing to earn my trust. Somehow it relates to that all-or-nothing, Good Amazon/Bad Amazon mind-set being wrongheaded...

But I told Jess I thought Theryn was telling the truth. I just don't know how we can use that.

❖

As Brenna closed the notebook she caught a glimpse of unfamiliar handwriting. She opened the journal again and read the lines Shann had written on its last page. She studied the map beneath Shann's entry, then gasped loudly when Jess touched her hair.

"Easy, lass." Jess lowered herself to the straw and winced as her arm draped across Brenna's blanketed shoulders. "We're still sneaking up on you, eh? You look cold."

"So do you." Brenna rested her head against Jess's shoulder. She was aware of Dana and the other City soldiers, but their presence felt immaterial. She slipped the journal into the inner pocket of her jacket and zipped the flap.

They sat quietly for a while. They couldn't possibly say everything they both needed to say in these brief moments of privacy, so they chose the more primitive comforts of silence and touch. Jess scratched Brenna's scalp through her tousled hair, and Brenna snuggled more deeply against her.

Then she remembered Jess's painful wince she had seen earlier and sat up again. "Oh, damn. Sorry."

Jess blinked at her. "What? I'm okay."

"Well, I've learned that's a relative concept. Apparently an Amazon thinks she's 'okay' if no one's yanked out her liver yet." Brenna smiled and rested her palm very lightly on Jess's side, close to the taser's mark. "How's this?"

"Sore." Jess adjusted her shoulders against the railing behind them.

"Anything else that I can't see in this light?"

"I'm just real stiff." Jess caught Brenna's probing fingers gently in her own and held them to her lips. "Rest a while, Bren."

Brenna sighed and settled again against her shoulder. "I need to get you someplace I can look you over, Jesstin. Hakan and Vicar too. They both took some pretty bad hits today."

"We all did, querida, body and heart." Jess rested her cheek in Brenna's hair. "Kyla's taken the worst strike."

Brenna closed her eyes. "How is she?"

"How Shann was, I imagine, right after we lost Dyan. How either of us would be."

Brenna shivered. She squeezed Jess's waist a little.

"You did save my life, lass. I thank you for it."

Brenna nodded. "Cam forgave me, didn't she?"

"Aye, she did."

"All right, Amazons, everyone up." Dana's voice was low, but still jarring in the dawn stillness of the stable. "You'll be given a chance to wash, then you'll be fed. You need to be ready for the arena in two hours. Move sharp, please."

❖

Time started to telescope.

In the middle of the fighting field, Shann's warriors, led by Jess, waited in a rough semicircle, just as they had the day before. Theryn's Amazons, led by Myrine and Patana, faced them from their position below the review stand.

Caster, Theryn, and Grythe sat in the stand with Shann and Kyla and two armed guards.

The cameras were all manned and ready.

Dana was watching her soldiers, and, judging from her expression, she shared Brenna's fears about them. The City mercs looked wired, as if their nerves were drawn tight as bowstrings.

The one difference between yesterday and today only increased Brenna's anxiety. The lower level of the stadium was filled with Amazons. Caster had ordered that every woman loyal to Shann's rule be brought in to witness this final war game.

Brenna saw Constance, Kas, Opal, and Teresias, four members of Tristaine's high council, clustered at one end of the risers. DeLorea and the thirty other Amazons who had been imprisoned in the warrior's barracks were spaced along the other side of the stadium.

More Amazons required more soldiers so, in effect, every human being in the village was in the arena or guarding its perimeter. If tension could be made visible, Brenna knew she would see sheets of it shimmer in the air around her.

Then Caster stood up, and time lurched sickeningly back into place.

"All right, Miss Dana, I'm ready for my close-up!"

The camera lenses whirred as they zoomed in.

"Roll film," Dana called tonelessly.

"Good morning, ladies and gentlemen." Caster placed both hands lightly on the stand's railing. "I reference, once again, Clinic Study T-714 and introduce this filmed record of the final, climactic battle for Tristaine!"

She paused. "Cut! Patana, distribute the weapons, please!"

Dana saw the bald Amazon trot quickly behind the wall of the stadium. She emerged carrying an armful of swords and crossbows.

"Come on, you lot," Patana called. "Myrine, Perry! Pass these out. I'll get the rest."

Dana's stomach clenched again. Obviously, Jesstin and her warriors were still expected to fight barehanded, only this time, against weapons that could kill. She looked up and saw that Caster was deep in conversation with Theryn, and their talk was growing heated.

Shann's warriors were watching Jesstin.

Jesstin was watching Shann.

Tristaine's queen looked like she had slept as little as Jess and Brenna. Shann sat erect on the cushioned bench in the review stand and held Kyla's hand. Kyla's eyes worried Brenna. They were unfocused and distant.

Theryn's Amazons all held weapons now. Most held crossbows, swords, and daggers, but two of the slightest fighters carried what looked like pistols.

Suddenly Theryn bellowed, "Caster, I forbid it!"

Brenna watched, dumbfounded, as Theryn vaulted from the review stand. She landed awkwardly, but apparently with ankles intact. The uneasy rumbling that had started to move through the watching Amazons in the risers subsided as she stalked toward Patana.

Wake up, daughtera. J'heika, rise!

"Tell me what to do," Brenna whispered. Yesterday, Camryn had been standing so close to her she would have heard the prayer.

"I said stand down, Amazon!" Theryn clenched the bunched fabric at Patana's throat. "I ordered *all* battles be fought without harm!"

"Caster changed that order, and she was right, Theryn." Patana gripped her mentor's arms. "Be honest, adanin, you knew this was coming! How else could it end?"

"What?"

"Let us *fight*, Theryn! Let's finish this at last, and give Tristaine the queen and the high council she deserves!"

Theryn shook off Patana's grip and wheeled on Myrine. "Has Caster poisoned *you* with this bloody swill, too?"

"No." Myrine looked as dazed as Brenna felt. "I mean, no, I didn't know anything about all—Patana, what—"

Theryn pushed Myrine aside and strode back beneath the review stand.

"Caster! I forbid the use of weapons! If we had to sacrifice Camryn, so be it. But I'll not allow *one more drop* of Amazon blood—"

"Your bosom heaves once again, Theryn." From the railing, Caster lifted a placating hand. "Now, think back. We have already filmed you on a horse in front of your triumphant warriors, yes?"

Theryn folded her arms, every line of her body defiant.

"Remember our story?" Caster coached. "A converted Jesstin tries to convince Tristaine to incorporate under the City. But Tristaine resists! Your warriors *defeat* Jesstin, Theryn! Then my protocol converts *your* warriors! Amazons become Citizens! City gets silver! You get throne!"

The mockery in Caster's tone registered with Grythe, who cast a blistering glare at her. Brenna realized Shann was studying Theryn with intense interest.

"Yes, we defeat Jesstin's warriors, Caster," Theryn retorted, "but then, according to our truce, Shann and her Amazons are to be *exiled*. Not murdered! We risk more deaths if any warriors carry weap—"

"Oh, please, you'll have plenty of Amazons to spawn our New Tristaine, Theryn." Caster seemed nettled by the delay. "Remember, all the villagers who escaped us, or *migrated*, as you quaintly put it, will come back. You'll have your own followers down there. *And* you'll even have those Amazons in the stands, the less competent of Shann's warriors. That's practically all of old Tristaine to rule!"

"Everyone lives." Theryn's voice was strained. "Caster, there will be no more bloodshed."

"Just a little bloodshed," Caster corrected. "Just those ten little warriors down there, give or take a few. We did get Camryn's death on film yesterday, but that's hardly enough, Theryn. The film must have *some* carnage if it's to be authentic!"

Caster turned a glowing smile on Shann. "And Tristaine's barbarian queen must see it, if she's to be humbled."

Brenna had never wanted to do anything but heal others, but now she realized she was capable of killing even if she wasn't physically threatened. She would think about that unpleasant revelation later.

"All right, get ready to fight, you people!" Caster snapped her fingers. "Roll 'em, Miss Dana!"

"Wait!" Theryn's cape swirled as she spun and walked toward Jess. "Dana, stand down!"

"At ease!" Dana yelled to her troops. Her mouth was dry. The damn stadium seemed to be teeming with hostile Amazons and spooked soldiers with rifles. "Lower your weapons, I said!"

"Theryn, get back up here!" Now Caster's voice was ominously shrill. "Dana, I am paying your commission, not that ridiculous Amazon queen wannabe!"

Brenna moved to Jess's side as Theryn reached her, and she felt that strange spiraling down of energy again.

Theryn hesitated, and her struggle for self-control aged her face a decade. Brenna sensed waves of outrage radiating from her, and something heavier, more like defeat or despair. Jess's own dark energy broadcast her grief and wariness.

Brenna realized with a jolt that she was, for god's sake, *reading energy waves*, and she looked up at Shann. Tristaine's queen stood at the railing now, just as she had yesterday, but try as she might, Brenna could read nothing in her pale features.

"All right, Jesstin." Theryn won her struggle for restraint, and her eyes on Jess were cold as slate. She spoke quietly, so only Jess and Brenna heard her. "I'm going to order my warriors to break ranks. We'll try to keep Caster's mercenaries off you. You and your Amazons, get Shann and her council out of the village. Then blow the dam and send that bitch up there to hell!" She smiled without mirth. "I don't care how many Amazons either of us have to lose to achieve *that*."

"Theryn!" Caster's fury was rising. "Get your pagan ass up

here! I *will* order your warriors to attack right now. Don't you *dare* test me!"

"Theryn, slow down." Jess's gaze was locked on Shann. "Things got real hot, real fast. Just watch me and follow my direction."

Theryn stepped forward into Jess's space, and Brenna knew that was not a wise move. "Do you imagine that you and your cohorts are the only Amazons in this stadium who love Tristaine, Jesstin? Sweet Gaia, the gall of the young and righteous! *We have no time to plan*, so spare me your indignation. Caster knows nothing of the dam, Jess."

"All right, Dana! Get those cameras rolling!" Caster was snapping her fingers, rapidly. "And you, you, bald Amazon! Attack! All of you, *attack!*"

Pulsing silence filled the arena.

"I'll get the women I love to safety, Jesstin. You do the same." Theryn's eyes flicked to Brenna. "Once they're safe, Shann can send Tristaine to a cold but righteous sleep. If you have a better strategy, I'm listening."

Jess looked at Brenna.

Brenna nodded. "We can trust her, Jess. She means it."

Then Grythe screamed. It was a raw, ugly sound that ripped the air and triggered the destruction that followed.

Brenna didn't remember Elodia's promise to Camryn until she saw the dagger in her hand. Elodia was racing across the arena toward them, targeted on Theryn. Brenna knew no Spanish and so didn't understand exactly what she was shouting, but one thing was clear. From the names Elodia screamed, she believed killing Theryn would avenge Camryn and free Tristaine's queen.

Time telescoped again.

"Elodia, stand down!" It was Shann's voice, but Elodia was too deep in her thirst for revenge to hear her.

Grythe leapt from the review stand and landed behind her wife like a frightened spider crazed to protect her egg sac. She emitted that soul-shriveling scream again and dashed toward Elodia.

Jess bolted after Grythe, and Vicar and Hakan were on a dead run to intercept them both.

Brenna didn't see which of Dana's mercenaries fired, but the first bullet hit Grythe in the back. Astonishment crossed her beautiful face as she crumpled into the dirt.

Elodia fell a bare second later, shot by at least two different rifles.

Dana was screaming hoarsely, racing from soldier to soldier, yelling orders into white faces. She saved the Amazons from an immediate bloodbath, but it was harrowingly close.

Vicar crouched beside Elodia's body and felt for a pulse at her throat. Brenna recognized the gesture as the formality it was. The girl was dead.

The Amazons on the risers, stunned by the sudden violence, began to step down onto the fighting field.

Caster still screamed orders, but she was largely ignored.

Theryn dropped to her knees beside her wife. Grythe still lived. Brenna could see the erratic lift and fall of her breast, but a small pool of blood was forming beneath her, soaking into the earth.

A surreal silence fell.

"Jesstin!"

Every eye flew to the review stand. Shann was staring down at Theryn, her hand poised over the railing, waiting. Her graceful fingers trembled.

Gently, Theryn let her unconscious wife come to rest on the ground. She got to her feet. She looked at Jess and at Brenna, and then she turned to address the Amazons who followed her.

"Hear me, sisters!" Theryn's voice rang through the stadium. "Caster seeks to violate the truce that would have preserved our clan!"

"Theryn!" Caster screamed. "My right hand to God, Theryn, I will order you shot where you stand!"

"We fight for Tristaine!" Theryn didn't even glance at Caster. She raised one hand to her Amazons. "We fight for Shann!"

Shann's fingers twirled, signaling Jess.

"Amazons, attack!" Jess shouted, and the battle for Tristaine began.

CHAPTER NINE

S everal soldiers fired blindly when the war cries erupted, galvanized by Caster's screamed commands. Four Amazons were hit immediately: three from Theryn's band, who lived, and Ayla, a warrior from Jess's side, who did not.

When Brenna dared throw a look at the review stand, it was empty.

Jess and Theryn led their separate cadres of warriors well, like warhorses pulling Shann's chariot in tandem. After the first outbreak of gunfire, the smoky fighting field was cleared fairly quickly and the wounded Amazons carried to the stadium's inner chambers.

Within minutes, Brenna was with the injured, kneeling between Perry and two other bleeding women she didn't know. She was coated with gore to the elbows for the second time in two days. The part of her that was calm also appreciated the efficiency of the Amazons, who kept her supplied with field dressings and fresh water, even in the full throes of battle.

"They're stable." Brenna turned to Amber, another of Jess's Amazons who had healing skills. She pulled her shoulder down to make sure Amber would hear her over the chaos of war cries and rifles. "Keep them here. This hallway's pretty safe!"

Amber shouted something back that sounded like agreement, but Brenna had already hit top speed on her run back toward the arena. The heart of the battle still centered there, though Amazons and soldiers alike had begun to branch out into the village itself.

Brenna burst out of the stone archway leading into the stadium. Two seconds later she was hit by what felt like a semitruck, and the ground came up and smacked her, hard. A bullet whistled above her head to career off a far wall, and Brenna realized the semitruck was an angry Amazon.

"Brenna, you brainless dolt!" Vicar snarled in her ear. She was lying full-length on top of Brenna. "You do *not* race pell-mell onto a flaming battlefield!"

"Well, excuse me, Vicar!" Brenna twisted over onto her back. "This is only my *second* flaming battle! I don't know all the rules yet. Where's Jess?"

"She sent me after you. Move with me, now!" Vicar clamped Brenna's wrist in one hand and hauled her to her feet. They ran together, in a half-crouch, toward the side wall of the stadium, and then Vicar hauled her bodily around a high log partition.

Brenna coughed dust and smoke out of her lungs; then she could see the five women gathered in the shadow of the log wall. Vicar patted her on the back until she recovered. She seemed a bit chagrined at her earlier roughness.

"Over here, Bren!"

Brenna saw Jess. "Ah, man." Her shoulders sagged in relief, and then she saw Shann and Kyla. "Ah, *man*," she repeated, and walked into Shann's open arms and hugged her, hard.

"You all right, Brenna?" Hakan was peering cautiously around the log wall, keeping a close eye on the still frenetic activity in the stadium.

"I'm fine." Brenna's pulse began to settle again as she went to Kyla and studied her face. She was still drawn and pale, but her eyes warmed for a moment as she took Brenna's hands.

Shann said, "Jesstin, report, please."

"Tristaine's high council is safe. They're under Amazon guard in the stables." Jess put her arm around Brenna's shoulders. "Our warriors fight side by side with Theryn's. They're holding off Caster's mercenaries. We're still outnumbered and outgunned, but the soldiers are a mess. No organization."

"We need to blow the dam, lady." Vicar ducked as another shot whined through the air to strike solidly into the arena wall yards away. "But we need to get you out first."

"Yes, well, here's the problem." Shann rummaged in a pocket of her robes. She held up a cracked plastic box and sprung wires.

With an unpleasant jolt, Brenna realized it was the remote detonator.

Jess's jaw dropped. "What happened to it?"

"I hit Caster with it." Shann sighed. "We're going to have to set off the timer by hand, Jesstin."

"You *what*?"

"I had to hit her with something."

Jess raked her hand through her dark hair, twice, before she could speak. "Shann, our detonator, the detonator you called Tristaine's greatest treasure, you used it as a *club*?"

"Caster went down like a sack of beets," Shann insisted. "She's still out, for all I know."

"Lady, I'll start the timer," Vicar volunteered. "I can run faster than any of us."

"That's debatable, Vicar," Hakan said.

"Later," Jess broke in. "Vicar, I need you and Hakan to get Shann and our council out of the valley. Take as many of the others as possible. Where shall we meet, lady?"

"The large glade, south of the pass," Shann answered at once.

"Shann, we need to warn as many of the City soldiers as we can." Brenna felt compelled to say it. "A lot of them are just poorly paid kids. This isn't their fight."

"Agreed, Blades." Shann nodded. "Good point. Vicar, I want you to find Theryn before we leave and have her spread the word. Tell her they must use every minute to get out before Jesstin triggers the blast."

"Jess is blowing the dam?" It was the first time Kyla had spoken. "Are you steady enough on your feet to do that, Jesstin? You look like hell."

"It won't be a matter of fitness or speed, adanin." Hakan's immense hand was gentle on the girl's shoulder. "Once Ziwa is freed and her waters join Terme Cay, no Amazon on Gaia's earth could outrun them. Jess won't have to rely on her own spindly legs." She inserted two fingers in her mouth, and an amazingly sharp whistle cracked through the air.

Before Brenna could ask what they were whistling at now, Shann drew her aside. They stood close together, and that veil of privacy fell around them again.

"On the stand, Blades, when I said I had Tristaine's greatest treasure, I didn't mean the detonator."

"I know. It's right here." Brenna patted her inner pocket. "I'll keep it safe, I promise."

"Thank you." Shann smiled. "Now listen carefully, Bren. Go with Jesstin. I've already convinced her that it's vital you do. Leave your journal by the dam, out of reach of the flood, but protected and somewhere *visible*, adanin. Do you understand?"

"Yes, I do."

Shann's eyebrows lifted. "You're not going to argue with me? No questions?"

"Probably, just not now." Brenna grinned. "We'll see you at the glade, lady."

Shann's smile acknowledged that Brenna had used her title for the first time. She kissed her forehead, then went to Kyla and took her hand. "Little sister. Do you want to bring Camryn with us?"

There was silence again in their small party. Even the war cries and shouts of the battle around them faded as they waited for Kyla's answer.

"Once we wash Caster off this mountain, our valley will be sacred again." Kyla's eyes were clear and tearless now. "Let Camryn rest here with the bones of Dyan and our other lost sisters."

Shann nodded. "As you wish, Ky."

"*Omboleza*, adanin," Hakan added.

"My sorrow," Jess translated softly for Brenna.

Brenna was startled by a drumming of hoofbeats, and then Hakan's beautiful warhorse, Valkyrie, loped into the arena. Another sharp whistle from Hakan turned the huge mare toward them.

"We're decided, then?" Shann waited to hear any dissent.

"We're ready, lady." Hakan steadied her big horse.

Shann looked at Jess and lifted one eyebrow.

Jess turned to Brenna and grasped her cold hands. "Hakan was right about the route we'll take, Bren. After I set the timer on the dynamite, we'll have twenty minutes to ride back through the village and get out of the valley. You've never been on a horse in your life. This is going to be pretty high drama, querida. You ready?"

"Of course not, but you have the hard part, Jesstin. All I have to do is hang on." Brenna went up on her toes and quickly kissed Jess. "We'd better hurry."

Without further ceremony, Jess ran three steps across the ground and jumped gracefully up onto Valkyrie's back.

Brenna's mouth fell open.

"You can get up there like a normal person if you prefer, little sister." Hakan grinned and offered Brenna her arm.

Being lifted to the broad back of an Amazon warhorse felt like cresting a mountain. A warm, hairy mountain that breathed. Even Vicar looked short from this height. Brenna wrapped her arms tightly around Jess's waist, careful to avoid the taser marks.

I could be in the Clinic's pharmacy filling out prescriptions for Caster, she reminded herself. She didn't know if her inner voice sounded relieved or incredulous. She thought she might be a bit hysterical.

"Remember, Jesstin." Shann's voice carried sure and certain command. "I consider both of you *irreplaceable.* Understood?"

"Aye, lady."

"Ride bloody fast, Stumpy." Vicar handed Jess a coiled rope and nodded at Brenna. "Find us at the glade tonight."

Jess leaned down to accept Shann's hand. "Your blessing, lady?"

Brenna watched the Amazon queen inhabit their elder sister again in the blink of an eye.

"Jesstin, Brenna, you ride for Tristaine. May Artemis shield you. Come home safe. Now *hurry!*"

Shann released Jess's arm as the big mare leapt forward. Brenna had thought there'd be a need to kick a horse to make that happen. Luckily, she was stuck to Jess's back like a burr.

She looked over her shoulder, and just before Shann and their sisters disappeared behind the log partition, Brenna saw Kyla lift her hand in benediction.

As they rode out of the stadium, Brenna had time to notice that it was almost twilight. The short winter day had given way to the golden sunlit hour that sometimes blessed the mountains just before dusk. Tristaine's village square was beautiful in the honeyed light.

But in jarring contrast to nature's peace, the scene was anything but serene. Shrill cries and shouts still split the cold air, and figures ran everywhere, both Amazons and City soldiers.

"Jesstin, no! Go that way!" It was an Amazon Brenna didn't know, one who had fought on Theryn's side. She was crouched in the grass at the east corner of the neat log infirmary, pointing. "Toward the lodges of the trades guild! The barracks of the warriors is overrun!"

"My thanks, Frost!" Jess nudged Valkyrie with one knee, and the mare charged back around the stadium and past it.

Brenna adjusted quickly to Valkyrie's even gait. There was something both alien and familiar about the horse's rhythms beneath her. She loosened her arms around Jess and found it easier to balance sitting upright.

"You all right?" Jess called to her as she hitched the coiled rope higher over her shoulder.

"I'm having fun!" she called back and spit a flying tendril of Jess's hair out of her mouth.

She heard Jess laugh as they rounded the first of the four long lodges used by Tristaine's tradeswomen.

Valkyrie was fast. They pounded down the grass strip that ran between the weavers' lodge and that of the woodworkers, heading toward the river that ran through Tristaine.

Toward Terme Cay, Brenna amended. It was beginning to look as if they would make it through the confusion unchallenged. Then, as they rounded the last lodge, she realized she was looking down the barrel of a rifle pointed right at them.

Rodriguez held it, the mercenary Brenna had introduced

herself to with a punch to the genitals. She started to shout a warning to Jess, but the words died in her throat. A dagger appeared, as if by magic, buried to the hilt in the man's chest. Rodriquez dropped the rifle, and blood exploded around the embedded blade. Brenna stopped watching.

"Briggs!" Jess saluted the warrior who had thrown the dagger, as Valkyrie carried them on a dead run past her.

"For Shann!" Briggs called, and Brenna heard several scattered Amazon voices echo her shout of fealty.

"Oh, lordy."

Brenna's stomach hadn't quite been ready to cross the footbridge. She trusted Tristaine's carpenters, but this was a half ton of horse carrying them across, and then Terme Cay was behind them, and Valkyrie churned up the low rise that led to the Amazons' private cabins. She felt for the journal in her pocket and was reassured by its solid presence.

They rode up the mountain now on the broad path that led to the dam. It *was* broad, at least, when you were walking on it alone. But even alone, it had terrified her only days ago. When riding an Amazon warhorse at top speed, possibly to your death, it was…

Bloody harrowing, Brenna thought, narrating the action in her head to record later in her journal. For the first time since she had left the City, Brenna barely noticed the natural beauty of her surroundings. There was little room in her mind for the colors of the rugged canyon off the path to their left, or even the dark blue glory of the lake that loomed ahead. Brenna could focus on only three things: following Jess's instructions, obeying Shann's command, and making sure they both got out of there alive.

When they reached the lake, Valkyrie slowed to a walk, steam puffing into the cold air. They studied the dam's shadowed surface and the small platform secured to its main support. The neatly wrapped bundle of dynamite looked undisturbed.

Jess lifted one knee over the horse's neck and dropped to the rocky ground. Brenna accepted her assistance with her own dismount, which felt like sliding off the roof of a building.

"Do you need me?" Brenna asked.

"Always." Jess's eyes sparkled at her. "But do I need you immediately? No, not until I'm finished on the platform. I'll make it back up faster with your help."

"I'll be there in five minutes. Jesstin, do *not* get hurt!" Brenna ordered.

"Yes'm." Jess shouldered the rope again and jogged toward the catwalk that topped the dam.

Then she turned around and jogged back. "Lass?"

"What, is anything wro—?"

Jess bent Brenna over one arm and kissed her, long and sweet and deep. Then she set her on her feet again and tapped her nose with one finger, gently.

"Wanted to make sure we took time for that," Jess explained, and jogged back toward the catwalk.

"Good. Thanks. Yes. Good idea. Okay." Brenna closed her mouth, unzipped her inner pocket, and scanned the rocky area around her. "Somewhere safe," she muttered.

She looked out over the lake, an ominous blue expanse in the twilight, then at the dam. This ground where she and the horse stood now was out of the projected path of the flood. Brenna spotted a sapling that seemed pretty well anchored to the bank.

She opened her journal and checked the last page to read Shann's note again, then scanned the map below. She made sure the folded paper was carefully inserted and wrapped the notebook in Jess's waterproof jacket. The bright red color would be eye-catching. Brenna fit the bundle securely in a "V" of branches and tied the sleeves tightly around the strongest one.

She took a step back, whiffing her bangs off her forehead, and studied the parcel that contained Tristaine's greatest treasure. It looked safe, and it was the best she could do. Brenna whispered a benediction of her own as she turned toward the lake.

The catwalk that spanned the top of the dam looked perilously narrow, and Brenna found, to her displeasure, that the urgency of their mission hadn't zapped her hatred of heights. Hatred, she reminded herself, as she trotted toward the center of the dam, not fear. She just didn't understand why Amazons who could design pyramids couldn't build a simple railing on a catwalk.

Jess was crouching on the platform halfway down the dam's face. She shaded her eyes to see Brenna above her. Brenna knelt and checked the rope that tethered her to the catwalk.

"We're set, Bren," Jess's voice echoed strangely in the silence. "Say a prayer, please."

"What? What prayer?"

"Doesn't matter. We're drowning our land, lass." Jess knelt and touched the switch of the timer. Then she looked into the canyon before her—the channel of the flood to come—and beyond it. They couldn't see Tristaine from here, but Jess gazed in that direction.

Brenna waited, in case any spectral voice wanted to whisper the right words to her. She couldn't hear what Jess was saying to the valley and to the village that was her childhood home. No words sounded in her mind, but she found she didn't need coaching.

"Thank you," Brenna whispered, "for Jesstin and for giving me this life with her."

Jess flicked the timer's switch. She climbed to the top of the dam in record time and without incident with Brenna's help. Jess still looked like she hadn't slept in a week, but she moved as efficiently and gracefully as ever.

"Twenty minutes until the blast?" Brenna took Jess's hand as they started back for the bank. "Then ten more before the flood hits the village?"

"More or less," Jess replied, and Brenna almost throttled her.

They walked the dam's catwalk quickly but carefully.

"Are you sure you can't be just a wee bit more specific about that timer?" Brenna asked.

"Shann and the others should be out of Tristaine by now," Jess said. "But not out of the valley. So aye, querida, we're counting on a solid twenty minutes."

Brenna didn't see the quarrel from Patana's crossbow, but she heard it. It fell short, shattering the edge of the beam an inch from Jess's boot. Jess stiffened instinctively and lost her balance.

Jess barely had time to shake Brenna's desperate fingers loose before she toppled off the dam and fell fifteen feet, to hit the cold water of the lake below.

"Jesstin!" Brenna almost followed her off the catwalk.

The deep lake swallowed Jess whole for a horrifically long time. Then she burst up heaving for air, and Brenna remembered winter, and mountain lakes, and hypothermia—

Another crossbow quarrel ricocheted off the face of the dam, yards from Jess's right arm. Brenna whirled and saw Patana at the other end of the catwalk, already inserting a fresh bolt into place. Her small eyes were pinned on Jess, her square jaw clenched.

Jess surged up out of the water; her hands scrabbled for any purchase on the smooth surface of the dam.

J'heika, rise!

Brenna swiftly tied the rope to one of the brackets on the side of the catwalk and tossed the other end down to Jess. She would become too weak to climb if she stayed in that water another second. She could be too weak even now, but Brenna had to stop Patana before she could worry about that. Once the rope left her hands, she shot to her feet and ran.

Patana didn't even glance Brenna's way at first. She fired another quarrel, then finally looked up. A wave of shock passed over her flushed face, and she flipped the crossbow into the sling on her back and faced her.

A calm voice whispered to Brenna. *Don't worry about Jesstin now, lass. You've achieved your first goal. Your enemy stopped shooting. Now, listen well.*

Brenna ran, staying to the center of the narrow catwalk, and listened. *Take her down. You can't win standing. She'll knock you off your feet. She'll fight to keep from falling off the dam. You fight to get her down and hold on to her until Jess can reach you.*

It wasn't the same inner voice that kept calling for J'heika, but it offered the sanest, most thorough advice she had received from Wherever yet, and Brenna intended to follow it. She adjusted her speed, aimed for Patana, and just kept going until she plowed into her.

Patana barked in surprise and flew backward to land on her back on the catwalk. Brenna sprawled on top of her and held on, and, so far, she was letter-perfect.

But Whoever was advising her should have taken into consideration that Patana was the second-best wrestler in Tristaine.

Grunting, Patana flipped Brenna off her with a sharp jerk of her hips and used the momentum to wrench her to one side. Brenna scrambled in terror, already feeling the abyss of the canyon that yawned below.

Patana kneed Brenna in the stomach and kicked her over the side.

Brenna finally stopped falling off the catwalk when she was caught short by a vicious jerk around her waist. The blue shawl Dorothea had given her had snagged on one of the catwalk's cleats. She dangled by it, the edge of the catwalk a good two feet over her head.

Stop kicking, young dolt! The voice roared, but Brenna's primal mind ignored the brilliant advisor who had gotten her into this. She flailed in helpless terror, expecting any second to hear the sickening rip of fabric tearing, then her own scream as she plummeted.

Stop kicking, the voice suggested calmly, and Brenna forced herself to hold still. She could hear the dry creaking of her makeshift sling. She stared down at her boots, rocking back and forth above the dizzying drop.

"This is *not* how to get me over a fear of heights!" she screamed to no one.

Brenna heard footsteps come to the edge of the catwalk, and Patana's breath rasped above her. She couldn't see her, so she didn't know if the Amazon had reloaded the crossbow. She assumed she had.

"We'll all die in a few minutes, *bruja*." Patana was breathing hard. "I'm just sending you and, more important, your smug bitch of a wife into the arms of our Grandmothers a bit early. I'll give you a moment. Tell your gods you're coming, Brenna."

Jess's face flashed through Brenna's mind, and then Shann, Kyla, Camryn, Sammy. But Brenna had no more time for preparation or anything else. She heard the distant twang of a bowstring and tightened spasmodically as she heard the arrow strike home.

She didn't know it was an arrow instead of a crossbow bolt until she heard Patana's guttural cry. She toppled off the catwalk and fell past Brenna, the feathered shaft of an arrow protruding from her neck.

Brenna instinctively lunged to try to catch Patana before she vanished forever, and the shawl securing her to the bracket ripped. She dropped a full three inches before very cold, wet fingers snatched her wrist.

"Brenna." Jess grunted with effort as she caught her full weight. Soaking wet, she was lying on top of the dam, one arm extended, her fingers locked like a vise around Brenna's slender wrist.

Jess is alive. The second bolt Patana fired didn't kill her. She's out of that freezing water. Brenna registered all of that first. She wondered, briefly, who had shot the arrow that killed Patana since Jess had no bow. But, mostly, she clung to Jess's wrist and turned to brace herself as well as she could on the surface of the dam. There were virtually no footholds. She looked up and saw Jess's white face.

"I've got you, Bren." Jess sounded insanely calm. "I won't let go."

"Good," Brenna gasped. She resisted a powerful urge to look over her shoulder at the canyon below. "C-can you? Hold on? But you can't pull me up, Jess."

"Help's coming," Jess said. Myrine's ashen face appeared beside her.

Myrine lowered herself to the catwalk beside Jess and reached down to grasp Brenna's arm. "All right, Jesstin, pull!"

Together, the two warriors pulled Brenna up, by inches. Gasping and struggling, Brenna made it over the top of the catwalk and sprawled on its cold plywood surface beside them.

Brenna groped for Jess and found her, then folded her into her arms.

Myrine got to her feet and looked down at them silently, her eyes filled with tears. Then she stepped to the edge of the catwalk and gazed down into the canyon below. For a horrible moment, Brenna thought she would jump.

"I knew why she was coming here when I saw her ride out of the village," Myrine said quietly. "I followed her as soon as I could find a horse."

Brenna looked past Myrine and saw two other horses cropping grass beside Hakan's Valkyrie.

"Myrine," Jess said. "Adanin—"

"Patana loved Tristaine, Jesstin, in her way." The scar on Myrine's face was livid against her pallor. "She loved me, in her way."

"Myrine," Brenna murmured, "I'm so—"

"We have fifteen minutes tops!" Jess yelled.

Myrine helped them up and they dashed for the three horses.

By the time they rode back into Tristaine, Brenna figured they had less than five minutes before the blast. She was plastered against Jess again, and no doubt her arms squeezed far too tightly, but Valkyrie's speed coming back down the mountain had been almost as frightening as dangling off the catwalk.

No. Untrue. Nowhere near.

Rifle fire still rose from the village, but the volleys were becoming more isolated. Brenna saw people running. Too many people. Some were Amazons, and her stomach did a sickening flip. Most of Tristaine's horses had gone with the migration. It was too late to get out of the valley on foot.

The flood would kill more than animals and trees.

The three horses clattered into the stadium, Myrine leading Patana's mount. The arena was all but deserted, but it wasn't empty. Brenna saw Theryn just as Jess veered Valkyrie toward her. She knelt in the dirt of the fighting field beneath the empty review stand. Grythe lay before her, covered to the chin with a beautiful blanket, her limbs peacefully arranged.

"Theryn, come on!" Jess pulled Valkyrie to a dancing stop. "Patana is dead. Take her horse!"

"Caster's alive, Jesstin." Theryn looked up at them. "She's probably in the main lodge, directing her mercenaries from there.

Some of her soldiers left, but some stayed. Some of my Amazons stayed, too, to fight them. And some of yours."

"Theryn," Jess was obviously struggling to match her calm tone, "we have no time! Get on your horse."

"If by some miracle Caster makes it out of here, you know she won't give up, Jess." Theryn rose and gazed down at Grythe's wild, beautiful face, peaceful at last in death. "We can't risk her survival. Caster would come for Shann, no matter how deep in the mountains she builds our new Tristaine. I'm staying to see Caster dead."

"Oh, Theryn, *please* don't be an idiot!" Brenna realized she was being less than diplomatic. "You'd be throwing your life away!"

"My life is over." Theryn looked down at Grythe. "I won't find a new one, not in Shann's Tristaine, where I'd be reviled as a traitor."

A flat, ugly percussive sound reached them. It was faint, but it shook Brenna to her core.

"Jesstin…" she whispered, and Jess's cold hand covered her own.

The dam was crumbling. Ziwa was free.

Brenna saw it happen, in her mind's eye.

The impact of the explosion shattered the main support beam and blew a substantial hole through the dam. The massive lake began surging through the breach in the wall that had held it back for generations. The crushing velocity of the water widened the hole, then shattered most of the dam, surging into the canyon below.

While the blast of the dynamite was faint, the death of the dam, and the release of Ziwa herself, were not. The riotous clamor of that initial first wave faded at first, but it did not disappear. It would grow deafening soon, as the flood reached Tristaine.

Behind Brenna, Myrine barked, "Jesstin, get out of here!" She slipped off her horse. "Seeing Caster dead is worth drowning for."

Brenna felt Jess's shoulders slump in pain. "Myrine—"

"Remember what I said, please, young Brenna." Theryn smiled grimly at Myrine as she joined her and took her hand. "If you ever write about the death of this village, little sister, be sure you record the truth. Shann and Jesstin and their followers were not the only Amazons who loved and honored their clan."

Brenna's eyes were filling, so it was hard to see them, but she nodded.

Jess still couldn't move, and finally Myrine sighed harshly. "Give my adanin my love, Jesstin. Now get your adonai out of here. *Go!*" She slapped Valkyrie's rump, hard.

Brenna felt the warhorse lunge for the exit, and Jess didn't stop her. The crashing of the flood grew closer. She gave her physical survival entirely over to Jess and did what she could not to throw off their balance.

Terme Cay was still calm as they clattered back over the footbridge, but Brenna's worst nightmares told her this was just the prelude. She heard cries of terror rising behind them, and more gunfire.

Jess wove the horse through the private lodges of the Amazons at a quick trot. "We're almost out of rifle range, Brenna. It's time to run. Can you hold on?"

Brenna rested her face against Jess's dark, wet hair. "Absolutely."

She remembered enough of that wild ride to record a chilling account in her next journal, and she didn't have to exaggerate a word.

Brenna and Jess rode the warhorse out of the darkening valley at a dead run, chased by impending doom in the form of a ravenous wall of water. Valkyrie leaped over a shallow but wide ravine, and Brenna almost lost her seat. Jess snaked one arm back to brace her, and she steadied herself. She buried her face again in Jess's hair and squeezed her eyes shut. That ravine marked the boundary of the valley.

They were out of danger now, but she could still see it happening. And not just see it...

Brenna smelled it first. A flood through a mountainous forest washed a gust of air before it, a cold wind filled with the stench of the dying. She smelled that wind first, and then she felt it, a foul buffet of air in her face.

She was standing on the arched footbridge that spanned the village's river. She'd heard the flood for several minutes now, and at any moment, the first crashing waves would course down Tristaine's peaceful stretch of Terme Cay. Brenna couldn't believe the growing roar could grow louder before the flood finally appeared, but it did.

Terme Cay was a river, and then she was a rushing wall of water, forty feet high. Anyone standing on Tristaine's footbridge would see a shadow, and then they'd see their death coming. The screams were everywhere by then, and Brenna heard them.

She shut down. *Really*, she prayed, *please, that's all I can take*. And to her vast relief, the images and sounds and smells all stopped. Brenna didn't have to watch the village drown.

They met Shann and the other survivors of Tristaine in the southern glade before the moon rose.

CHAPTER TEN

Dana sat cross-legged on a blanket in the grass, close to one of the campfires. Several such small blazes dotted the glade around her, in areas cleared for that purpose. She had been fed and left alone for the most part, which is what she fervently wanted at this point.

She thought about thirty Amazons had escaped the flood, counting Jesstin and Brenna. Those two had ridden in an hour ago, on the biggest animal she had ever seen. A circle of Amazons had surrounded them at once. They appeared to be all right, thank god.

So far, no one seemed inclined to take Dana on for tasering Jesstin. Dana remembered watching Brenna tend Jess after it happened. She remembered thinking no one had ever touched her with such love.

She was the only City soldier among the Amazons. She wasn't the only mercenary to escape the flood, but all the others had insisted on their own stubborn course, down into the foothills. She had almost gone with them.

Shann, the Amazon queen, and dozens of her followers, had run past Dana on their way out of Tristaine. Shann stopped and called to her. Dana had hesitated, and in the kind of split-second decision that changes lives, she ran to her.

She still wasn't sure why.

Soft laughter filtered through the circle of women around Jesstin and Brenna; then they began to get up and drift back toward their blankets. Dana could see the queen kneeling beside Jess, her palm on her breast to monitor her heartbeat. Shann straightened and smiled at Jess, then looked straight at Dana, as if her gaze called to her.

"Dana, come join us, please."

Shit fire. She felt a jolt of unease, certain the Amazons had decided to kick her out. She put on a neutral expression and shuffled over to the group.

Dana recognized the two big Amazon warriors, Vicar and Hakan. They both looked like war goddesses this close up, one black and one white. They sat protectively on either side of young Kyla, and Dana noticed neither of them looked at her as she joined them. She settled stiffly beside Jesstin and avoided her appraising eyes.

"I'm glad to see you." Brenna leaned across her reclined lover to touch Dana's knee. "Are you all right?"

"Yeah, I'm okay." Dana cleared her throat and finally met Brenna's friendly eyes. "How about you two?"

"I wish we had some bloody proof, Jesstin," Vicar broke in. She had her long arms coiled around one raised knee. "None of us will sleep a full night until we see that witch's corpse."

"Vicar? Courtesy, please." Shann nodded at Dana. "Yes, little sister. Given rest and warmth and decent food, Brenna and Jesstin will both heal and be well."

Little sister? Dana's brows rose.

"I know you have to be exhausted, Dana. We all are, so I won't keep you long." Shann curled her legs gracefully beneath her before continuing. "We're assuming Caster is dead and her vendetta is over. The silver the City wanted is gone. We feel the Military won't bother to pursue our clan if we establish our new holdings deeper in the mountains. Do you agree?"

"Me?" Dana was puzzled. "I'm not in on any Military plans, Shann. I'm not a Government soldier. Uh, I mean Queen Shann."

Hakan and Vicar and Jess all snickered, and Shann raised an eyebrow at them.

"Shann will suffice. I know you can't give us inside information, Dana. We're just asking your opinion. You've lived in the City more recently than any of us, so you know the atmosphere down there even better than Brenna."

"Oh." Dana wished mightily that everyone would find something to look at besides her face. "Well, let me think. The City paper did mention the closing of Caster's program at the Clinic this last summer. But it sure didn't mention any escaped prisoners or Amazons. Tristaine is hot gossip, but that's nothing new. So there won't be any public pressure, or even public knowledge, that you guys still exist. I guess I really don't see any big advantage for the Military in coming after you."

"After us," Shann corrected. "Good, Dana, thank you. Those are our thoughts, too."

"Ma'am?"

"Yes?"

"How high, exactly, into the mountains will we be going?" Dana asked.

She saw Shann smile at Brenna, for some reason, the lines around her eyes crinkling.

"Our first stop will be the southern meadows, where we'll join the sisters who migrated a few days ago from our mountain village. We'll pass the winter there, then begin the search for our new home in the spring."

A low, chanting music filtered through the chilly air, and Dana peered over her shoulder into the glade. She saw the other Amazons gather into a circle around the largest of the campfires. They were humming something, a melodic, lonely sound.

"Sisters, join the storyfire," Shann urged them. "Give me a moment, please, with Kyla, Jesstin, and Brenna."

"Lady." Hakan got smoothly to her feet. She clamped one broad hand on Dana's shoulder and pulled her up, too. "Come on, youngster, and stop looking like a skittish hare. Vic and I will keep the others from spitting you on a mesquite branch and roasting you for dinner."

Dana smiled weakly and stumbled after Hakan toward the storyfire.

"So…" Vicar unwound to her full height and put her hands on her hips. She nudged Jesstin's foot with her own. "You need anything, Stumpy?"

"Shorter, more humble cousins," Jess grumbled. She was nestled against Brenna. "Nice work tonight, mate."

"You too. Both of you." Vicar winked at Brenna and followed Hakan and Dana.

"Kyla?" Shann held out a hand, and Kyla obediently shifted closer to her. Shann put an arm around her shoulders and looked down at Jess. "I think you'll be fine to travel in the morning, Jesstin, if we make it a light day. Are you in much pain?"

"Yes," Jess growled. "My back hurts, my belly hurts. Also my left shoulder, and my entire right arm. Also my left knee."

"I've been talking to Jess a lot about being a little less stoic about her injuries," Brenna explained. She ruffled Jess's hair. "Unfortunately, I don't think she's exaggerating."

"A plant called talwin grows between here and the southern meadows." Shann pursed her lips. "We may need to dose all our warriors with it. Your women fought well, Jesstin, and you all have the bruises to prove it. Why would I want to be careful, Blades, with a tea boiled with talwin leaves?"

"Because talwin has a mild narcotic effect, so it can be addictive," Brenna answered, and then she and Jess both blinked. "How did I know that?"

"How did you know Patana would try to assassinate Jesstin yesterday?" Shann asked. "Or that Caster's soldiers had ambushed Tristaine? Or all the sacred promises made in a Queen's Blessing? Really, honey, how much more proof of your sight do you think you're going to require?"

"You did tell me about the Blessing yourself, Shann." Brenna had also known when Camryn began to die, but she couldn't say it aloud.

*And my voices...*Brenna was afraid she was starting to sound psychotic, even in her own mind. *The voices didn't warn me before Elodia snapped or before Patana got off that first shot on the dam.*

"Bren..." Jess ventured, watching her. "You in there?"

"I'm right here." Brenna smiled and brushed Jess's tumbling hair off her brow.

"And what about you, little sister?" Shann's arm was light around Kyla's slender shoulders. "How are you?"

Kyla smiled, but it hurt Brenna's heart to see the effort it took. "I'm broken up inside. But I'm alive. And I'm real glad we got almost everyone out." Her eyes closed for a moment. "So many faces are gone, Shann."

"Yes…" Shann rested her lips on Kyla's pale forehead for a moment. "We have mourning to do. And a new Tristaine to build come spring."

"What's next for us, lady?" Jess stared up at the dazzling canopy of stars overhead. "Our clan has been diminished, and there'll be no more new Amazons from the City. They wouldn't know how to find us."

Shann glanced at Brenna and smiled before she answered. "Well, if our line is meant to die out at last, Jess, then it will. I have a feeling Gaia has other plans for us."

"Yeah?" Kyla looked almost hopeful. "You do?"

"I do. For one thing," Shann said, "I have a feeling Gaia might want us to finally learn the lesson She set before all Amazons a thousand years ago. Not a single generation of Tristaine has learned it, under any queen. Including me, it seems, at least not yet."

"I'm sorry?" Brenna asked. "What lesson was that?"

"*'Amazons must be unified, if the Clan is to survive,'*" Shann recited to them. "That's one of the challenges our Seven Adanin left us, Blades. Sounds simple enough, doesn't it?"

"Aye, but another challenge was, '*All women must live free,*'" Jess responded from her relaxed position against Brenna. "Remember what Dyan always said, Shann. It's never simple for a clan to live with both unity and freedom."

"You still quote Dyan at Shann all the time, Jess." Kyla's smile wasn't as forced this time. "Except when it suits you. Dyan also yelled at you to take less risks when you fight."

Jess winked at her, but her eyes on Shann were grave. "Lady, Theryn's betrayal wasn't your fault. You worked yourself to death in high council last spring trying to bring her faction around."

"I'm not blaming myself, Jesstin." Shann patted Jess's shoulder. "My own particular challenge has always been Jocelyn's favorite, '*Don't push the river,*' so that's what I intend to practice. Now, let's listen to the dirge for a while. They're singing for Camryn and the other sisters we've lost."

They fell silent, and the low, musical chant of the larger circle reached them. Brenna felt her heart fill with a deep, pure sadness. She looked at the Amazons seated around the distant storyfire and watched as Dana lowered her head.

Dana's eyes kept filling with tears, which mystified her, because she rarely cried. Given her choice, she would rather *not* bawl in front of dozens of Amazon warriors.

Some of the faces around her wore stony expressions as they sang. Some mourned only with their chant, while others wept openly. They all grieved for their lost village, Dana knew, and for the Amazon warriors who had died. She just didn't understand why *she* cried, too. She didn't even know these people, so why was her throat so tight with grief?

The dirge eventually wound down. The storyfire in the center of the circle finally burned down to glowing coals. Dana got up to limp off to her blankets, and she glanced toward Shann and the others.

Jesstin dozed, her head pillowed on Brenna's lap. Kyla had fallen asleep, leaning against her queen. Shann's fingers drifted through the girl's auburn tresses. She smiled at Dana, who waved vaguely, then lay down and pulled a blanket over her face.

"Um, lady? A question," Brenna asked, her voice low so as not to disturb Jess or Kyla. "Do you know who they are? These voices I keep hearing? They're the Grandmothers? I guess that's three questions."

"Yes, I believe you're hearing Amazon voices." Shann sounded pleased by Brenna's question. "I've never heard them in the way you do, so I can't say who any of them are. But they may be our Seven Adanin, as well as other sisters from past generations of our clan."

"Shann." Brenna cleared her throat. "Did Dyan speak with a thick brogue?"

"Thick as maple syrup." Shann looked surprised. "Why, Blades?"

"Because I think I heard her on the dam," Brenna said. She didn't know if this would be painful news or simply absurd.

But after a moment of silence, Shann sounded excited. "That's wonderful, Bren, honestly! Yes, it might have been our Dyan. What did this voice say?"

"Duck, ye young dolt," Jess burred softly, in what sounded like a spot-on imitation of the voice on the dam, and both Shann and Brenna stifled laughter.

"Ask Shann about that name, Brenna," Kyla said sleepily.

"Oh, good, thanks, Ky," Brenna said. "Shann, who is Jaheeka?"

A line appeared between Shann's brows. "What did you say?"

"Ja-heeka? Was there such a person? I've heard a voice calling her for days now."

"So did Camryn," Kyla added. Her shadowed brown eyes were focused on the flames of the fire. "Camryn said that name right before she died."

"Are you sure, Ky?" Shann's voice was quiet, but something in her tone made Kyla look at her.

"Are you all right?" Brenna asked. In the flame's low light, Shann had grown pale.

Alarmed, Jess sat up, as did Kyla. "Shann?"

"You're sure that Camryn said the word 'j'heika,' before she died?"

Kyla nodded in confirmation. "Yes, lady. She said it to Brenna when she asked her for the Queen's Blessing."

"I hear that name every time I hear the Grandmothers." Brenna realized her throat was dry. Shann's expression was an extraordinary mixture of surprise and consternation, and much else that Brenna wasn't sure she could interpret. "Shann, who is J'heika?" Concern colored her question this time.

"Brenna, sisters, everything's all right." Shann let out a long breath. Brenna found her shoulders lowering as Shann relaxed. "I'm sorry. I was just a bit surprised. Brenna, there's something you might need to know."

"Are you sure?" Brenna swallowed. "Judging by your look, maybe ignorance would be better."

"Ignorance is never better," Shann corrected, and pressed Brenna's hand. "J'heika isn't a proper name, Blades. It's an honorific, a title."

They didn't sleep for a very long time.

Nine Months Later

"Amazon Lake."

The reverence in Lee Ann's tone would be understandable, Karen figured, even if this beautiful lake had no spiritual legends behind it. They had never seen anything as flat-out gorgeous as all this mountain scenery in their lives.

Karen rested her foot on a stump and gazed out over the lake, a wide expanse of twinkling blue, dotted here and there with small, inviting, islands—the tops of hills, she realized, when this had been a valley. Only last fall. Only last fall, there might have been a village here, some kind of women's community. She shivered and turned away.

Attuned as always to her shifts in mood, Lee Ann squinted up at her. "What?"

"It's a beautiful graveyard."

"Well, yeah." Lee Ann looked out over the lake again. "Women did die here, if they couldn't get clear of the avalanche in time. Think of it, Karen, those women were Amazons, if this was really Tristaine. This lake is a shrine, honey."

"Yeah, well, trespassing here is two years in Prison, honey." Karen's teasing was kind. She knew how much this illicit trek meant to Lee Ann, who had dreamed of Amazons since she was a girl. "The place looks completely deserted, so I'm fine with camping here tonight. But we shouldn't stand out here in the open, okay?

Just because there's no Military patrol around now doesn't mean there won't be."

"I don't think anyone's been through here in weeks." Lee Ann accepted Karen's hand up and slapped the dust from her jeans. Karen helped her with that, too, ending with a lecherous pinch that made them both grin.

Then Lee Ann stepped away and scanned the ground curiously. "Look, love. There's only one path in here, and the only footprints I can see were made by the three of us. It hasn't rained that much this month. There should be more tracks, shouldn't there?"

"Well, maybe the paper was as bullshit inaccurate as ever, and patrols never come here." Karen scanned the empty blue sky overhead for copters, nonetheless. "I still don't want us to take any chances. Where the heck did Sly go?"

Lee Ann nodded toward the largest hill. "She took off up that way. Want to see what she found?"

"Sure." Karen drew her close for a quick kiss before taking her hand.

It was a pleasant day for a romantic stroll. The warmth of summer had reached high enough into the mountains that shedding clothing seemed feasible. "Any chance Sly might lay her sleeping bag a bit farther away tonight?"

"I will make that request." Lee Ann smiled.

Karen liked Sly well enough, but if she was going to travel with them, they were going to have to put their foot down about a few things. Her smoking, for instance.

Karen knew what Lee Ann's friend had been through in the Prison, and no one could begrudge her a few vices. But it wasn't just the stink of the smoke. Sly was starting on a real hacker's cough, and she was barely twenty. Both Karen and Lee Ann were trying to get her to cut down.

She saw Sly up ahead, reaching up into a smallish tree that stood on a bluff looking out over the lake. The view on either side of the bluff was breathtaking, and Karen had to keep coaxing her dazzled lover on with gentle tugs of her hand.

By the time they reached their taciturn friend, Sly had seated herself in the grass at the base of the tree. She was unwrapping a swath of red cloth.

"Hey, what's that?" Lee Ann crouched, her lively eyes sparkling. "Where did you find it?"

Sly gestured vaguely up into the tree. Her rough hands slipped a worn spiral notebook out of the red cloth and held it for a moment. She looked up at them, her green eyes wary, then opened the notebook. A folded piece of paper fell out, and Karen knelt and retrieved it.

"Is that a note, Sly? Is it from *them*?" Lee Ann was making an obvious effort to sound casual, but Karen's hands were trembling as she unfolded the paper. "A map? You're kidding. Is that a *map*?"

"Yeah." Karen held the sheet up to the fading light. "It looks pretty readable. I think. From what I know of mountain maps, which is nil."

"Where's that trail go, the one that's marked?" Lee Ann leaned over Karen's shoulder.

"Uh, south. Right? It goes somewhere south. That's the best I can do."

"The map leads to the southern meadows." Sly had been skimming through the spiral notebook, and her gaunt features were expressionless as she read the last two pages. "Whatever the southern meadows are," she added.

"It says that in there?" Lee Ann crouched beside Sly. "Who was that notebook left for, Sly. Do you know? And who left it?"

"It's a woman's diary. It was left here for anybody who finds it, I guess." Sly turned to the last page and read aloud.

> *If you have searched long enough to find this journal, you can find Tristaine, wherever we rebuild Her.*

"Oh, lord." Lee Ann sounded breathless. "Lord, Karen, the Amazons left this! We were right. Some of them *did* survive."

*Read this notebook, and guard it well. Bring it
with you to the southern meadows. You'll find
another map there.*
*But, first, you must make a copy of this first
map and leave the original here. Return it to its
hiding place for other lost sisters to find.*
Follow us if you will.
Shanendra, daughter of Elaine

"This was brilliant," Lee Ann said softly, accepting the worn notebook from Sly at last. "That second map the note mentions must lead us to wherever the Amazons have gone. But how did they know anyone would find this one?"

No one answered her, but the question was forgotten as Lee Ann and Karen pored over the notebook's first entries.

Sly got stiffly to her feet and limped to the edge of the bluff to stare down at the lovely, placid blue of the lake. She unshouldered her heavy pack and knelt to rummage through it. "Are you two game?"

"Oh, *hell,* yes." Lee Ann's voice held that overtly reverent note again, but Karen was so excited about the journal, she didn't care. "Are you kidding? Of course we're going. Sly, we didn't even hope for something like this!"

"There's definitely nothing in the City we have to stay for." Karen looked up when Sly made no reply. "The same is true for you, Sly, right?"

"That's right." Sly zipped up her pack.

"Hey, pal." Lee Ann touched Sly's shoulder. "You're still coming with us, aren't you? You know you can't go home."

"Yeah, I'll come along." Sly fished a pack of cigarettes out of her breast pocket. "Why don't you two set up some kind of camp down by the lake? This bluff is kind of exposed. I'll help after a quick smoke."

"Sheesh, you're right. Anyone could spot us up here." Karen flushed, mad at herself. She closed the notebook like it was a sacred tome and secured it inside her shirt. "Don't stay on this bluff too long, Sly, okay?"

She waved and blew out smoke in agreement; then Karen and Lee Ann made their way quickly back down the hill.

Alone, she gazed down at the lake once more, then around her at the timeless beauty of the surrounding mountain peaks. She took a long, satisfying pull, which helped mask her constant companions, pain and loss.

Sammy hadn't seen her sister's handwriting in over a year. Funny how the sight of that slanted hand in the pages of the notebook brought Brenna's face back to her. She'd stopped being able to picture her at all in Prison.

She rocked slightly with her eyes closed and moved her hand across her belly in a desolate caress. She had named her daughter for Brenna. Matthew hadn't lived to see his baby born, and Samantha knew she would never see her again. Prisoners were not allowed to parent, and the child had been taken at birth. She was told the baby died soon afterward.

When they were young, Brenna had been all she knew of safety. Her older sister had been her shelter and protection, and now, again, she was the only family Sammy had. In the stark chill of her grief, she still yearned for the early, familiar comfort of Brenna's voice. She had brought Sammy through a nightmarish childhood; then she brought Caster into their lives.

It seemed she might see Brenna again. She tried to feel happiness.

She rolled the map carefully and wrapped it in the slick red cloth. She ground her cigarette out beneath her boot heel, then went back to the tree. After reaching up and replacing the package securely in the branches, "for other lost sisters to find," she walked down the hill to join her friends.

Epilogue

**Article in that week's *City Gazette*
Section D, page 4, June 30:**

Natural Mountain Lake

Formed By Avalanche

Rumors of clandestine activity in the mountain range east of the City proved categorically false last week. Government surveillance teams have confirmed that a large lake, newly discovered high in the range, was formed by natural processes. An avalanche caused the collapse of an earthen shelf holding back a river, which drained into a valley, forming the lake. Citizens are reminded that any unauthorized travel beyond City limits is punishable by imprisonment.

Scarred fingers reached for a pair of scissors and painstakingly clipped the article for a scrapbook.

About the Author

Cate Culpepper is a 2005 Golden Crown Literary Award winner in the Sci-Fi/Fantasy category. She grew up in southern New Mexico, where she served as the state lesbian for several years, before moving to the Pacific Northwest almost twenty years ago. She now resides in Seattle with her faithful sidekick, Kirby, Warrior Westie. Cate supervises a housing program for homeless young gay adults. She is the author of the Tristaine series: *Tristaine: The Clinic, Battle for Tristaine*, and *Tristaine Rises*. She can be reached at Klancy7@aol.com.

Books Available From Bold Strokes Books

Too Close to Touch by Georgia Beers. Kylie O'Brien believes in true love and is willing to wait for it. It doesn't matter one damn bit that Gretchen, her new and off-limits boss, has a voice as rich and smooth as melted chocolate. It absolutely doesn't. (1-933110-47-3)

100th Generation by Justine Saracen. Ancient curses, modern day villains, and a most intriguing woman who keeps appearing when least expected lead Archeologist Valerie Foret on the adventure of her life. (1-933110-48-1)

Battle for Tristaine by Cate Culpepper. While Brenna struggles to find her place in the clan and the love between her and Jess grows, Tristaine is threatened with destruction. Second in the Tristaine series. (1-933110-49-X)

The Traitor and the Chalice by Jane Fletcher. Without allies to help them, Tevi and Jemeryl will have to risk all in the race to uncover the traitor and retrieve the chalice. The Lyremouth Chronicles Book Two. (1-933110-43-0)

Promising Hearts by Radclyffe. Dr. Vance Phelps lost everything in the War Between the States and arrives in New Hope, Montana with no hope of happiness and no desire for anything except forgetting—until she meets Mae, a frontier madam. (1-933110-44-9)

Carly's Sound by Ali Vali. Poppy Valente and Julia Johnson form a bond of friendship that lays the foundation for something more, until Poppy's past comes back to haunt her—literally. A poignant romance about love and renewal. (1-933110-45-7)

Unexpected Sparks by Gina L. Dartt. Falling in love is complicated enough without adding murder to the mix. Kate Shannon's growing feelings for much younger Nikki Harris are challenging enough without the mystery of a fatal fire that Kate can't ignore. (1-933110-46-5)

Whitewater Rendezvous by Kim Baldwin. Two women on a wilderness kayak adventure—Chaz Herrick, a laid-back outdoorswoman, and Megan Maxwell, a workaholic news executive—discover that true love may be nothing at all like they imagined. (1-933110-38-4)

Erotic Interludes 3: Lessons in Love by Stacia Seaman and Radclyffe, eds. Sign on for a class in love…the best lesbian erotica writers take us to "school." (1-933110-39-2)

Punk Like Me by JD Glass. Twenty-one year old Nina writes lyrics and plays guitar in the rock band, Adam's Rib, and she doesn't always play by the rules. And, oh yeah—she has a way with the girls. (1-933110-40-6)

Coffee Sonata by Gun Brooke. Four women whose lives unexpectedly intersect in a small town by the sea share one thing in common—they all have secrets. (1-933110-41-4)

The Clinic: Tristaine Book One by Cate Culpepper. Brenna, a prison medic, finds herself deeply conflicted by her growing feelings for her patient, Jesstin, a wild and rebellious warrior reputed to be descended from ancient Amazons. (1-933110-42-2)

Forever Found by JLee Meyer. Can time, tragedy, and shattered trust destroy a love that seemed destined? When chance reunites two childhood friends separated by tragedy, the past resurfaces to determine the shape of their future. (1-933110-37-6)

Sword of the Guardian by Merry Shannon. Princess Shasta's bold new bodyguard has a secret that could change both of their lives. He is actually a *she*. A passionate romance filled with courtly intrigue, chivalry, and devotion. (1-933110-36-8)

Wild Abandon by Ronica Black. From their first tumultuous meeting, Dr. Chandler Brogan and Officer Sarah Monroe are drawn together by their common obsessions—sex, speed, and danger. (1-933110-35-X)

Turn Back Time by Radclyffe. Pearce Rifkin and Wynter Thompson have nothing in common but a shared passion for surgery. They clash at every opportunity, especially when matters of the heart are suddenly at stake. (1-933110-34-1)

Chance by Grace Lennox. At twenty-six, Chance Delaney decides her life isn't working so she swaps it for a different one. What follows is the sexy, funny, touching story of two women who, in finding themselves, also find one another. (1-933110-31-7)

The Exile and the Sorcerer by Jane Fletcher. First in the Lyremouth Chronicles. Tevi, wounded and adrift, arrives in the courtyard of a shy young sorcerer. Together they face monsters, magic, and the challenge of loving despite their differences. (1-933110-32-5)

A Matter of Trust by Radclyffe. JT Sloan is a cybersleuth who doesn't like attachments. Michael Lassiter is leaving her husband, and she needs Sloan's expertise to safeguard her company. It should just be business—but it turns into much more. (1-933110-33-3)

Sweet Creek by Lee Lynch. A celebration of the enduring nature of love, friendship, and community in the quirky, heart-warming lesbian community of Waterfall Falls. (1-933110-29-5)

The Devil Inside by Ali Vali. Derby Cain Casey, head of a New Orleans crime organization, runs the family business with guts and grit, and no one crosses her. No one, that is, until Emma Verde claims her heart and turns her world upside down. (1-933110-30-9)

Grave Silence by Rose Beecham. Detective Jude Devine's investigation of a series of ritual murders is complicated by her torrid affair with the golden girl of Southwestern forensic pathology, Dr. Mercy Westmoreland. (1-933110-25-2)

Honor Reclaimed by Radclyffe. In the aftermath of 9/11, Secret Service Agent Cameron Roberts and Blair Powell close ranks with a trusted few to find the would-be assassins who nearly claimed Blair's life. (1-933110-18-X)

Honor Bound by Radclyffe. Secret Service Agent Cameron Roberts and Blair Powell face political intrigue, a clandestine threat to Blair's safety, and the seemingly irreconcilable personal differences that force them ever farther apart. (1-933110-20-1)

Protector of the Realm: Supreme Constellations Book One by Gun Brooke. A space adventure filled with suspense and a daring intergalactic romance featuring Commodore Rae Jacelon and a stunning, but decidedly lethal, Kellen O'Dal. (1-933110-26-0)

Innocent Hearts by Radclyffe. In a wild and unforgiving land, two women learn about love, passion, and the wonders of the heart. (1-933110-21-X)

The Temple at Landfall by Jane Fletcher. An imprinter, one of Celaeno's most revered servants of the Goddess, is also a prisoner to the faith—until a Ranger frees her by claiming her heart. The Celaeno series. (1-933110-27-9)

Force of Nature by Kim Baldwin. From tornados to forest fires, the forces of nature conspire to bring Gable McCoy and Erin Richards close to danger, and closer to each other. (1-933110-23-6)

In Too Deep by Ronica Black. Undercover homicide cop Erin McKenzie tracks a femme fatale who just might be a real killer…with love and danger hot on her heels. (1-933110-17-1)

Erotic Interludes 2: Stolen Moments by Stacia Seaman and Radclyffe, eds. Love on the run, in the office, in the shadows…Fast, furious, and almost too hot to handle. (1-933110-16-3)

Course of Action by Gun Brooke. Actress Carolyn Black desperately wants the starring role in an upcoming film produced by Annelie Peterson. Just how far will she go for the dream part of a lifetime? (1-933110-22-8)

Rangers at Roadsend by Jane Fletcher. Sergeant Chip Coppelli has learned to spot trouble coming, and that is exactly what she sees in her new recruit, Katryn Nagata. The Celaeno series. (1-933110-28-7)

Justice Served by Radclyffe. Lieutenant Rebecca Frye and her lover, Dr. Catherine Rawlings, embark on a deadly game of hide-and-seek with an underworld kingpin who traffics in human souls. (1-933110-15-5)

Distant Shores, Silent Thunder by Radclyffe. Doctor Tory King—and the women who love her—is forced to examine the boundaries of love, friendship, and the ties that transcend time. (1-933110-08-2)

Hunter's Pursuit by Kim Baldwin. A raging blizzard, a mountain hideaway, and a killer-for-hire set a scene for disaster—or desire—when Katarzyna Demetrious rescues a beautiful stranger. (1-933110-09-0)

The Walls of Westernfort by Jane Fletcher. All Temple Guard Natasha Ionadis wants is to serve the Goddess—until she falls in love with one of the rebels she is sworn to destroy. The Celaeno series. (1-933110-24-4)

Erotic Interludes: *Change of Pace* by Radclyffe. Twenty-five hot-wired encounters guaranteed to spark more than just your imagination. Erotica as you've always dreamed of it. (1-933110-07-4)

Honor Guards by Radclyffe. In a wild flight for their lives, the president's daughter and those who are sworn to protect her wage a desperate struggle for survival. (1-933110-01-5)

Fated Love by Radclyffe. Amidst the chaos and drama of a busy emergency room, two women must contend not only with the fragile nature of life, but also with the irresistible forces of fate. (1-933110-05-8)

Justice in the Shadows by Radclyffe. In a shadow world of secrets and lies, Detective Sergeant Rebecca Frye and her lover, Dr. Catherine Rawlings, join forces in the elusive search for justice.(1-933110-03-1)

Love's Masquerade by Radclyffe. Plunged into the indistinguishable realms of fiction, fantasy, and hidden desires, Auden Frost is forced to question all she believes about the nature of love. (1-933110-14-7)

Love & Honor by Radclyffe. The president's daughter and her lover are faced with difficult choices as they battle a tangled web of Washington intrigue for...love and honor. (1-933110-10-4)

Beyond the Breakwater by Radclyffe. One Provincetown summer three women learn the true meaning of love, friendship, and family. (1-933110-06-6)

Tomorrow's Promise by Radclyffe. One timeless summer, two very different women discover the power of passion to heal and the promise of hope that only love can bestow. (1-933110-12-0)

Love's Melody Lost by Radclyffe. A secretive artist with a haunted past and a young woman escaping a life that has proved to be a lie find their destinies entwined. (1-933110-00-7)

Safe Harbor by Radclyffe. A mysterious newcomer, a reclusive doctor, and a troubled gay teenager learn about love, friendship, and trust during one tumultuous summer in Provincetown. (1-933110-13-9)

Above All, Honor by Radclyffe. Secret Service Agent Cameron Roberts fights her desire for the one woman she can't have—Blair Powell, the daughter of the president of the United States. (1-933110-04-X)